Voyagers of the Lost Earth

Voyagers of the Lost Earth

Saratchendra Nitturi

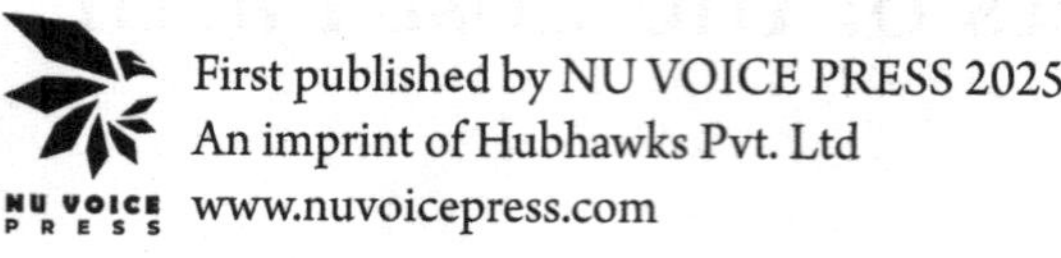

First published by NU VOICE PRESS 2025
An imprint of Hubhawks Pvt. Ltd
www.nuvoicepress.com

This is a work of fiction. Space and time have been rearranged to suit the convenience of the book. Except for public figures, hotels, and institution names, any resemblance to persons living or dead or the real events are purely coincidental. The opinions expressed in the book are those of the characters, and should not be confused with that of the Author.

ISBN: 978-81-993531-7-6
Typeset by Pooja Sharma
Published by Nu Voice Press

Prologue

"Is this on?"

The young girl sitting on the leather sofa seemed to be curious about everything around her. Her eyes darted around, wide and interested in the way the boom mike hung over her head, the way the harsh lights that resembled umbrellas kept being adjusted, the half a dozen people hastening around her, adjusting the décor, dabbing makeup on her, and adjusting the interviewer's hair.

Finally, the interviewer smiled at the girl in a practiced way and began. "Why don't you get us started, Tara?"

Tara didn't need further encouragement. She'd already decided what she was going to say, where she would start—she'd listened to the stories her parents, her grandparents, extended family, colleagues of her family, and even random strangers on the streets had told her, for a very long time.

"This isn't the world I was born in," Tara began. "My world was small. Tiny, really, in comparison ... but for me, it was endless. It was home. This place ..." she smiled as her gaze went to the windows, where the massive maple tree stood just outside, its leaves gently rustling in the breeze.

"This place *is* beautiful. But the world my parents were born into, the one they grew up in, was *suffocating*. Too much sun, barely enough shade, and the air seemed to choke the life out of everyone.

"But that world was once beautiful, too. Humans ... *ruined* it. Ruined the only home they had. They polluted it, weaponised it, broke it, till nothing but ashes remained.

"That's why people like my parents decided that they had to find a new home. Somewhere ... they hopefully wouldn't leave pain, fear, and death behind. Somewhere *habitable*."

The interviewer leaned in. "Will you tell us, Tara?" she asked. "Tell us how your parents tried to find another home for us?"

Tara smiled widely, making dimples appear at the sides of her mouth. *Just like your Ma's*, her grandmother always said.

"I'll tell you everything I know."

Chapter 1

In the year 2000, in the backyard of a small bar, the quiet of the night was interrupted in staccato beats at the sounds of angry men jeering, fists pounding at the door—yet not a single soul moved in the backyard. The stars twinkled overhead, their distant light casting a faint glow on the rustic surroundings. It was a typical balmy night in Merritt Island, Florida, with mosquitoes buzzing through the air, filling the silence with an incessant droning.

From inside the bar, the voices of impatient customers grew louder, shouting for someone to open the door and let them in. There was an odd odour of sweaty bodies mixed with the heady sweetness of whiskey emanating from the bar. The wooden walls of the bar seemed to groan in exasperation—they'd barely had time to let the fresh air in before the stink of alcohol, cigarettes, and humans was to be absorbed once again. The atmosphere seemed to almost crackle with electricity as the promise of a night of revelry hung just as heavy in the humid air.

Amidst this commotion sat Harry, a 12-year-old boy, at a weathered wooden table, his gaze fixed upon the sky. He was lost in the beauty of the evening, seemingly unaware of the growing impatience of the customers. The boy's breath formed small puffs of mist in the cool air as a cold breeze swept through the yard. He shivered slightly but remained undeterred, captivated by the celestial display above. His mind wandered, lost in the vastness of the universe, as he contemplated the mysteries of the cosmos. In his considerably short life, this is all he had ever wanted—to be away from the reality of his world here on Earth. And instead, he wanted to fly, weightless, in the vast sky, untethered to anyone and anything.

Suddenly, a stern voice broke through the noise. Harry's grandad strode over and delivered a firm but gentle slap to the boy's shoulder. Harry jumped at the touch, but didn't get up. He simply cocked his head to his side to look at his grandfather's sun-burnt, wizened face inquiringly.

"Harry, what are you doing?"

Harry didn't have to ask what his grandfather meant. It was opening time at the bar, with customers waiting impatiently. He still didn't move. *What if,* he wondered, *I just stayed here forever, gazing up at the stars?*

His grandfather rudely interrupted Harry's trance yet again by grabbing him by the collar of his t-shirt and dragging him off the table.

"Time to work!" he said brusquely. Without looking back, he walked into the bar, leaving a dejected-looking Harry in the backyard.

Harry blinked for a few seconds and then, resigning himself to his fate, walked into the bar. He left the evening sky behind and joined his grandad in attending to the impatient customers. As Harry and his grandad approached the bar's entrance, the shouts from the impatient customers waiting outside grew louder and more aggressive. They were knocking on the door, and one of them, in a fit of frustration, yelled, "Open the door, you son of a bitch!"

Harry's grandad, now even more agitated by the commotion, hurriedly fumbled for the keys, trying to unlock the door as quickly as possible.

With the door now open and the frustrated customers inside, Charlton, Harry's grandad, stepped forward to address them. He apologised for the delay and extended a warm welcome, saying, "I'm sorry for the wait. Please feel free to order whatever you'd like."

Charlton's tiny bar was financially unfavourable due to debt. Despite the challenges, the bar attracted patrons thanks to its unique and eclectic atmosphere. Charlton had added a casino area to the bar to increase the entertainment options, where patrons could try their luck with various games such as poker, slot machines, and blackjack. The bar also boasted a charming, albeit compact, bowling alley. A beautiful chandelier hung from the ceiling, providing a touch of elegance to the otherwise cosy and intimate setting. It cast a soft, warm light over the space, creating a welcoming ambience. Adorning the walls of the bar were decorative animal heads of various species.

As the night wound down, the customers had mostly departed from the bar. Charlton wearily leaned against one of the tables, taking a moment to rest. Harry diligently cleaned and tidied all the tables, making sure everything was in order before joining his grandad. Due to the labour laws, Harry couldn't legally work at the bar, so while the bar was open, he mostly kept to the back, stocking up the alcohol and doing inventory. When all the customers had left, he came out to the main bar and helped with cleaning.

Sipping his drink, Charlton watched Harry with a wistful expression. "You know, Harry, your dad left us a long time ago and left behind all these debts and unpaid bills for this bar. But I'm working hard to clear them all. Soon, we're going to own this bar, and you'll have to look after it."

He took another sip of his drink, his gaze distant, and continued, "I don't know how long I'm going to live, but I want to clear all these debts before I pass on. This bar is our only livelihood, and I want to make sure you have a better future, son."

Harry listened attentively, understanding the weight of the situation and the responsibility that lay ahead. As they sat together on the floor, Harry stayed quiet, intermittently stealing glances at his grandfather. He decided not to tell Charlton that day that he had no intention of chaining himself to a mundane life of serving alcohol in the place where the ghost of his father's betrayal hung heavy in every corner.

*

The next day, delegates of various countries assembled in the Apollo Centre Conference Room at the Kennedy Space Centre. Some people talked amongst themselves, while some rifled through the briefs placed before them, and the rest looked around. The opulence of the conference room –its triangle-shaped table, carpeted floors, and golden ceiling lights was jarring in comparison to the sight outside. Past the ceiling-to-floor windows and palm trees was a vast expanse of empty land, with a giant space shuttle waiting patiently in a corner at the launch site.

At the head of the table was Professor Steve Meyers, Director of Propulsion Mechanics at NASA. He glanced quickly at his own brief and then got to his feet, adjusting his tie. When he cleared his throat, silence fell across the room, every eye now focused on Meyers.

"Good morning, ladies and gentlemen," he began, his tone serious and focused. "Today, we have gathered here with an urgent agenda." He reached for a remote control and activated the projector, illuminating a screen at the front of the room.

On the screen, a news channel called *World News Telecasts* (*WN*) began broadcasting a 'breaking news' report. The reporter's voice filled the room as they delivered a sobering message.

"Earth's condition has been deteriorating," echoed their voice in the conference room. "Natural calamities are striking with increasing frequency. Mountain glaciers are melting, leading to flooding in various regions. Acid rains are affecting parts of the world, and global warming continues its relentless march. If these trends persist, there's a grim possibility that the Earth will, sooner or later, succumb to freezing temperatures, leaving only debris and threatening the extinction of mankind."

Meyers turned off the projector, and a hushed silence fell over the room. The gravity of the situation and the urgent need for action were palpable among the delegates as they prepared to discuss how to address these pressing global challenges.

Turning to Michael Clark, Space Operations Mission Director, Meyers asked, "Director Clark, would you be willing to take the lead in addressing this crisis?"

Clark stood up, nodding solemnly. "Good morning, ladies and gentlemen. I've been closely monitoring these developments for years," he began. "Our primary focus now must be to find a sustainable solution, and that may lie in exploring the possibility of inhabiting other planets."

Meyers nodded. "What do you have in mind, Professor?"

Clark activated the projector again, casting a detailed schematic onto the screen. "We've initiated Project Inhabitation, P-I, for short," he explained. "Our dedicated team is working to assess other planets as potential destinations for long-term human survival."

A murmur spread across the room. While a few heads nodded, others exchanged wary glances.

"That's promising," said Delegate Ludwig. "But what approach are you planning to take, Michael?"

Before Clark could respond, a sharp voice cut through the silence. Dr. Elaine Kumari, Senior Aerospace Engineer, leaned forward, frowning. "With all due respect, Director, are we certain this isn't premature? We've barely scratched the surface of reliable data. What if we're rushing into the unknown?"

"And what about the resources?" added Dr. Youssef, a planetary climatologist. "Even if the data suggests potential, the logistical nightmare of establishing life-support systems on another planet is monumental. Are we really prepared for that?"

Clark kept his gaze steady. "These concerns are valid. But we've trained a specialised team of astronomers, exobiologists, and engineers. Their mission will be to collect precise, on-ground data about atmospheric composition, geological stability, and sustainability indicators. We've been preparing for this quietly for years."

Dr. Kumari still looked unconvinced. "Preparation doesn't guarantee success. If we send teams into unstable planetary systems without conclusive data, we're risking lives and our already stretched resources."

A tense pause followed.

Clark exhaled slowly, then continued, "Over the past decade, our research divisions have been analysing data from satellite imaging, unmanned probes, and telescopic observation. The signs are there. Certain exoplanets show promising conditions: some with oxygen traces, others with water in frozen or vapour form. We believe these worlds could support life, or at the very least, offer critical resources to support ours."

There was a beat of silence before Dr. Youssef said, more quietly, "Belief is not certainty."

"I agree," Clark replied. "But waiting for certainty may be a luxury we no longer have. Earth's climate systems are collapsing faster than predicted. This mission isn't about abandoning Earth. It's about buying time. And options."

At the head of the room, Meyers glanced around at the tense faces. "Enough," he said firmly. "The risks are high, yes, but so are the stakes. Do we have an alternative?"

Everyone was quiet. Meyers then rose slowly from his chair. "I've reviewed the preliminary reports. There are holes, yes, but also potential. We move forward cautiously, but decisively. Granted. Proceed with Project Inhabitation (P-I). Our future depends on your team's success, Clark. Make it count."

Clark nodded once, his jaw tight, eyes scanning the room full of sceptics. He knew the real battle was only beginning.

With the project officially approved, the assembly of delegates and scientists left the meeting with a sense of purpose, knowing that the future of humanity may hinge on the success of their efforts to find a new home beyond Earth.

*

In the year 1990, just one week before the highly anticipated launch, employees of the Space Research Centre (SRC) gathered in the Space Launch Control (SLC) room. The atmosphere is charged with excitement and anticipation as everyone prepares for this historic moment.

In the front of the room stood Clark, a dynamic figure in his mid-thirties. He was wearing a sharp, tailored suit and ran his hand through his straw-coloured hair. Although he had the presence of a confident man, if anyone noticed him closely, they'd see the sheen of sweat on his forehead, how sweaty his palms were, and how his heartbeat seemed to be going a million beats a second—a chink in the armour. He stood before a projector displaying detailed blueprints of the spaceship and rockets. Meyers, along with space centre delegates and employees, listened intently to his explanation.

Clark began, "Ladies and gentlemen, thank you for assembling here today. As we prepare for this momentous launch, let me walk you through the design and functionality of our spaceship."

He stepped to the front and gestured towards the projector screen as it hummed to life. A sleek blueprint of the spacecraft glowed in electric blue.

"Our spacecraft, *Echolight*, is equipped with three powerful engines," he said, his voice cutting through the hush of the room.

The diagram was zoomed in and two large thrusters flared to life in animated detail, flames licking the edges of the frame.

"These two will handle the initial propulsion," Clark continued, tapping the image. "They're designed to generate an immense burst of force and speed during liftoff."

Lines of data and speed vectors swirled around the engines on screen, the numbers climbing rapidly.

"We've calculated every inch of thrust needed," he said almost proudly, "to break Earth's grip and launch us into the void."

The room was filled with focused attention as everyone absorbed the technical details. Clark continued, "Once we're in the sky, the backup engine comes into play. This space shuttle is designed for its voyage to the first planet on our exploration mission, where our team of dedicated astronomers will begin their planetary exploration."

A murmur of awe rippled through the room as Clark spoke. One engineer leaned forward, eyes fixed on the screen, lips parted in silent calculation. Meyers folded his arms, a rare smile tugging at the corner of his mouth. Across the table, a delegate scribbled furiously in a notebook, while another tapped their pen against their knee, barely containing their energy. Someone at the back exhaled sharply, almost a whistle, before biting their nail to the quick. Heads nodded, some slowly, some with sharp, eager movements—every face lit with the weight and wonder of what was coming.

As part of the comprehensive space exploration mission, leading up to the launch of the spaceship, the Space Research Centre (SRC) implemented a unique approach. Before sending astronauts and the main spacecraft to the planets, they launched specialised space vehicles to each of the target planets in the year 1985. These vehicles were designed as towering structures, housing advanced equipment, and a significant innovation known as the Cataract Disc.

Each space vehicle was equipped with a Cataract Disc, a cutting-edge data collection and storage device. The disc contained a vast repository of information about the particular planet it was sent to explore. It included details about the planet's geology, atmosphere, climate, potential resources, and any other relevant scientific information.

The launch of these space vehicles marked the first phase of the mission, allowing scientists and researchers to gather crucial preliminary data from various planets in the solar system. This data served as a foundation for planning and decision-making for the subsequent stages, including the manned mission onboard the spaceship.

The Cataract Discs, with their comprehensive planetary data, were instrumental in ensuring that astronauts and scientists had the essential knowledge needed to conduct successful explorations and research on each planet. This groundbreaking approach represented a significant step forward in space exploration and laid the groundwork for humanity's continued journey beyond Earth.

*

Four days before the launch, with preparations in their final stages, the three astronauts set aside some precious moments to bid their families farewell.

One of the astronauts who lived in Florida, Bill Andrews, went back home after being called out of a week-long gravity testing exercise. He stood in front of the door, took a deep breath and rang the doorbell. His wife, Susan, opened the door. She gasped in delight, but her brow immediately furrowed in confusion.

"Bill? What are you doing home? You weren't supposed to be here till ... Monday, right?" Susan said, unsure herself.

Bill smiled warmly, "They let me come home early, hon."

Before Susan could ask why, Bill pulled out a bouquet of red roses from behind him. She gasped once again and took the flowers with a huge smile on her face.

"Happy anniversary, sweetheart."

*

Susan ran around the kitchen, flustered, and Bill watched on with a fond smile as she kept saying that since she wasn't expecting him so soon, and she didn't have any fancy food in the house to prepare. But Bill calmed her down and convinced her that hot dogs sounded divine, and they'd have a candle-lit dinner in their backyard. A bottle of sparkling wine hidden deep inside a dusty cupboard saved the day, and Bill and

Susan sat down to eat, savouring the moment and each other's company.

As they gazed at the stars and the beautiful moon in the night sky, Susan sighed. "Look at the stars and the beautiful moon. How romantic it is, Bill!" she said, resting her head on his shoulder.

"Yes, it is."

"I want to freeze this moment," Susan said with a smile.

Bill smiled in agreement, and they both continued to admire the celestial display above.

Then, with a mix of excitement and surprise, Bill dropped some life-changing news. "What if I tell you that I got a chance to travel to another planet?"

His wife was momentarily stunned, taking in the revelation. "What?" she said, her voice trembling with a mixture of astonishment and pride.

"You heard it right. I am going to fly to another planet."

Susan was overwhelmed by the news and instead just stared at Bill, lost for words. She was, of course, proud and excited for Bill—he had been working for a chance like this for years and years. She had seen how much of himself he had poured into his work. But at the same time, she was *terrified.* It was a necessary expedition, of course, she knew that, but what would it mean for Bill? For herself? For them? What did they *truly* know existed in the vast space of the universe? And how long would it be till Susan would see the love of her life again?

But, like always, she composed herself. Blinking back tears, she squeezed Bill's hand. "Your dream has finally come true."

Deeply moved and grateful for her understanding, Bill leaned in and kissed her affectionately. Their wedding anniversary had become a momentous occasion filled with love, dreams, and the promise of an extraordinary adventure in the vastness of space.

As the reality of Bill's imminent departure set in, his wife couldn't help but express her concern. "When are you leaving?" Susan asked, her voice tinged with sadness.

Bill gently replied, "I am leaving tomorrow, and the rocket launch will be in a couple of days."

Tears welled up in Susan's eyes as she processed the fact that Bill would soon be embarking on this extraordinary journey. "And you will leave me too," she said, her voice quivering with emotion.

Standing face to face, their foreheads touching, they locked eyes, finding solace and understanding in each other's gaze.

"I'll come back."

*

The next morning, with a heavy heart, Bill kissed his wife and quietly said *good morning*, after which he turned to pack his luggage. The early light spilt through the curtains, casting long, golden shadows across the floor. His wife stood silently by the doorway, arms wrapped around herself, watching each careful movement he made. Her heart was racing against her chest, as she didn't know whether, or even *if*, she would see Bill again.

She wandered into the living room, fingers trailing across the frames on the mantelpiece. Their photos smiled back at her—beach trips, birthdays, quiet Sundays filled with laughs. A lump rose in her throat as she sat down, the worn leather couch creaking under her. Pride shimmered behind her eyes, but it was swallowed by the ache of longing. Their home, once forged in everyday moments, now had to withstand silence, distance, and the terrifying unknown of space. Each of them was about to embark on a journey—Bill into the stars, Susan into the hollow quiet of waiting.

*

The second astronaut, Uday, arrived at his home and rang the doorbell. He could hear the familiar sound of his dog barking excitedly from the inside. When his mother opened the door, Uday greeted her with a warm smile and lifted his beloved dog in his arms.

"How are you doing, Amma and Appa?" Uday asked.

"We are good," Appa replied, taking a sip of his coffee. "How about you?"

Uday responded, "Not bad."

His mother, brimming with enthusiasm, showed Uday a photo and declared, "We have decided for you to get married. Her dad is a successful businessman, and she is an engineering graduate from Harvard."

"I have something to say," he announced, straightening his back like he was about to deliver a presidential address. "I'm flying to another planet."

There was a beat of silence. His parents blinked.

"Another excuse?" his mother asked, arms already crossing. "Last week it was an allergy to commitment, now it's interplanetary travel?"

"No, Amma, really!" Uday insisted. "This time, I actually *can't* get married. I'll be ... unavailable. Possibly unreachable."

His announcement left his parents in shock. His mother's jaw dropped open in disbelief as she realised that Uday was not joking. Unable to form any words, she turned to her husband for support, but confusion blurred the edges of his face, too.

"What? Why on earth would you go to space and leave us here? This is ridiculous," Amma exclaimed.

His father, though visibly concerned, remained silent, shaking his head in incredulity.

Uday, sensing their disapproval and knowing he didn't have time for a lengthy discussion, said hastily, "Let's talk when I am back."

*

As the third astronaut started his car engine and began the journey toward his home, he couldn't help but be overwhelmed by a sudden surge of emotions. He was halfway through his journey when he abruptly stopped the car on the roadside. With a heavy heart, he took out a photo of his family from the dashboard and gazed at it.

Tears welled up in his eyes as the weight of the mission settled heavily on his chest. It wasn't just the danger or the unknown, it was the cost. The photograph in his hand trembled slightly as he stared at it. His wife's beautiful smile was frozen in time, radiant and full of quiet joy as she held their baby boy to her chest. The child's tiny hand was curled against her collarbone, his eyes half-closed in sleep, unaware of the world or the future that loomed ahead.

A lump formed in his throat. That moment, captured in perfect stillness, reminded him of everything he was about to leave behind: bedtime stories, shared laughter over dinner, the feel of his son's fingers gripping his own. The room around him faded, replaced by the echo of a life he would soon only carry in memory. The mission ahead was historic, monumental. But this ... this was his home.

In a moment of deep reflection, he made a difficult decision. He turned the car around, heading back in the direction of the space centre. The call of duty and the weight of the mission weighed heavily on his mind, and he knew that he must return to complete the preparations for the extraordinary journey that lay ahead.

*

As the launch day drew near, the astronauts were wholly focused, immersed in final preparations for the journey ahead. With just a day remaining, they underwent a final round of intense physical and psychological evaluations designed to ensure they were in optimal condition for the mission.

Inside the medical facility, doctors and technicians performed exhaustive health assessments: monitored vital signs, tested muscle strength, and reviewed each astronaut's physical readiness with meticulous precision. Every detail was scrutinised; nothing was left to chance.

At the same time, psychologists and mental health specialists were conducting one-on-one sessions, gauging emotional resilience and providing tailored strategies to help manage the intense psychological demands of space travel. It wasn't just the body that must endure the unknown, it was the mind, too.

Elsewhere, the crew reviewed mission protocols, conducted comprehensive equipment checks, and ran high-pressure simulation drills, rehearsing every possible emergency scenario. Each procedure was committed to memory; every variable accounted for. Years of training converged into these final moments of preparation.

As the countdown entered its final hours, a charged sense of anticipation filled the space centre. The atmosphere was electric: an emotional blend of pride, nerves, and focused energy. Years of innovation, sacrifice, and hard work were about to culminate in one defining moment.

Technicians and engineers swarmed the launchpad, conducting last-minute diagnostics to ensure *Echolight's* systems were operating flawlessly. In mission control, eyes were glued to the monitors, voices low and urgent as teams ran through final checklists and contingency plans.

Dressed in their suits, the astronauts gathered for their final checklists and contingency plans. Their faces revealed a mixture of exhilaration and the solemn awareness of the risks ahead. They exchanged quiet words of encouragement, nods of understanding, united not just by mission, but by purpose.

Soon, they would leave the Earth behind. But in those final moments, they carried with them the collective hopes of all those who had prepared them for this journey into the unknown.

Outside, the launchpad stood tall, ready to propel the spacecraft into the great unknown. The sky above the space centre was streaked with shades of pink and orange as dawn broke– nature's own drumroll for the historic event to come. A growing crowd had gathered at the viewing site, their eyes fixed on the towering rocket silhouetted against the morning light. Among them stood Bill's wife, clutching their son to her chest, Uday's parents holding hands tightly, and dozens of other spectators wrapped in blankets, binoculars in hand, hearts thudding with the ticking clock.

Loudspeakers echoed the countdown: "T-minus ten minutes". Each second shaved off sent ripples through the gathering. Children perched on their parents' shoulders, journalists murmured into microphones. Even the wind seemed to hush in reverence.

The tension in the air was electric, like static before a storm. In the control room, rows of monitors blinked to life, casting a cold glow on the focused faces of mission control.

Fingers danced across keyboards, voices crackled through headsets, and Michael Clark stood behind the engineers, arms crossed tightly. He tried to appear calm, but his pacing gave him away. His thoughts raced, every equation double-checked, every risk calculated–but still, anything could happen once those engines fired.

Back on the launchpad, the astronauts climbed into a specialised vehicle that would take them to the rocket. Inside, silence reigned at first, broken only by the soft hiss of oxygen tanks and the mechanical *click* of suit adjustments. Then, a few whispered words passed between them–encouragement, camaraderie, even a quiet joke to steady their nerves. They were strapped in now, eyes scanning details and readouts, minds steeled for the mission ahead.

The countdown clock ticked down into its final minutes. Engines rumbled beneath the earth, a low, growing growl that vibrated through the soles of everyone's feet. Spectators held their breath. A bird took flight from the nearby marshes as if it too felt the moment approach.

Cameras were positioned at multiple angles–most of them were focused on *Echolight* itself, while others swivelled between reporters, the crowd around the launch site, and the vast landscape and them. In the sky, a safe distance from the spaceship, were drones and helicopters, providing aerial views of the launch site.

As the moment of launch arrived, the astronauts were inside the spacecraft, their suits pressurised, and their hearts pounding with a mix of excitement and trepidation. Inside the control room, the space centre crew members are in close communication with the astronauts, conducting final checks and receiving their confirmations.

"Engine," said one crew member, her voice steady and resolute.

The chief engineer responsible for the propulsion systems responded, "Go."

"Booster," another crew member announced.

The engineer in charge of the boosters echoed, "Go."

"Electrical," said the third crew member.

The electrical engineer confirmed, "Go."

The countdown to launch continued, and the automated voice seemed to boom louder as the numbering reached the ten-second mark. The frenzied atmosphere seemed to almost vibrate with anticipation and excitement.

T-minus 10 seconds.

The engines were primed, and final checks were underway.

T-minus 9 seconds.

All the systems were announced "go". The astronauts braced themselves inside *Echolight* for the intense G-forces that would accompany liftoff.

T-minus 8 seconds.

The control room was now filled with hushed voices and the clicking of keyboards as the engineers monitored *Echolight's* systems in real time.

T-minus 7 seconds.

The astronauts exchanged glances, despite the fact that the glare from the equipment lights and ignition made their faces hide behind their helmet visors. The spaceship's engines rumbled, and the vibrations could be felt throughout the entire pod.

T-minus 6 seconds.

The astronauts collectively took a deep breath and gripped their seats—all the systems were ready.

T-minus 5 seconds.

The control room seemed to hum with activity as the engineers and mission control personnel monitored every detail.

T-minus 4 seconds.

The crowd surrounding the launch site, which till now was full of voices and excited sounds, seemed to exist in pin-drop silence, as though every single person was holding their breath.

T-minus 3 seconds.

Echolight's engines roared to life, sending tremors through the launchpad.

T-minus 2 seconds.

Even the control room fell into a hushed silence, with everyone focused on every single monitor around them, looking for any complication that might pop up.

T-minus 1 second.

"Ready for liftoff," announced Launch Director, Laura Andrews, her voice filled with determination.

While the astronauts were on their exhilarating journey into space, far away from the space centre and the launchpad, young Harry was having a simpler yet magical experience of his own.

Chasing a butterfly near the barn, Harry found himself at the end of the barn's structure. He watched in awe as the butterfly gracefully landed on a fence nearby. Just as he was about to reach out and gently touch it, both the butterfly and the spaceship took flight into the sky.

While the butterfly fluttered off in perfect silence, in an explosion of power and fire, the spacecraft lifted off the launchpad with an incredible burst of speed and force. The Earth shook, and the astronauts were pressed into their seats.

Clark was overwhelmed by the marvel of the spacecraft's capabilities. "She's even more beautiful than I thought she'd be."

His words resonated with everyone on board, and a wave of enthusiasm swept through the spacecraft. The astronauts, engineers, and mission control team exchanged high-fives and joyful glances, celebrating the success of the launch and the incredible speed and power of their vessel.

The spacecraft had launched flawlessly. Numbers on the screen danced in perfect alignment, and all systems were green. But then–

BEEP. BEEP. BEEP.

The sharp sounds of alarms sliced through the jubilation. Red lights began flashing on the main console, interrupting the celebration with a chilling urgency. One by one, the monitors blinked red. Propulsion System: UNSTABLE. Pressure Readings: SPIKING. Containment Integrity: COMPROMISED.

"Wait, what's going on with Engine Module 2?" one of the technicians shouted, typing furiously.

"Control to *Echolight*, do you copy?" Laura barked into her headset, voice tight with worry. "We're getting erratic readouts on propulsion. Can you confirm the status on your end?"

A brief, calculating silence. Then the astronauts' voice came through, faint and laced with static.

"This is *Echolight*. We're reading some instability ... trying to run diagnostics now. Pressure's ... hold on, pressure's rising in the aft chamber. We're ..."

BEEP. BEEP. BEEP.

"*Echolight*, evacuate the propulsion corridor immediately!" a voice shouted from ground control. "Repeat, clear the aft chamber now. You're in critical breach!"

"Copy, we're ..."

The signal was suddenly cut. For a second, all was still. The room held its collective breath.

Then, it happened.

High above Earth, in the silence of space, a brilliant burst of light flared from the rear of the spacecraft. The propulsion system failed catastrophically, sending an enormous inward surge of energy through the ship's core. The containment hull around the astronauts' chamber couldn't hold. In a blinding instant, the breach tore through the craft.

An inferno bloomed within the ship, consuming equipment, walls and lives in a flash of fire and pressure. The screen feeds at ground control erupted into static. A deathly silence followed.

***

Chapter II

In the Space Centre, everybody was seriously looking at Clark, treating him as a culprit, and taking him to a conference room. Meyers expressed his profound disappointment and frustration over the catastrophic failure of the spaceship.

"We spent around a million dollars on this spaceship, and it collapsed with a bloody propulsion effect. What is this nonsense?" Meyers exclaimed, his voice filled with anger and disbelief.

He turned his attention to the team responsible for the mission, including Clark. "I admire your dedication, but this is not acceptable," he says, his stern tone emphasising the gravity of the situation. "An investigation team will interrogate you."

Inside the interrogation room, Clark, Laura and the other team members found themselves facing a gruelling process. They had to provide justifications and explanations for the propulsion effect and the catastrophic failure that led to the loss of the spaceship and its crew.

Clark, in particular, was tasked with defending the decisions and actions that were taken in the mission's planning and execution. He had to navigate the intense scrutiny and pressure as he attempted to shed light on the tragic events that unfolded in space, providing insights into the propulsion system and the circumstances that led to its failure.

In the space centre, a meeting was convened by the Director of NASA, James Wong, attended by Clark, Meyers and Laura. The board members and space centre delegates decided on their service.

Wong delivered the news, stating that they had decided on a soft suspension of their services within the space centre. This shocking announcement left Clark, Meyers, and Laura in disbelief.

Meyers expressed his frustration, emphasising the unfairness of their dismissal. He pointed out the years of hard work and dedication that went into building the spaceship and training astronauts, making their dreams come true. Clark joined in, highlighting the long years of struggle they endured to reach this point in their careers. Both men were upset by the decision and found it difficult to accept. Laura was quiet throughout it all; she was the closest to the astronauts as compared to the others. She just muttered something about the captain rightfully going down with the ship.

Wong, however, emphasised that the decision was not his alone and assured them that an investigation was underway. The focus of the inquiry was the propulsion effect and whether there was any malfunction in the booster engine, which resulted in flames eroding the shields of the booster and spreading throughout the spaceship before separation. The investigation was ongoing, leaving the fate of Clark, Meyers, and Laura uncertain.

*

That day, when Clark picked up his daughter Ruma from school, she immediately knew that something bad had happened. Her father had always been a quiet person, and his face was always a picture of concentration. But something was different that day—he was quiet, but his face was blank, like all the emotion had left his body. And then Ruma spotted a large cardboard box on the back seat with photo frames and a plant that she knew Clark kept on his desk at work.

Ruma, of course, knew about the tragic events that unfolded during *Echolight's* launch—she'd watched the news, alongside her classmates at school, and had felt a horrible sinking feeling when she realised that not only had people died, but the mission was her father's baby, and he had failed.

"Dad, why did the spaceship collapse?" Ruma asked, unable to bear the silence in the car anymore.

Clark took a deep breath. "There was an issue with the engine, Ruma."

"How many astronauts were there in the spaceship?" Ruma inquired further.

"Three," Prof. Clark responded.

Innocently, Ruma whispered, "Oh my God, they're all dead."

A heavy silence fell over the car as they both grappled with the weight of the tragedy. Clark, finding it difficult to continue the drive, decided to make a stop at a nearby bar.

"Ruma, come with me," Clark said as he exited the car. They walked inside the bar, and Ruma felt immediately unsure of her surroundings. Clark never took her to places like this. In fact, the only time she'd seen her father drink was in the safety of their home. But she was too concerned about her father's emotionless face and quiet voice to question why they were there. He took off his coat and placed it on a chair before they sat down.

Harry approached their table and asked, "What would you like to have, sir?"

Clark noticed that Harry was too young to work at a bar, but he found that he didn't give enough of a damn at that moment to question it. He asked for a double whiskey on the rocks while Ruma looked around, taking in the surroundings of the bar.

Ruma's presence distracted Harry as his gaze shifted towards her. He found her adorable as he looked into her expressive eyes, soft cheeks, and blonde hair.

After serving drinks to Clark. Harry, still holding the tray with steady hands, asked Ruma, "What would you like to have?"

Ruma, at that moment, lifted her head and looked at Harry. Her gaze met his, and the first thing she noticed was that they both seemed to have a similar skin tone—a warm caramel colour that glowed under Harry's light blue eyes. He was tall for his age and had messy hair that seemed to half cover his eyes. Harry felt an odd sense of comfort when he saw Ruma and felt as though he'd known her in a previous life. She had worn a neat little blue dress and clung to Clark like she was expecting him to run away and leave her any second. Harry couldn't explain the immediate feeling of protectiveness that took over him towards Ruma.

Ruma, with a sweet and slightly bashful smile, said, "Um, can I have a glass of apple juice, please?"

"Sure," Harry said.

Once Harry left, Ruma turned back to look at her father. His face was drooping, his eyes fixed somewhere in the distance, although by the glazed look in them, she knew he was somewhere far, far away. She couldn't bear to look at him this way—broken, distraught, nursing his whiskey like it was the only thing that was giving him a sense of being alive. She decided to get up from her seat, keeping her eyes on Clark. Once she realised that he didn't care about her presence, she walked away from their table.

As she walked around, one of the customers yelled at the older gentleman serving drinks at the bar counter, "Hey, old man. I ordered a scotch. How long does it take?"

His eyes then went towards Ruma, and an awful grin spread across his face, like he'd spotted his favourite dish at a buffet. He angled his body towards her, and she felt even smaller than usual as she tried not to focus on his yellowed, pointed teeth and how his tongue kept flicking against his dry, chapped lips as though he were a lizard and she were a tasty fly. Ruma decided to step back from the man, yet she didn't watch where she was going and nearly crashed into an already drunk man who upturned most of his drink just inches away from Ruma's toes.

Feeling scared and overwhelmed, Ruma began to run back towards the bar table. At that moment, Harry swiftly reacted. He grabbed her wrist gently but firmly and guided her away from the commotion, leading her to a quieter space.

Harry hushed her by placing his palm over her mouth and reassured her, saying, "Shh, don't be scared. My name is Harry. I work here, help clean up and stuff. This is my grandpa's bar." He then removed his hand from her mouth. "What's your name?"

Ruma didn't answer for a few seconds. Her heartbeat was still going a million miles per hour, but there was something calming and reassuring about Harry's presence. "My name is Ruma Sharma. My dad is a scientist who works at the space centre."

Harry's eyes widened. "Wow, that's amazing!" His expression turned wistful, and as Ruma watched him, it was as if he'd disappeared into a different world. Before she could say anything, he snapped out of his reverie, gently placed his hand on her wrist and lifted them up. "Come with me, I'll show you something."

Leading her to his closet, Harry shoved all the clothes aside to reveal a mural on the wall. The mural was a beautifully hand-drawn depiction of a spaceship; the sky was filled with stars, planets, galaxies, and the entire solar system.

Ruma, with wide-eyed wonder, gazed at the fantastical artwork and asked, "Did you draw all of this?"

Harry nodded bashfully, watching as Ruma admired his work. He couldn't help but feel slightly proud at her reaction—he'd never shown these to anybody, not even his grandfather, who would probably berate him for wasting time on such things.

"Which school are you studying at?" Ruma asked.

Harry's pride immediately dissolved into a deep-seated embarrassment as he avoided Ruma's eyes. "I ... I don't go to school. This is my part-time job. My full-time job is as a mechanic's assistant, although to be very honest, most of the work I do there involves cleaning." He smiled warmly.

He fully expected Ruma to ask more questions or look strangely at him. Instead, she just returned his smile, and her eyes went back to her father. There were now three empty glasses in front of him, and his shoulders were sagging more and more. She sighed and felt a horrible sadness seep into her bones as she wondered how and if Clark would ever be okay again.

Harry noticed all of this, and he was bowled over at the look of sadness on Ruma's small face. He then placed a hand on her wrist gently, led her out of the room, leaving Clark to his thoughts as he continued to drink.

They found a secluded spot under one table. “Look at this, Ruma,” Harry said excitedly.

Under the table, a hidden world of imagination unfolded. Harry pointed to a bowling ball hanging from the table, exactly at the centre of a tambourine with a single row of jingles. He had created a miniature solar system, with the bowling ball representing the sun and the table tennis balls inside the tambourine serving as planets.

Above the tennis balls, there was a dart symbolising the spaceship, and a deer horn served as the pilot’s control wheel. The planets revolved around the sun while the spaceship appeared to travel through the system.

With a flourish, Harry switched on a blue light, transforming the top of the table into a dazzling night sky, complete with twinkling stars.

He took hold of the deer horn, mimicking the actions of a pilot, and turned to Ruma. “Look, Ruma, this is how I’m piloting the spaceship.”

Ruma, enchanted by the miniature solar system and the simulation of space travel, exclaimed, “This is amazing!”

Harry, still excited, continued, “You know, in space, we’ll be weightless. We’ll float. There’s no gravity at all.” He raised his hands in the air and pretended to float.

But the duo’s childish joy at Harry’s creation was short-lived as their conversation was interrupted by Clark, who, in his inebriated state, yelled out that this would be his final drink. He mumbled for the bill, and Charlton responded promptly.

“Sir, $35,” Charlton stated.

Professor Clark placed $40 on the table and said, "Keep the change."

"Thank you, sir," Charlton replied gratefully.

Ruma and Harry decided to move on to another activity. They made their way to the roulette game, where Harry turned on the roulette wheel and released the ball.

"Choose a number," Harry suggested to Ruma. The roulette wheel spun, and the ball began its unpredictable journey. With smiles exchanged between them, Ruma decided to choose the number 4 as the roulette game began. Harry activated the roulette wheel, and as the ball spun, it miraculously landed in the slot marked with the number 4.

Ruma could hardly contain her excitement, exclaiming, "I'm lucky! I'm lucky!"

However, a few seconds later, to her surprise, the ball moved to number 18. She looked at Harry with an expression that was part confusion and part betrayal, as though the game had purposefully cheated her.

Harry leaned in to explain, "It's a gambling game, Ruma. The ball has a magnet built into it, and I control its movement with another magnet that's inside the roulette. That's how we play this game."

Ruma smiled slyly at Harry. "So, that's how you cheat people?"

Harry, with a playful grin, offered his perspective, "It's a part of the game, Ruma."

Ruma and Harry then made their way to the dartboard game, nestled conveniently beside the roulette table. As she took the dart, Ruma instinctively gripped it like a pen, awkward and unsure. Harry noticed, and with a quiet, guiding gesture, repositioned her fingers, his hand brushing against hers. Their eyes met briefly, a silent moment of connection passing between them. He stood behind her, helping her draw back her arm and guiding the release. The dart sailed cleanly through the air and struck the centre of the board. Ruma's face lit up with pure exhilaration, her body practically vibrating with joy. In a spontaneous burst of excitement, she threw her arms around Harry, hugging him tightly as laughter bubbled between them.

Their evening carried forward to the bowling alley, where Harry patiently demonstrated the correct grip and technique. Ruma struggled at first—the ball felt heavy in her small hands—but determination flickered in her eyes. Mimicking Harry's instructions, she took a few careful steps, bent her knees and released. The ball spun down the lane and crashed into the pins with a satisfying clatter as every single one toppled. They erupted in celebration, their high-fives echoing like small explosions of glee, and their feet stamped in joy. Their laughter came easily now, unfiltered, and free.

*

After closing the bar, Charlton leaned wearily against the table. Harry took care of the closing routine, turning off all the lights in the bar except for the one at their table.

Harry brought a drink and set it down beside his grandfather. Charlton took a sip from his glass and let out a heavy sigh. "Ha, I am tired. I am tired of serving those fucking idiots." His words were laced with anger, and he took another drink, visibly distressed.

Charlton then poured all the money and coins they earned today onto the table he was sitting at. He took another sip of his drink. "This is what we earned today. God knows if we'll ever have enough money."

Harry listened quietly to his grandfather's words, the same underlying accusation evident. He was used to Charlton saying these words on a daily basis; Harry had made peace with the fact that there was nothing *he* could do about it. *But why should I have to answer for my father's recklessness? Why do I have to be punished for my deadbeat father's actions?* These were the questions that shuttled around Harry's mind every day, especially when Charlton would start grumbling about the bar and the debt.

Harry was *twelve*, for crying out loud. People his age were going to school, complaining about homework, getting skinned knees after playing football. And here he was—wiping sticky countertops, cleaning alcohol-stained glass after glass, and building a vocabulary of solely swear words, thanks to the quality of people that came through the doors every night. Where was the normal childhood that he was entitled to?

Charlton, with a mixture of weariness and resolve, told Harry, "Go, kiddo, go to bed."

*

The night took a tumultuous turn for Clark and Ruma as he drove recklessly, displaying rude and aggressive behaviour. His erratic driving terrified Ruma. She pressed her small body against the seat of the car with so much pressure that she was bound to leave a mark. Her fingers were like claws as they held onto the seats. At every hairpin turn that Clark took, Ruma's widened eyes went to her father's, hoping to make him look, make him see how frightened she was. But he just stared ahead, eyes looking glazed and dead. Ruma had an awful feeling that he wouldn't even know if they died in a fiery car crash. Eventually, they arrived home, and Clark turned off the car engine. As he got out of the car, he hobbled, swaying from side to side.

Clark and Sameera were not married, but they had Ruma together. They had a tumultuous relationship, and Sameera never trusted Clark because he was barely at home and was always too busy to spend time with his own daughter. On official documents and in school, Ruma took her mother's name because Sameera insisted that her father was barely present in her life, so why should she carry his name? In his inebriated state, Clark urgently knocked on their house's door. It was almost midnight when he repeatedly called for Sameera to open it. Barely conscious, he leaned his head against the doorbell, causing it to ring even louder.

Sameera, hastily descending the stairs while tying her nightdress, opened the door to the chaotic scene. Clark, in his drunken state, leaned against her and greeted her with slurred words, "Hey, Sameera, my darling. How are you doing?"

Sameera's lips pressed into a thin line at the sight of Clark's state. "Are you drunk?"

Ruma intervened, saying, "Mom."

Sameera looked to her daughter for confirmation. "Is your dad drunk?"

Reluctantly, Ruma responded, "A little bit."

Sameera said nothing and stared at the duo for a while instead. She looked at Clark, who was swaying so violently that he was sure to pass out there and then. She, of course, knew why he was acting this way—she had seen how much of himself he'd poured into *Echolight*, only for it all to burst into flames right in front of his very eyes. But what hurt her the most was the sight of her daughter, Ruma, still in her school uniform, eyes wide with anxiety and fear, trembling slightly and smelling faintly of alcohol. *That bastard took her with him to some horrible bar to drown his sorrows in. Just when I think he couldn't be a worse father than he already is*, Sameera thought.

Ruma was filled with relief as her mother let her and Clark pass. It was a great relief to be back in the safety of her home. She watched as Clark wrapped an arm around Sameera for support as she led him upstairs to their bedroom.

Ruma was told to sleep in her room downstairs, a quiet command masked as routine. But as the walls weren't thick enough to muffle the chaos above. From her bed, she could hear the sharp rise and fall of voices coming from her father's deep, clipped tone rising in frustration, her mother's voice brittle and defiant in response. The words were muffled, but the anger was unmistakable, echoing through the house like a slow-building storm. Furniture scraped against the floor, and something slammed. Then came the *crack*–sharp, sudden, and the unmistakable sound of a slap. Ruma froze, her body going rigid under the covers. Shame, fear, and helplessness coiled tight in her chest. She pressed the pillow over her ears, but it was no use. The room grew quiet again, only to be replaced by the rhythmic creaking of the bed.

It was always like this. Violence bleeding into intimacy. Rage dissolving into panting, muffled gasps. Ruma would lie awake, paralysed by the knowledge of it, each sound etched into her memory like scars she couldn't see. She didn't understand completely yet, but something about it made her feel hollow and small. As if the world was shifting in a way that left no space for her. She would clutch her blanket tighter and count backwards from a hundred, desperately trying to block out the noises, to hold on to something steady in the middle of the storm.

***

Chapter III

Ten years later

In the year 2010, Michael Clark found a new home in Alabama, where he became a faculty member at Marshal Academy, a prestigious part of NASA Academy. His lessons specialised in space, spaceships, and the significance of space exploration. He passionately encouraged his students to dream big and reach for the stars, emphasising that the sky was not their limit. He instilled in them the belief that, with advancing technology, they could aspire to fly to other planets and explore the cosmos.

Among the students at Marshal was also Ruma, who was pursuing her education in the field of aeronautics. There was a part of Ruma who had thought long and hard about not following her father's footsteps. She knew how much hard work a job in aerospace involved, how much you had to sacrifice. And this feeling of doubt had made its root into Ruma's bones after *Echolight's* explosion. Clark had gone completely underground after that. Even though he was employed a year later after his suspension, he still carried that guilt and shame. For Ruma, it was painful to look at her father like that, and she was too afraid of how *she would* react if something similar happened when *she* led a team.

Yet Ruma knew that she was deeply passionate about the world that existed beyond the Earth. Every little facet of information she'd learnt through her father over the years had filled her with a longing to go to outer space so strong that she could almost taste it.

So, she pressed the brakes on her fears and decided to work every waking hour to fill her father's shoes. She didn't just start training to be an astronaut; she also took up specialities in AI engineering and taught herself how to write code.

*

Still in Merritt Island, Florida, Harry had turned twenty-two and was now working as a mechanic in a domestic airline. It was through his uncle, Richard, whom he was the assistant of when he used to work for as a child, that he got this job. Harry knew that it wasn't the best job in the world, but he saw it as a win–it kept him away from the dankness of his grandfather's bar and the memories it brought, and brought him closer to the world of aviation.

Furthermore, the fact that the airline was involved in astronaut training, which included tests, piloting, and mechanics, presented exciting opportunities for Harry and also provided the opportunity to meet people who worked at NASA. He sometimes hesitated to pick their brains, but everyone he had met from NASA, including scientists, engineers, and pilots, had all been extremely patient and indulgent as they explained different projects to him. They would also be very impressed by Harry's passion for aerospace and the work that he conducted on the Earth-bound machines.

The Helicopter and Spaceship Maintenance Hangar was bustling with activity. Technicians were inspecting and working on various aircraft, including a helicopter and a spaceship. Harry, now a seasoned mechanic, was engrossed in examining the helicopter's engine.

Harry scratched his head, "There's room for improvement here. The rotor blades seem slightly misaligned, and the engine could use a tune-up for better speed and efficiency."

The helicopter technician, Marcus, approached Harry, "Well, you're always full of ideas. What do you suggest?"

Harry thought for a few seconds, "Well, first, let's adjust the rotor blades' angles to ensure better lift and reduced drag. That should help with speed." He walked in circles around the helicopter, still examining its components. "Also, consider fine-tuning the engine's fuel injection system. We might need to recalibrate the air-fuel mixture for optimal combustion."

Marcus nodded in agreement and took notes of Harry's suggestions, instructing the junior mechanics to implement the changes. Harry was always bemused at the fact that Marcus never validated this information for himself and trusted Harry's judgment beyond anyone else's.

They then walked to another part of the hangar, where a spaceship was undergoing maintenance. Harry always felt a wave of respect pass over him whenever a piece of machinery or equipment was sent over from NASA. No matter how big or small, Harry treated it with the utmost reverence, like a chariot of the Gods themselves had descended down to him to take care of and mend. Richard was inspecting the spaceship's propulsion system.

He called Harry over, "Hey, take a look at this. I've noticed some irregularities in the propulsion system. It's been causing minor malfunctions during test flights."

Harry went into his trance once again. "I see what you mean, Uncle Richard," he said quietly, making his hands dance over the exposed wires as though they were the bones of a loved one. "The plasma injection nozzles appear to have carbon deposits. That's affecting the thrust efficiency." He then turned back to his uncle. "We should schedule a thorough cleaning and consider adding an automatic carbon deposit cleaning mechanism to prevent this in the future."

Richard, as always, was impressed by Harry's quick diagnosis, "Excellent observation, Harry. And the ignition timing for the plasma chamber—it might need some adjustment. Your insights could significantly enhance the spaceship's performance."

When Richard turned his attention towards some paperwork that a previous client had sent over, Harry turned back to the spaceship. He traced the NASA logo and exhaled deeply, a small, slightly sad smile on his face.

*

Harry was sitting cross-legged on the ground in the Aeroplane and Spaceship Design Lab. This particular lab was a lot fancier than the rest of the hangars and labs in the office, specifically because it had been built and funded by NASA and was to be used solely for any mechanical repairs required on the NASA machinery sent over.

He was engrossed in analysing blueprints and designs of the spaceship he had just examined, making sure he memorised the construction of the craft to memory. He looked up when he heard footsteps and saw Richard approaching him.

"Hey. What do you think so far?"

Harry turned his attention back to the schematics of the craft in front of him, "One thing that stands out is the aerodynamic profile. We could reduce drag by incorporating a more streamlined nose cone, and perhaps reconfigure the wing shape for improved lift-to-drag ratio."

Richard nodded in agreement. "We need to maximise the spaceship's aerodynamic efficiency. What about the propulsion system? Any ideas to enhance thrust?"

Harry pointed to the engine layout. "The current propulsion system is impressive, but we might consider integrating a variable geometry nozzle. It would allow us to adjust the exhaust flow depending on the spaceship's speed and altitude, optimising thrust across a broader range of conditions."

"Variable geometry, that's a smart addition. Now, let's talk about materials. We want a balance between strength and weight. Any suggestions?"

"I'd recommend looking into advanced composite materials. They offer excellent strength-to-weight ratios and can withstand the stresses of space travel. Carbon nanotube composites, for instance, could be ideal for the spaceship's structural components."

"Carbon nanotubes, yes, they're incredibly strong and lightweight. And what about the spaceship's control systems? Are there any innovations we can implement?"

"We might explore integrating AI-assisted flight control systems that continuously analyse data from onboard sensors. This AI could provide real-time adjustments to optimise the spaceship's trajectory, ensuring smoother flights and precise landings."

Richard smiled widely, "As always, Harry, your insights are invaluable. AI-assisted control systems would indeed elevate the spaceship's precision."

They continued to discuss technical aspects, delving into power sources, shielding materials, and advanced navigation systems. They talked about the scope of redesigning the spaceship for enhanced speed, efficiency, and safety. When they got started talking about these things, oftentimes more than not, they barely breathed as they picked each other's brains, excited about the prospects of their innovations.

Richard then told Harry that he had a surprise for him. Curious, Harry followed him along. He knew every part of the hangars inside and out, so it was very unlikely that Harry would see something that would surprise him. Yet when Richard turned them towards the Private Aircraft Hangar, Harry's heart started thrumming faster.

Richard turned to Harry with a sly smile. "I have something special to show you tonight." He grabbed the edge of the curtains with a flourish, then yanked them aside in one dramatic motion.

Behind it stood a sleep, silver beast of a machine. Its fuselage gleamed under the hangar lights like liquid mercury. The nose of the jet sloped into a sharp point, and its wings stretched out, wide and commanding, edged with the sharpness of a predator's blade. The emblem of their airline was painted near the cockpits, its colours bold and proud.

Harry froze. His breath caught in his throat as his eyes locked onto the jet.

"My god," he whispered, stepping closer. "That's ... that's a P-10 Mustang, isn't it?"

Richard chuckled, a satisfied gleam in his eyes. "Indeed, Harry. Built in Russia, assembled in Germany, and now part of our very own fleet. This jet's a marvel of engineering. One of the fastest in the world. She clocks in at 916 kilometres an hour, and she can soar higher than most birds, 25000 metres up."

Harry moved slowly, reverently, until he stood right beside the aircraft. He reached out and ran a hand along the cool metal of its flank. Every curve, every rivet told a story of speed, power and impossible precision. To him, it wasn't just a machine–it was a childhood dream made real.

"I've seen pictures," he said, softly, almost to himself. "But this ... this is something else. It's magnificent. Like it could slice through the sky without even trying."

Richard stepped up to the side and reached for the cockpit canopy. With a smooth *hiss*, it opened.

He grinned, "What do you say, Harry? Want to take her for a spin?"

Harry looked at the jet again, eyes wide with disbelief and excitement, the hum of adrenaline already beginning to course through him.

"Hell yes," he breathed.

Harry eagerly climbed into the cockpit of the jet, and Richard followed suit, sitting beside him. Richard proceeded to give Harry instructions on how to pilot the helicopter, carefully guiding him.

"First, fasten your seat belt, Harry," Richard said, checking the systems.

Harry secured his seatbelt as Richard demonstrated how to start the jet's engine. Harry followed his commands, enabling the GPS and other necessary systems.

"I can't believe I'm about to fly this jet!" Harry said excitedly.

The jet taxied onto the runway, ready for take-off. Richard opened a small pocket flask of liquor and took a sip, smirking. "This jet is faster and more thrilling than you can imagine, Harry."

As the jet accelerated down the runway and took off, Harry couldn't contain his excitement. He pushed the jet's capabilities, even flipping it upside down, which caused some of Richard's liquor to spill.

Harry whooped, "Richard, this is amazing!"

"Easy there, Harry. Let's enjoy the view," Richard chuckled.

The jet soared gracefully through the sky, slicing through the clouds with ease. Below them, Merritt Island unfolded like a living canvas. The Atlantic shimmered in the distance, its endless blue stretching to the horizon, while the Indian River snaked alongside the land like a ribbon of molten silver.

The ground they were flying over now looked like a painting. Tiny houses dotted the earth, their rooftops catching the sunlight and glittering like scattered diamonds. Palm trees swayed gently in the breeze far below, their shadows cast long and soft over sun-drenched lawns. Neatly plotted roads criss-crossed the island like a child's scribble, winding through suburban neighbourhoods, wetlands, and stretches of untouched greenery.

To the east, Cape Canaveral gleamed faintly, its launch pads and towers a quiet reminder of how close they were to history and the stars. The sight of it made Harry's stomach flip for some inexplicable reason. The whole world seemed hushed from this height, bathed in golden light, beautiful and still.

After a painstakingly short time, they started to descend. Richard kept his eyes on Harry, whose adrenaline was still rushing as he manoeuvred the flight lower and lower. "Always remember—a soft landing is key."

Harry nodded, frowning in concentration as he expertly piloted the jet back to the hangar, executing a smooth landing. When they touched down, he grinned lazily at Richard, "Soft as a feather, just like you taught me."

*

The Marshal Academy Laboratory in Alabama buzzed with energy, with low hums of machinery, the occasional beep from diagnostic consoles, and the steady clack of keystrokes created a rhythm all their own. Glass-panelled walls enclosed the space, allowing sunlight to streak in and bounce off sleek metal surfaces.

Inside rows of long workbenches brimmed with cutting-edge technology: microscope arms governed over glowing petri dishes, complex circuitry snaked across disassembled hardware, and translucent cables pulsed faintly with data. Some students were bent over microscopes, jotting notes in frantic shorthand, while others typed rapidly at their stations, brows furrowed in concentration. Overhead, a holographic globe spun lazily from the ceiling, a mounted projector displaying satellite feeds in real time.

Near the far end of the lab were Professors Clark and Peter Williams; the latter was the Head of Department at the Rocketry and Spacecraft Propulsion Research Centre at the Marshal Space Flight Centre. They were hunched over a device no larger than a box of UNO cards. It sat on a raised pedestal between them, its polished black casing gleaming under the overhead lights. Intricate wires fed into its core like veins, and a small, lens-like projector on top blinked in readiness.

"There," Clark said, his voice low with anticipation. "William, this is it. we've finally cracked it."

Clark tapped a panel on the side of the device. The machine came to life with a soft whir, followed by a crystalline chime. Lights flickered at its apex, then poured upward in waves as shimmering pixels danced mid-air. A holographic city street slowly materialised before them, stretching out across the lab's open floor. Yellow taxis zipped past, pedestrians walked into hurried strides, and the muffled echo of car horns filled the space.

Students nearby looked up, gasping quietly as they saw a slice of Manhattan brought vividly to life. Clark gestured toward the machine. "All it needs is the right data input, and it renders the world; any world around you."

William nodded, already keying in a new set of coordinates. "It's like a virtual passport," he said. "Only better."

The cityscape dissolved into a swirl of light. In its place, a lab now appeared, submerged in a tranquil reef–sunlight danced about, casting rippling shadows over coral outcrops teeming with fish. Neon-coloured angelfish darted past William's elbow, dissolving into pixels when they neared the real-world boundary.

Clark's fingers flew across the console. "Let's go further."

With a flicker, they were no longer underwater. Ancient sandstone walls towered around them, casting long shadows across the simulated sands of Giza. Hieroglyphs glowed faintly on the stone as a figure in traditional robes walked by, murmuring in ancient Egyptian.

One more sequence ran, and the lab was suddenly floating in orbit. A holographic astronaut hovered before them, conducting an experiment as Earth turned slowly behind him. The room held its breath, marvelling at all the different images being conjured out of seemingly thin air.

"But it doesn't just stop at places. It can replicate humans too, making them visible and interactive," Clark said excitedly.

They fed the device with more data, and a holographic version of William appeared in the room, complete with his mannerisms and expressions.

The real William laughed in amazement, "I'm seeing myself, Clark! This is surreal!"

Clark approached the holographic William, and they engaged in a conversation, their holographic selves interacting seamlessly.

Clark turned back to the students with a wide smile on his face, "With this technology, a person can walk, talk, and explore the world without actually being there physically. It's like teleportation without the need to move an inch!"

"And the best part? Others can see you, talk to you, and experience your presence. It's like being in two places at once!" William added enthusiastically.

"The world is at your fingertips with this technology. It's not just about exploration; it's about expanding the boundaries of knowledge and experiences. The possibilities are endless, and we're just scratching the surface."

They continued to fine-tune the hologram, amazed by the endless possibilities that their invention held. The holographic world continued to expand around them, offering a glimpse into the future of exploration and connection as the students gathered closer, wanting to try a simulation for their own. Everyone's faces were brimming with amazement and intrigue, and Clark watched it all with a proud smile on his face.

*

The lecture hall was shaped like a shallow amphitheatre, its curved rows of seating descending gradually toward a central dais where Clark stood. The room was spacious, built to accommodate over a hundred students, yet designed with an intimacy that made even the back rows feel close to the action.

High ceilings arched overhead, fitted with recessed lighting that cast a warm glow across the space; not too harsh, but bright enough to make every chalk mark on the board clearly visible. A massive, digital projection screen dominated the wall behind the professor, currently displaying a rotating 3D model of a multistage rocket, its inner components labelled and colour-coded. Each rotation was accompanied by a soft mechanical hum and the occasional whir of the ceiling-mounted projector.

The chalkboard, a rare hybrid of traditional and modern design, stretched across half the front walls. It was already crowded with equations of fluid dynamics, escape velocities, and thrust-to-weight ratios in Clark's precise, looping handwriting. Alongside them were sketches of engine nozzles and schematic cross sections of launch vehicles, drawn with a clarity that betrayed years of practice.

Students filled the room, sitting shoulder to shoulder in wide rows. Some leaned forward eagerly with notebooks in hand, while others tapped away at tablets and laptops, their screens glowing faintly in the dimmer light of the upper tiers. The air buzzed with anticipation and quiet concentration, broken only by the occasional rustle of paper or the clack of a keyboard.

At the front, Clark stood like a conductor before an orchestra, gesturing fluidly as he paced. His eyes shone with enthusiasm, and his voice carried easily across the room.

"Today," he began, his voice vibrant, "we're delving into the exhilarating world of rocket science. This is the discipline that launched Sputnik, carried humans to the Moon, and continues to propel our dreams beyond the stars."

He tapped the chalkboard with a knuckle, where a key formula was written: $F = ma$.

A student at the front couldn't hold their excitement in as they whispered, "This is where the magic begins!"

Clark smiled. "Indeed, it is! The foundation of rocket science is based on Sir Isaac Newton's Third Law of Motion: 'For every action, there is an equal and opposite reaction.'" He continued gesturing to the chalkboard as the students feverishly took notes. "The key principle here is that the combustion of rocket fuel generates action—force—directed in one direction, typically downward, expelled as exhaust. Now, according to Newton's law, there's an equal and opposite reaction, and that's what drives the rocket forward."

He drew a rocket on the board, showing the fiery exhaust pushing downward.

"So, the rocket goes up because the exhaust goes down?" a student from the back of the class asked.

"Precisely!" Clark nodded. "What's truly fascinating is that this principle works not just in Earth's atmosphere but also in the vacuum of space. Rockets can propel spacecraft to incredible speeds and distances, all thanks to this fundamental law."

He moved on to explain more complex concepts, detailing the intricacies of propulsion systems, stages of rocket launches, and orbital mechanics.

The student at the front gained more confidence as the class moved on, and they had a huge smile on their face. "It's amazing how everything comes together to make space travel possible."

"I agree! It's a symphony of physics, engineering, and mathematics. Each piece contributes to the grand orchestra of space exploration. And as future scientists and engineers, you'll play a vital role in advancing our understanding of the universe."

Clark was getting to the conclusion of his lecture when one of the university's attendants entered the classroom. He smiled nervously at Clark as the latter looked a little irritated at the interruption.

"Excuse me, Professor Clark, but there's an urgent call for you."

Clark was surprised. One of the best (and sometimes not) things about his appointment at Marshal was that he was barely disturbed. "A call? Very well, thank you. I'll be right there."

He nodded to the students and followed the attendant out of the classroom. The latter handed Clark a cell phone and stepped away a polite distance to let Clark have his privacy.

"Hello?" Clark said into the phone in a cautious tone.

A deep, authoritative voice issued, "Professor Clark, can you please come to the space centre?"

Clark baulked at the person's words, "The space centre?" he repeated.

"Yes, in Florida, at the ..."

"Yes, yes, I know where the centre is," Clark interrupted, "but who are you, and what's the matter at the space centre?

The voice was firm. "That's not important right now. What matters is that we need you here, urgently."

There was a pause as Clark processed the request. Resigned, he muttered, "Very well, I'll be there."

The voice on the other end of the line merely muttered *a thank you* and abruptly ended the call.

What could this be about? Clark thought. He handed the phone back to the attendant, who walked away wordlessly. After staring after him for a few seconds, Clark sat on one of the benches across the corridor and rubbed his chin as he pondered about this unexpected summons and the mysteries that awaited him at the space centre.

***

Chapter IV

Clark stepped out of the car, his polished shoes clicking softly against the pavement as he approached the front gates of the Kennedy Space Centre. The NASA insignia loomed overhead, gleaming in the sunlight like a memory reborn. He hadn't been here in five years, not since he was reassigned to the Marshal Academy because he couldn't walk through these corridors without people whispering behind his back. But now, as the Florida air pressed warm against his suit, he felt at home.

A uniformed security guard stepped forward, intercepting him just before the checkpoint.

"Good morning, sir," the guard said politely. "May I see your ID?"

Clark reached into the inner pocket of his jacket and handed over the card. The guard examined it carefully before speaking into his walkie-talkie.

"This is Gate Three," he said. "Requesting security clearance for Professor Michael Clark. Do you copy, Hannah?"

As Clark waited, a sadness washed over him as he remembered the countless days he'd walked through these halls, not requiring double-checks for security clearance. He would just show his NASA employment ID and go wherever he wanted to in this beautiful building. And now, he was being treated like an ordinary visitor.

A short burst of static crackled from the walkie-talkie before a voice responded, firm and clear.

"Copy that, he's clear, let him through. He's been requested to be at the Space Mission Memorial."

The guard muttered an acknowledgement and turned back to Clark, handing him his ID back, "Professor, you'll walk through these doors and see a blue ..."

But Clark interrupted him by raising his hand, "That's all right, I know the way. Thanks."

The guard returned Clark's small smile and pressed a panel beside the glass doors. They slid open with a quiet *hiss*, revealing the bright, expansive atrium of the centre beyond. Clark stepped inside.

It was as bustling as he remembered—scientists and engineers crisscrossed the polished floors, voices low and urgent, monitors glowing with telemetry and mission readouts. The air hummed with a low murmur of focused energy, the kind that only ever lived in places where the future was being built in real time.

He paused for a moment, taking it all in. The curved ceilings, the flashing control panels, the holographic models suspended midair—it was the same place, and yet not. Updated, upgraded. Still, the pulse of it, the ambition and awe, still remained.

Clark allowed himself a small, almost imperceptible smile as he made his way to the Space Mission Memorial. Once the novelty wore off, the confusion came back. Why the Memorial? And who was he supposed to even be meeting? What was with all the espionage-like mystery element? And the main question of all—what was he supposed to be doing here?

He stood at the bridge connecting the Memorial to the rest of the building, unsure where to go. People barely came to this part of the building, unless for some event or an arranged visit. He was about to turn back and go ask where he was supposed to meet this stranger when he heard a voice from behind him.

"Hi, Professor Clark. I've been waiting for you."

A man, previously in shadow, stepped forward into the light. The man was tall, dark-skinned, had close-cropped hair and wore thick glasses. He was clearly at least a decade younger than Clark, but without even saying anything, he seemed to command a presence that made Clark stand up straighter. It was when the man came within touching distance of Clark that the latter realised who it was.

"Karthik? Karthik Duvedi?" Clark confirmed.

Karthik's stern expression softened as he smiled, shaking Clark's hand. "Hello, Michael, it's good to see you."

"Likewise. It's been almost ..."

"Ten years," Karthik finished for Clark, who nodded. There was an awkward, painful silence as Clark once again recalled the day *Echolight* exploded. It wasn't as though he ever stopped thinking about that day–it was always hidden in a dark corner of his mind, ready to come out like some horrible, parasitic demon.

"I didn't know you moved here. Weren't you at the Johnson Space Centre?" Clark said.

"It's fairly recent. I've been appointed the new Director here at the Kennedy Centre."

Clark smiled in response, but remained quiet. Ten years ago, when *Echolight* was launched, Karthik was a Systems Engineer and used to follow Clark around like a puppy–over-eager, aiming to please, but still clearly brilliant. Clark had an odd feeling in him. He couldn't call it as envy, not really, but it had seemed like in the past ten years, while he had been stuck in a never-ending loop of grief and regret, everyone else had moved on and up with their lives.

Karthik then immediately launched into business. "Well, Michael, I'm sure you're aware of the fact that our days are getting numbered more and more. We've seen that planet Earth is deteriorating day by day. Natural calamities and technological disruptions are becoming more frequent." He had a grave look on his face as he gestured for them to walk across the bridge.

"Sooner or later, we will need to find another planet to inhabit," Clark concurred.

Karthik nodded. "Indeed, and that's why we are here today. There has been a significant technological advancement." He stepped closer to Clark. "Our primary goal now is to launch another spaceship for habitation."

Clark was quiet. *Another spaceship?* He knew that technology had advanced multi-fold in the past ten years. NASA had also had multiple space missions that went by seamlessly, brilliantly successful launches to the planets nearest to Earth. But he couldn't help but feel an odd foreboding. Was he prepared to jump back into it if asked?

Karthik tactfully understood Clark's silence and decided to change the subject slightly, with a small smile on his face, "Any new inventions from your side, Michael?"

Clark smiled indulgently at Karthik and pulled a small device from his coat pocket. He activated the device, causing it to hover in the air. The device emitted a soft, illuminating light.

"This is the hologram technology. If you feed it with the right data, it can create a virtual reality world that allows you to explore anywhere in the world."

Karthik's face was illuminated by the light from the hologram box, and Clark smiled as he saw the ghost of the young, excited engineer he knew. "This is remarkable!"

He then got distracted as his phone started to buzz. He excused himself politely and ducked into the dark corner he was previously in. Clark watched him and then suddenly had a streak of mischief run through him, making him smile. He fiddled with the hologram box and stepped away slightly.

After a few minutes, Karthik came back to find Clark watching the view from the massive glass windows. "Sorry about that, Michael, it was the office."

"Oh, it's all right."

Karthik extended his hand, "Thank you for being here, Professor Clark."

However, as Michael reached out to shake hands with the Director, something unexpected happened. Michael's hologram suddenly disappeared, leaving Karthik surprised and puzzled.

"What just happened?" He looked around and only saw the hologram box on the floor, sitting innocently. Then, with a beam of bright light, a holographic image of Clark appeared from the box, smiling politely.

"Thank you, Director Duvedi. The hologram experiment has been tested live."

Karthik took off his glasses, looking around the room in astonishment. "What ... how is this possible?"

Finally, a laughing Clark came out of a door in the corner of the corridor. His glee increased at the sight of Karthik's baffled face. Karthik realised what had happened and shook his head in bemusement.

"Very funny, Michael. Glad to see you've still got your sense of humour."

"Couldn't help it, Karthik," Clark said, still chortling, feeling an innocent, unbound sense of happiness after a long time.

***

Chapter V

After a brief discussion about the imminent launch, Clark was sent home to get some rest and gather his thoughts while looking over the mission programme.

He had been given an apartment near the space centre, quite similar to the house he used to share with Sameera and Ruma. When he walked in, the quiet loneliness of it made his heart hurt. The apartment had been equipped with every amenity that one could think of, but Clark missed his family. Sameera had left him a couple of years after *Echolight* had exploded. They remained in touch, but this too fizzled out once Ruma turned eighteen and they no longer had to deal with custody shifts every week. The only time he'd hear from Sameera was through his daughter.

And Ruma. Beautiful, brilliant, courageous Ruma. Although she, too, spent most of her time at Marshal, she and Clark had drifted away. She looked at him like he was a stranger whom she had to be polite to—closed smiles, monosyllabic answers, comments muttered under her breath. He missed his daughter, not her physically, but missed the way he was with her—Dad and Ruma against the world.

And yet, in a way, Clark's wish had come true. Ruma had been selected to be one of the astronauts to undertake PI Beta. She had excelled in all her tests, proving herself to be a worthwhile asset, with her quick response to emergencies, AI system handling expertise and prowess with coding. Clark was proud of her, of course, he was, but it terrified him beyond belief. During *Echolight*, he'd worked with the astronauts for so long in such close contact that they had become like his own sons. But this? This was his flesh and blood—his baby girl, and he didn't know how to stop her from risking her life without stopping her from fulfilling her dreams.

Clark sighed as he sat on the comfortable couch and held the mission programme open on his lap. He hadn't yearned for a glass of whiskey like this in so long, but he knew he must not. Seven years of sobriety and counting couldn't be thrown away right before he was going to be responsible for a mission that was to send his daughter and three other astronauts into outer space.

Mission Statement - Tarayana. The words loomed out at him. Expect it of Karthik Duvedi to assign the spaceship a Sanskrit name. Clark made a mental note to ask him what it meant. He took a deep breath, quickly cleaned his glasses and decided to peruse the programme—no stone must be left unturned—the fate of humanity rested on it.

*

The next morning, Clark arrived at the Heroes and Legends Conference Facility at the Kennedy Space Centre. Karthik was already there, dressed impeccably as always. Just as Clark walked in, he felt a pat on his back. He turned to see Peter Williams.

"Peter! When did you arrive?"

"Just today morning," he said and gave a tight smile to Clark. "You doing okay, Michael?"

"No other way to be, right?"

The duo walked up to Karthik, and Clark introduced Peter. "Morning, Karthik. This is Peter Williams. He is the Head of Department at the Rocketry and Spacecraft Propulsion Research Centre at Marshal."

"Good morning, Director Duvedi. Thanks for having me here," Peter said politely, holding out his hand.

But Karthik took a step back and looked at William up and down warily, "Are you real or a hologram?"

Clark chuckled, and the others followed after they saw Karthik's suspicious expression, "We are all real here, Karthik."

But Karthik stepped slightly forward like he was approaching a growling animal. He extended his hand to shake Williams'. The latter appraised his hand with a bemused expression, and, snickering, shook Karthik's hand.

"No holograms here," Williams assured him.

Karthik had a look of relief wash over his face and smiled, joining the others in laughter, "Alright then, let's proceed."

*

The medical wing of the space centre buzzed with the quiet urgency as the four astronaut candidates underwent their final round of tests. These evaluations were designed to push both body and mind to the limit. Every heartbeat was monitored, every reaction timed with precision. But what had begun as routine quickly spiralled into an emergency.

One of the astronauts suddenly showed signs of distress. His pulse spiked, his blood pressure rose, and his breath became ragged and shallow. Alarms blared on the monitors as the medical team rushed to his side, administering oxygen and hooking him up to advanced diagnostic equipment. The ECG readings were erratic, the beeping growing frantic with each second. Within minutes, it was clear: he was suffering from a severe asthma attack.

Despite rapid intervention, his condition worsened. The team struggled to stabilise him, but the stress and instability of the test had already taken their toll. He was declared medically unfit to proceed; disqualified not by lack of skill or preparation, but by the fragility of the human body under extreme strain.

News of the accident quickly reached mission supervisors Karthik, Michael, and Peter. Their concern wasn't just for their colleague's well-being; it cast a shadow over the entire crew selection. If one candidate could break under pressure, who was to say others wouldn't?

The leadership at the space centre found themselves facing a critical decision. With the mission timeline tightening, a replacement had to be identified and tested immediately. The clock was ticking.

*

The scent of oil and hot metal lingered in the hangar air as Harry adjusted the hydraulic lift under the tail section of a modified Falcon jet. The sun slanted through the open hangar doors, lighting up a halo of dust around him. He was elbow-deep in the engine assembly when he heard footsteps behind him.

"Harry Charlton?" a voice called out.

Harry wiped his hands on a rag, turning to see a man and a woman in dark suits, flanked by a third figure wearing a NASA badge.

"That's me," he replied cautiously.

The woman stepped forward and extended a hand. "I'm Laura Andrews. NASA."

Harry shook it, a flicker of curiosity in his eyes.

"You've worked on three of our refit vehicles, I believe?" Laura said, and Harry nodded. "Your notes on the thermal shielding overhaul caught our attention. Your understanding of our systems without formal aerospace training, mind you, is ... rare."

"I've always loved figuring things out," Harry said modestly. "Books, schematics, test flights –I read everything I can get my hands on," he then added hastily, "of course, only things I'm *allowed* to read."

Laura gave him a measured look. "We may have a situation. One of our primary astronauts has failed medical clearance due to a severe asthma attack during testing. We need a replacement, fast. Someone who understands spacecraft inside and out, and can be trained quickly to function in low-Earth orbit."

Harry's eyebrows shot up. "You want me to go to space?"

"We want to test if you *can*. If you're willing, we'll take you to the space centre immediately. You'll undergo a full battery of tests, including physical, mental, and physiological. If you pass, we'll talk about next steps."

Harry hesitated for only a second before nodding. "Let's do it."

*

The boardroom buzzed with tension. A large monitor displayed the failed astronaut's medical profile with erratic ECG, oxygen desaturation, and a final note: *Unfit for Mission*. Peter leaned back, frowning. "We're cutting it too close. We need someone who can match the team's dynamic and contribute technically."

Laura cleared her throat. "I'd like to propose a name–Harry Charlton. He's a senior mechanic who's worked extensively on our vehicles. Unorthodox, yes, but brilliant."

"You want a mechanic on a space mission?" Clark asked, incredulous.

"Not *just* a mechanic," Laura said calmly. "Harry has a deep, intuitive grasp of our spacecrafts. He's diagnosed failures that our engineers couldn't, using nothing but raw skill and pure instinct. He's passed preliminary clearances. Let's give him a full test protocol."

"That's highly irregular," Karthik muttered.

"So is losing a crew member *days* before launch," Laura countered. "We can't afford a systems failure in orbit. Harry can fix problems others can't see."

There was a pause, and everyone looked to Karthik for an answer. His face was furrowed in thought, and after a few painfully long seconds, he said: "I trust your opinion, Laura. You're Ground Mission Commander, it's your call."

*

Harry underwent days of rigorous evaluation. Endurance runs in zero-simulators, stress tests, isolation channels, and logic puzzles under timed conditions. The medical team watched in growing disbelief.

"Jesus," one of the technicians muttered, watching his vitals. "His oxygen retention levels are better than half the crew."

When the final reports landed on Karthik's desk, the room fell silent as he flipped through the results.

"He's not just passing," Laura said. "He's *exceeding* mission standards."

Karthik looked up and gave her a nod of approval, and Laura allowed herself a small, proud smile.

*

Harry sat outside the boardroom, leg bouncing nervously. The door then finally opened, and Karthik came out. He beamed at Harry with a genial smile like a favourite uncle, and extended his hand.

"Hello, Harry. I'm very pleased to meet you. I'm Karthik Duvedi, Director of the Kennedy Space Centre."

Harry shook his hand and gulped. "It's great to meet you, too, sir."

"Come on in, and call me Karthik, please."

The men walked inside the boardroom, and Harry was slightly nervous to see all the expectant faces turning to look up when he walked in. Karthik turned back to Harry.

"We've reviewed your performance. Under all criteria, you've surpassed all thresholds. Laura's endorsement wasn't misplaced. You've got what it takes."

Harry blinked, stunned.

"We're officially selecting you as a candidate for the mission," Karthik continued. "Training begins immediately. It won't be easy, but if you commit, we believe you can be a vital part of this team."

A grin broke across Harry's face. "Thank you, sir. I, I mean, thank you, Karthik. I won't let you down."

Laura then came up to Harry and clapped him on the back, a bright smile on her face. "Told you."

***

Chapter VI

As Harry walked out of the conference hall, he was filled with a newfound sense of purpose and excitement for the journey ahead. The whole mission was beyond anything he had ever imagined. All those nights spent in the backyard of his grandfather's bar, gazing up at the stars, could he have ever imagined that he'd not only get to live his dreams fully, but also get to make a difference in the history of humankind? He felt like wanting to skip ahead of all the preliminary activities and tests they'd have to undergo before the launch, and just be in the sky, adrift, weightless, ears filled with an endless silence.

Yet there was another part of him that was *terrified.* Looking up at the night sky was a beautiful image, but Harry knew all too well about the risks involved. After all, the crew of *Echolight* had barely left the Earth's stratosphere before they imploded in a fiery ball. And once Harry did get to outer space, any small malfunction, anything overlooked, could cause a pressure gauge to malfunction, a door jamb to break, fuel to inexplicably run out, and there would be no part of him that could be brought back for his grandfather to mourn over.

And of course, there was Charlton. Could Harry leave his grandfather behind and be gone for who knows how long? Could Charlton—bitter, angry, lonely Charlton—survive on his own? And would he be angry at Harry for abandoning him, or would he be proud, urging him to live his dreams?

With Harry's selection confirmed, the preparations for the space exploration mission kicked into high gear. Over the following weeks, Harry underwent rigorous training alongside the astronauts. He learnt about spacecraft systems, navigation, emergency protocols, and more. He also spent significant time with Richard, who imparted his extensive knowledge about the starship's mechanics and maintenance.

As the mission's launch date approached, tensions ran high, and the excitement was palpable. After their individual training was finished, Laura introduced Harry to the rest of the crew, who had, of course, known each other a lot longer than Harry had.

"Harry, I'd like you to meet the core team members who will be embarking on this mission with us. First, we have Ruma, your Team Leader. She's a remarkable young woman with a sharp mind and unwavering determination. Ruma will ensure that our crew operates at peak efficiency."

Harry's eyes widened when he heard Ruma's name. There was a part of him that rationally told him that it could be someone else, but when he saw the woman step forward and smile at him with the same dimpled smile he'd seen under a sticky bar table ten years ago, he felt his heart melt. She was there—the girl who, seemingly like stardust, had appeared in his life, a frightened, anxious girl and left with a wide smile on her face. She was here, actually here. And not only were they reunited, but they were about to take a long-term mission that involved spending an extensive period of time together in close quarters.

Ruma's face didn't betray much, but the wide smile and the warmth behind her eyes were enough to tell Harry that she remembered him, too. Harry cleared his throat and nodded in acknowledgement, wanting to grab her hand and get a quiet corner to ask a million questions. *There will be time for all of that later*, he told himself, and turned to the next astronaut.

"Next, we have Arthur Symmonds, our resident biological researcher. He'll be conducting experiments and studies related to any potential life forms or ecosystems we might encounter.

Symmonds is thorough and meticulous, which will be crucial for our mission's success."

Symmonds had a kind, round face and wore such thick glasses that they magnified his warm brown eyes to twice their actual size. He had messy light brown hair and was dressed so casually in a pair of sweatpants and a large sweatshirt that he looked like he'd just dropped off his kids at school and was now heading to grocery shopping. But there was something in his eyes—a glint that gave away the quiet intelligence of the man.

"And finally, we have Mikhail, a brilliant physicist and wave analyser. He'll be working on various scientific aspects of the mission, including analysing cosmic waves and phenomena. Mikhail's expertise will help us navigate the complexities of deep space."

Mikhail looked like someone who should be working as a bouncer outside a bar, not as an astronaut. He was wide and broad and towered over Harry, who was considerably tall. He had close-cropped, silver hair, and the fade alongside his ears gave a very military look to him. He had impeccable posture and stood ramrod-straight, arms crossed in front of his chest, tightly. But when Harry held out his hand, Mikhail's face immediately changed as he flashed a grin at him.

"Nice to meet you, Harry," Mikhail said with a strong accent, but a soft voice as he shook Harry's hand firmly. Now he came across as someone who spent his free time volunteering at an animal shelter.

"Each member of this team brings unique skills and knowledge to the table. Together, we're going to push the boundaries of human exploration and unlock the mysteries of the cosmos. Welcome aboard, Harry," Laura said.

***

Chapter VII

A couple of days before the launch, Harry decided to visit his home away from home—the local bar where his grandad, Charlton, still ran the show. The bar hadn't changed at all in all these years. It still held its eclectic décor, the tables were still greasy and sticky, Charlton's favourite genre of music, 80s rock, still blared from the staticky music system, and the lights flickered weakly. Yet it was a place of comfort for Harry. The moment he stepped inside, he felt like he was home, and he looked around at the regulars, slowly nursing their drinks with seemingly no jobs or homes to go back to.

As he walked through the familiar door, the chatter inside briefly subsided, and heads turned to greet him. His grandad, seated at the bar with a glass of beer in hand, noticed him immediately. Charlton's ruddy face lit up with a smile at the sight of his grandson. Immediately, he was reminded of how much Harry resembled his father, but his eyes were of his mother's—warm and kind. Charlton put down his beer on the counter and made his way out of the bar with a warm smile.

"Ahh, you're back," Charlton said as though Harry had just gone grocery shopping. Harry chuckled and hugged him, the smell of his grandfather—whiskey, sweat, and Florida, welcoming him.

He headed towards the bar counter and opened the refrigerator, grabbing a bottle of beer. As he opened it with the bottle opener, he glanced at his grandad. "Would you like to have one more?" Harry offered, holding the beer bottle invitingly.

Charlton grinned and nodded, his eyes twinkling with amusement. Harry handed his grandad another bottle and took a seat opposite him. They clinked their bottles together, and Charlton raised his beer in a silent toast. The bar came alive once more as conversations and laughter resumed around them.

Harry took a sip of his beer and, with a curious smile, prompted Charlton, "Sorry I haven't had the chance to reply to your voicemail, it's been a ... crazy few days. What is the good news you wanted to share?"

Charlton's eyes sparkled with excitement as he set his beer down, leaning in closer to Harry. "Ha! Our bar is finally out of debt," he exclaimed with a triumphant tone. "I cleared 'em all. I can now hand it over to you," he added, a sense of pride evident in his voice.

Harry's face lit up with genuine joy at the news. But almost instantly, a torrential wave of guilt poured down on him. How was he supposed to tell Charlton that he couldn't take the bar, which his own father had left them with; he couldn't take it now, maybe *never*? How could he let his grandfather down like that? "That's great news, Grandad," he said, his words laced with happiness. "Now I can drink as many beers as I can without worrying about the bills." Their laughter filled the bar.

After the laughter died down, Charlton took a sip of his beer and peered at Harry with a curious yet expectant look. He leaned in closer, his eyes narrowing slightly, "What's on your mind, boy?"

Harry looked at his grandfather, his throat suddenly dry. He couldn't lie to that face, he knew that. So he just sighed and took a big swig of his beer. When he finally looked up, Charlton was still watching him with an impassive expression.

"You know how NASA is working on launching Project Inhabitant again?"

"Uh-huh," Charlton grunted.

"Well. I know this sounds crazy, Grandad, and even I still can't believe it," Harry rambled nervously. "But they've selected me. They've selected me to be a part of the crew that goes into outer space."

Grandad's reaction was immediate and tangible. His emotion changed from wariness to seriousness in an instant. His eyes widened slightly, and he fixed a sharp, intense look on Harry as if trying to gauge whether this was a joke or a genuine revelation.

"What?" Charlton uttered in disbelief, his voice hushed and incredulous. Time seemed to stand still, and the weight of Harry's announcement hung heavily in the air.

Harry fumbled around with his bag and pulled out a few documents and his ID card that now had NASA's insignia stamped on it. "Look, grandpa. I am an astronaut and flying to another planet. This is the offer letter."

Harry's announcement hung in the air like a thunderclap, instantly transforming the jovial atmosphere of the bar into one of tense disbelief. His hand shook slightly as he extended the offer letter to his grandad, a tangible symbol of his impending journey into the unknown.

Charlton's eyes darted from the document to Harry's face, his features contorted by a mix of anger, confusion, and a hint of sadness. He slammed the empty beer mug on the table.

"I built this bar, and I cleared all the debts," Charlton's voice trembled with emotion as he spoke through clenched teeth. "And now you will go somewhere far beyond. Then who would look after this bar?" His words carried a heavyweight, not just of anger, but of the years of hard work and dreams that had gone into this place.

Harry knew this was a difficult moment, and his frustration and determination were mirrored in his grandad's eyes. It was a clash of dreams—one reaching for the stars, the other rooted in the foundations of the bar they both loved. The bar had been their anchor, and now Harry's journey threatened to disrupt that stability.

"The way you looked after *me* these many years," Harry retorted sarcastically, his tone dripping with bitterness. It was a moment of conflict between generations, dreams, and responsibilities. He sighed, "Look, Grandad, this mission, it's bigger than me, bigger than this bar."

Charlton crossed his arms. "That's easy for you to say when you are the one leaving it all behind."

"I didn't ask for this; it *chose* me. I've been trained for this my whole life!"

"Trained for what, Harry?" Charlton scoffed. "To abandon your family, your legacy?"

"No! To explore, to discover, to push the boundaries of human existence!" Harry exclaimed.

"Boundaries? Do you think you're gonna find answers out there in the void of space?"

"Maybe. Or maybe I'll find more questions, ones that challenge everything we know." Harry spat and slid off the stool. He grabbed his bag and headed towards the stairs behind the bar that led upstairs to Charlton's tiny apartment.

"Where do you think you're going?" Charlton demanded.

"I have to get the rest of my stuff and pack," Harry muttered and only turned back to shoot a venomous look at his grandfather. "Don't worry, I'll be out of your hair soon."

*

But going back to his childhood bedroom made Harry's anger slowly fade away. He looked around in the tiny, glorified broom cupboard. He sat on the small bed, which creaked under his adult weight and ran his eyes all over the NASA posters about the different images taken by the telescopes. He smiled at the solar system model he had made about ten years ago, which he had excitedly shown to Ruma. And then his eyes went to the bedside table where, alongside a lava lamp, was his toy aeroplane—the one Charlton had given him.

Harry sighed. He had known that coming to his grandfather with the big news wasn't going to be an easy experience. He also knew what kind of a man Charlton was—he talked a big talk, but inside, he was a kind, loving man. Circumstances had made him the bitter man he was on the outside. *Don't leave angry*, Harry told himself.

*

By the time Harry had finished taking the sparse belongings he had left behind, which included, most importantly, his toy aeroplane, he headed downstairs. There was no customer in the bar, and Charlton wasn't anywhere to be seen either. Harry dropped his bag on the bar and headed to the backyard, where he knew Charlton would be.

The sun had set now, and the balmy temperature had dropped a couple of degrees. The stars above were in full display, and under them, sitting on one of the rickety beach chairs was Charlton, taking frequent sips of beer. Harry walked up to him and noticed how Charlton stilled when he heard them.

"All done?" Charlton asked, his voice gruff but quiet.

Harry hummed in assent and sat down on the chair next to Charlton. The latter wordlessly handed him a bottle of beer, and Harry thanked him.

"I hope you have done me the favour of throwing away your old underwear," Charlton said dryly.

Harry snorted. "Yeah, don't worry."

"Some of them might even qualify as toxic material, y'know."

Harry chuckled and watched Charlton, who now had a small smile playing on his face. Harry felt embarrassed when he realised that his own eyes were now filling with tears. He cleared his throat, took a large swig of the beer and followed his grandfather's gaze, looking straight ahead.

"You know, Grandad, this backyard has seen a lot of stories," Harry said softly.

Charlton hummed in assent. "It sure has, lad. We've laughed here, cried here, and shared our lives."

They clinked their beer bottles together in a silent toast, acknowledging the memories they've created. Harry once again found himself looking up at the stars. "Soon, I'll be among those stars."

"Aye, you will," Charlton said, and at the sound of his voice, tinged with sadness and pride, Harry looked at him. Charlton reached over and squeezed Harry's hand. "And when you come back, you'll have even more stories to tell."

They took another sip of their beers. "Grandad, I want you to know that you're the reason who I am today. You taught me the value of hard work, perseverance, and always aiming high."

Charlton was quiet for the longest time. But when he finally spoke, his voice was brimming with emotion. "It's not easy for an old man like me to see his grandson venture into the great unknown. But I'm proud, Harry, so very proud.

Harry placed a hand on Charlton's shoulder. "I promise I'll make you proud up there, just like you've made me proud down here."

"I'll be waiting for your stories, lad. And remember, no matter how far you go, this old bar will always be here for you," Charlton murmured, smiling through his tears as they clinked their beer bottles once more.

*

As Harry darted from one room to the other, Charlton couldn't help but reminisce about the young, innocent Harry of years gone by. He still saw Harry as the small boy whose messy head of hair barely reached Charlton's waist. The soft-faced, kind-hearted boy, who, when he wasn't working off the debt his father had left, used to spend most of his time walking next to the Kennedy Space Centre, cycling past Cape Canaveral, or simply lying on the warm grass and staring up at the sky full of stars for hours on end.

Charlton could still remember when, on Harry's twelfth birthday, he'd gifted him a toy aeroplane. Nothing fancy like the ones with batteries and flashing lights, but completely ordinary, made out of plastic with cheap paint. But Harry's eyes had lit up like the candles on his tiny birthday cake. Charlton couldn't help but smile as he could see Harry, running around with the toy in the air, arm held up, screaming, "Grandad, this is my plane and I'm gonna fly it faster and higher than anyone!"

Charlton sighed. He didn't like keeping secrets from Harry—didn't then, and didn't now. But what choice did he have? Could he ever tell Harry the truth about his father? Would it stop him from living his dreams?

"It's time for me to get going, Grandad." Harry's voice jolted Charlton out of his reminiscing. Charlton nodded, unable to find any words. He awkwardly shuffled in space, rubbing his hand over his unshaven chin, avoiding Harry's eyes.

But Harry understood. He ran to his grandfather and hugged him tightly. Although he towered over Charlton now, he let his body envelop his grandfather's like he was a small boy. Charlton was taken by surprise, but in a couple of seconds, hugged Harry back too, fisting his hands onto Harry's back, grateful that he couldn't see the tears running down his face.

"I know, grandad, I know."

*

After Charlton watched Harry drive away on his bike, he came back slowly to the bar. It was too early in the day to receive any patrons, but it seemed to be even quieter than usual. Charlton found himself walking to the shelves on the bar. He didn't reach out for a bottle of alcohol; instead, he picked up the one photograph in the whole place. It was of him and Harry when Harry was a newborn baby; Charlton, too, looked young, happy, intensely vulnerable and grateful as he held the small baby in his hands. Charlton's hands shook as he looked at the photograph, and soon enough, one teardrop splashed down on the dusty glass.

Taking the photograph in hand, Charlton poured himself a glass of whiskey, not bothering to measure the amount that sloshed into the glass. He then sat at the bar, eyes still on the photograph and drank the contents of the glass in one desperate gulp. The bitter liquid burned as it went down his throat, but it was nothing compared to the burning ache in his heart.

***

Chapter VIII

The day before the launch was unlike any other—electric with anticipation, yet grounded in ritual. Inside the prep wing of the space centre, a quiet intensity pulsed through the halls. The four astronauts, dressed in standard-issue jumpsuits, moved from one checkpoint to the next with the solemn grace of seasoned professionals. But beneath their calm exteriors, hearts pounded, minds buzzed with the knowledge that within twenty-four hours, they would leave the Earth behind.

First came the health checks. Monitors beeped steadily in the background as doctors hovered over vitals, ran blood tests, and cross-checked every detail of each astronaut's medical history. Any anomaly, no matter how minor, could mean grounding. The physician's eyes were sharp, but so were their voices, offering quiet reassurance. It wasn't just about physical fitness. It was about trust. If something went wrong in orbit, they had to know their bodies wouldn't betray them.

Next was the suit up. The suits, custom-fitted, painstakingly engineered, hung like silent sentinels in the pressurisation room. Each astronaut stepped into their second skin, the *hiss* of sealed zippers and the soft *clunk* of the helmets echoing like a prelude. Their suits were more than gear; they were survival. Protection against the vacuum of space, extreme cold, unfiltered radiation; protection against an entire hostile world, held at bay by layers of technology.

The safety briefings followed. In a sealed chamber, they reviewed emergency procedures, evacuation drills, fire scenarios, and depressurisation protocols. No one spoke casually here. Every word could one day be the difference between life and death. The gravity of it wasn't lost on anyone.

Even the seasoned veterans among them sat straighter, their expressions hardened as simulations played out on-screen.

After a short break, they gathered again for the mission overview, as led by their Ground Mission Commander, Laura. The objective timelines, trajectory, and landing sites were all discussed. The weight of responsibility settling down on their shoulders felt like a silent co-pilot. Each crewmember reviewed their roles and reran every step in their heads. A mistake wasn't just failure. It could jeopardise years of planning, billions in funding and most importantly, lives.

Then came the equipment checks. Communication devices, scientific instruments, life support systems—every wire, every screw had to be double-checked. Redundant systems were tested, calibrated, and retested. Communication with Mission Control was established and rehearsed, voice lines bouncing from satellites with crisp clarity. Every payload was logged, verified, and stowed, leaving nothing to chance.

But beneath the procedures, there was humanity. A quiet psychologist sat with each of them for a final emotional check-in. No probing, just present as an anchor amidst the chaos. Nerves, excitement, and doubt were all normal and valid.

Then came the hardest part of the day—the goodbyes.

In a quiet lounge bathed in golden light, families gathered. Hushed words were exchanged. Children clung a little tighter, and partners fought back tears. Promises were made to return, to stay safe, to make it worth it. the astronauts smiled for photos, laughing gently, trying to mask the knot in their stomachs. There was no certainty in this line of work. Only hope.

Later in their bunker, the crew lay still and quiet. The world outside continued to turn, but for them, time had slowed. They stared at the ceiling and listened to their own breathing, knowing that soon, the only thing separating them from the stars would be a wall of metal and fire.

*

With three hours to go before the launch of *Tarayaan*, the atmosphere in Charlton's bar was abuzz with excitement as spectators passing through on their way to the space centre prepared to witness the rocket launch. People of all ages were grabbing beers and drinks to enjoy the spectacle.

"Hey, old man, can I get a beer?" a spectator inquired, gesturing toward the bar.

"Me too," chimed in another spectator, raising their hand.

Charlton nodded and hurriedly handed them their beers. One of the patrons waited to close their tab. "Me and the missus are heading down to Cape Canaveral for the launch."

"Got to be a great view," Charlton said.

"You should go too, close up the bar for a little while. It's not like you see something like this twice in your life."

Something sad flickered on Charlton's face. But he smiled and handed the patron his change. "Yeah, I'll definitely think about it."

*

As Harry and the others walked in silence towards the transport vehicle, the corridors narrowed into the gallery of faces. Framed portraits lined the walls—sepia-toned at first, then shifting into sharper colour with each passing decade. Glenn Philips, jaw set with Cold War resolve. Scott E. Stone, mid-laugh, helmet tucked under one arm. Annabel Jonassen, eyes fierce, as though daring gravity to try her. Aidan Klassen, gaze distant, already halfway to the stars.

The footsteps of the team slowed. No one spoke.

Harry's eyes lingered on the dates beneath each name. some of them had flown when missions still felt like gambles. Others had flown when the world had almost forgotten to look up. Each photo caught something unspoken–fatigue, courage, fear–and together, they pressed down on his chest like an invisible weight.

He felt his own reflection in the glass of the last frame. Soon, another picture would join this hallway. His, if they made it back.

As the clock ticked down to just one hour before the launch, the tension and excitement in and around the spaceship were palpable. The astronauts completed their final checks, ensuring that their suits and equipment were in perfect condition. The ground crew went through their last-minute preparations, making sure that everything was for the momentous event.

Outside the spaceship, spectators gathered in anticipation, their eyes fixed on the enormous rocket that stood tall on the launch pad. The setting sun cast a warm glow over the scene, creating a surreal atmosphere as people from all walks of life came together to witness history in the making.

Inside the spaceship, the astronauts exchanged encouraging words, reminding each other of the importance of their mission and the trust placed in them by humanity. They went through their pre-launch procedures meticulously, readying themselves for the challenges and adventures that awaited them beyond the stars.

As the countdown continued, the world held its breath, waiting for the moment when the rocket engines would roar to life and propel the spaceship into the unknown.

Spectators waved flags representing their nations, creating a sea of colours and patriotism. Music filled the air, its rhythm syncing with the pulsating anticipation of the crowd. Some spectators couldn't contain their excitement, breaking into spontaneous dances, their joy infectious. Amidst the celebratory atmosphere, some couldn't help but bite their nails in nervous tension, fully aware of the risks involved in space exploration. They held their collective breaths, praying silently for a successful mission.

As the clock inched closer to 7.30 a.m., the astronauts embarked on Tarayaan. They moved with precision, each step rehearsed countless times, ensuring that all the required switches and knobs were enabled as per the checklist. Inside the spaceship, a controlled chaos reigned as the crew finalised their preparations.

Back at the space centre, Clark's tension was palpable. He stood among the mission control team, his eyes glued to the monitors displaying vital information from the spaceship. Every heartbeat felt like an eternity as the seconds ticked away. The weight of responsibility bore down on everyone involved in the mission. But above everything else, he couldn't help but constantly be reminded of the *Echolight* incident. He knew he must not think about that, and instead focus on *Tarayaan*, but he kept finding his eyes drifting towards the propulsion engineer, as though waiting for the engineer to pipe up that there had been a system malfunction. *No,* Clark told himself. *Nothing like that can happen again. Ruma is on the spacecraft, for god's sake. Pull it together!*

The communication lines between the space centre and the spaceship remained open, a lifeline connecting those on Earth to those about to venture into the unknown. The countdown continued, and the world held its breath, ready to witness the next giant leap in human exploration.

Inside the spaceship, as the tension mounted, each astronaut coped with their thoughts and emotions.

Symmonds paused beside his bunk, fingers brushing the curling edge of a photo taped to the wall. The image had faded slightly, the colours dulled by time and distance, but the faces were unmistakable. His partner's lopsided smile, his daughter mid-laugh, arms flung around a chocolate coloured dog. He let his thumb rest on the corner of the picture, just long enough to feel the quiet hum of the ship beneath his skin. They weren't there. But somehow, they were.

Across the cabin, Mikhail shifted in his harness for the third time in as many minutes. Sweat gathered at his temples, catching the sterile overhead lights and trailing down his jaw. He ran a hand through his hair, then wiped it on his pant leg again. The recycled air felt too still, the metal walls too close. He inhaled deeply, as if to stretch the shrinking space inside his chest, but the breath caught halfway.

Symmonds glanced at him briefly, then turned back to the photo. They were all carrying something into the stars.

"Mikhail. Helmet," Ruma said curtly. Mikhail didn't wait for a second before he jammed the helmet back on his head. Ruma spared a brief glance to verify and then looked ahead, a steely look of determination fixed on her face.

Finally, Clark's voice came through the microphone. "Everybody, we are ready for the launch."

The Communication system team leader reported, "T-30 seconds."

"Booster," Laura confirmed.

"Ready to go," the leader of the Engine team affirmed.

"Everything is set up," the Communication team reported.

As the countdown reached the single digits, the spaceship began to tremble, and the tension in the room reached its peak.

"T-10 seconds ... T-9 seconds ..."

Symmonds, Mikhail, and Harry clung to their seats tightly as the spaceship began to tremble during the launch. The intense vibrations filled the cabin, making it hard to focus on anything else. Each second felt like an eternity as the countdown continued. Ruma, on the other hand, kept her eyes open, her expression determined and fearless. She was ready for the adventure that awaited her in the stars.

As the countdown continued, the tension inside the space centre grew dense, almost physical, like a storm brewing just beneath the surface. The seconds ticked away relentlessly, each one a drumbeat echoing through every heart in the launch facility.

T-8 seconds.

Harry gripped the armrests of his seat, feeling the vibrations humming through the capsule. His breath fogged the inside of his helmet for a moment before the ventilation kicked in. *We're really doing this*, he thought.

T-7 seconds.

A soft click in his earpiece signalled an update from Mission Control. Routine. But nothing about this moment felt routine. He glanced sideways at his crewmates, seeing only visors reflecting back his own nervous anticipation. Beneath them, a tower of fire and engineering genius waited to be unleashed. His pulse matched the rhythm of the countdown.

T-6 seconds.

Don't think about what can go wrong. Just breathe. The words belonged to his psychologist from the final emotional support session. Harry inhaled slowly, deeply. His suit felt tighter than usual. The pressure wasn't from the layers of Kevlar and polymers—it was from the weight of expectation, of dreams stretching across decades and generations.

T-5 seconds.

In the Control Room, Clark stood stone-still, knuckles white as he gripped the edge of the console. Laura flicked her eyes between data streams and telemetry, lips pressed into a tight line. Engineers whispered updates. The tension was a wire pulled taut, waiting to snap, to sing.

T-4 seconds.

Harry closed his eyes briefly. For a moment, it wasn't the capsule he felt around him. It was the soft, warm grass of the backyard of Charlton's bar. He lay there next to his grandfather, who pointed out the various constellations in the sky. The capsule smelled of metal and electricity, but to Harry, it was stardust and memory.

T-3 seconds.

The engines came alive beneath them with a low growl, like an awakening giant. Harry's fingers tightened reflexively around his armrests. Ruma's voice crackled over the comms, calm and confident: "Commander Sharma. All systems green."

T-2 seconds.

Harry heard someone, maybe himself, whisper, *please.* Whether it was the plea to the ship, to the stars, or to fate itself, he couldn't tell. Everything had led to this moment.

T-1 second.

The silence before ignition was louder than anything. In that sliver of suspended time, Harry thought not of his mission, but of the Earth—fragile, blue, spinning quietly behind his closed lids.

"Ready for liftoff!"

The rocket roared to life, its engines igniting with an incredible burst of power. Flames and smoke billowed from the launch platform as the spacecraft began its ascent into the sky. The spectators on the ground cheered, and emotions ran high as the rocket soared higher and higher, leaving Earth's atmosphere behind. The astronauts onboard felt the immense forces of the launch as they were propelled into space. The adventure had begun, and the journey to another planet was underway.

Clark turned to the countdown clock. The numbers fell one by one, each second dragging heavier than the last. No one spoke. Eyes flicked between monitors and control panels. Somewhere, a breath was held too long. Then, the first critical updates came in.

"Booster separation complete. Smooth."

"120 seconds. Acceleration stable."

"180. All readings nominal."

"240. Clear."

"300 seconds. Rocket is autonomous now."

Clark didn't realise his fists had been clenched till he let them go. His gaze stayed locked on the screen as the rocket pushed farther into the sky. Relief lit him in a wave. His eyes burned.

"It's a successful launch!" Williams shouted, nearly breathless.

Clark nodded, swallowing hard. "Yes, it is."

Monitors displayed a clean trajectory. No anomalies. No surprises.

"All systems green," one of the specialists confirmed.

"Trajectory is spot on," another added.

And just like that, the tension gave way to the quiet triumph. The mission was underway.

As the launch spectacle concluded and the spaceship disappeared into the vastness of space, the ground began to empty. Spectators gradually made their way home or to other post-launch activities, but Charlton remained seated, his gaze fixed upon the blue, cloudless sky.

***

Chapter IX

Inside the spaceship, once they were in the weightless environment of space, the astronauts took off their seat belts, allowing the buckles to float freely in microgravity. With practised movements, they gracefully pushed off from their seats, floating in the air within the spacecraft.

Harry, eager to demonstrate a feature of the spaceship, spoke up. "We have a special feature called Gravity Mode," he explained, reaching for a control panel. He confidently pressed the button, expecting the artificial gravity to activate.

However, instead of smoothly transitioning into a simulated gravity environment, there was a momentary confusion. The buckles, which had been floating, suddenly fell to the seats with a clatter, and the crew members dropped abruptly to the floor.

Harry scratched his head and chuckled. "My bad," he admitted with a sheepish grin. Despite the momentary hiccup, the astronauts continued to adapt to their surroundings. They began the process of removing their spacesuits and helmets, preparing for the tasks and experiments that lay ahead in the weightless realm of space.

As the astronauts adjusted to the weightlessness of space, they continued to remove their spacesuits. Carefully, they unzipped the suits, revealing the regular clothing they wore underneath. Each astronaut had a set of comfortable attire designed for their time aboard the spacecraft. With the suits removed, they felt more at ease and began floating freely in the spacious interior of the spaceship.

Ruma turned to them with a small smile on her face. "How is everyone feeling?"

Each one contemplated the question, their emotions running deep. Mikhail, always the scientist, responded first. "I feel a mix of excitement and curiosity."

Symmonds, who had been sweating nervously earlier, now looked calmer. "It's strange, but I feel strangely serene. I guess I'm just relieved that the launch went smoothly."

Harry, with his characteristic humour, chimed in. "Well, I'm feeling great now that I've figured out how to turn off Gravity Mode. But seriously, it's a once-in-a-lifetime experience, and I'm ready for the adventure."

Ruma nodded, satisfied with their responses. She was determined to lead her team through the challenges of space exploration, and she knew they were all in this together.

"Let's get to work, team," she said with resolve. "There's a lot to accomplish, and we've got a planet to explore."

"May I have your attention?" a familiar voice rang out, making them all jump. They then turned to see a hologram of Clark appear in the spaceship, and they turned their attention towards him. His presence, even as a hologram, provided them with a sense of connection to Earth and their mission's purpose.

"Welcome aboard," said Clark, smiling genially. "Now that I can see you, and I can easily monitor you virtually."

Before he could ask, Ruma chimed in with the status he was clearly looking for: "All good here, Professor Clark. *Tarayaan* seems to be functioning perfectly, and the crew is in good health."

Clark smiled softly at his daughter and nodded. "That's good to hear. You all should get some rest; it's been a long day. Good night, will speak to you soon."

The astronauts waved and bid Clark good night, after which his hologram disappeared.

*

Symmonds had taken on the job of providing a live interaction from space. It had garnered a significant audience from the people on Earth. The crew members inside the spaceship waved and smiled as Symmonds panned the camera to capture each of their faces.

"Hi, folks!" Symmonds continued, enthusiasm evident in his voice. "We're here in the spaceship with the Gravity Mode turned on, so it's not all floating around. We're on a mission to explore new horizons and make incredible discoveries."

As Symmonds continued to interact with the viewers, he provided glimpses of life inside the spaceship, showcasing their daily routines, the technology they used, and the breathtaking views of space through the spacecraft's windows. It was a moment of connection between the crew and the people back on Earth, a reminder of the shared human spirit of exploration and discovery.

The comments section of the livestream was flooded with messages of encouragement, curiosity, and wonder from people all over the world as they tuned in to witness this extraordinary journey.

Harry's call prompted the crew members to gather and embark on a tour of the different capsules within the spaceship. Symmonds, with his video camera still rolling, led the way as they explored each area.

"Now, folks, we're going on a space tour to give you a glimpse of what we have in this incredible spaceship," Symmonds announced with excitement.

The corridor opened into a spherical chamber at the end of the ship. Walls curved above and below them like a planet turned inside out. Light pulsed gently along the seams, illuminating the passageways that led outward like spokes on a wheel. No one said much as they started together, but drifted off to their separate explorations.

Mikhail hovered in place, rubbing the sweat from his brow. The recycled air felt thick in his lungs, heavier than it had in the shuttle. He drifted towards one of the spokes, drawn more by movement than intent.

Symmonds, meanwhile, caught sight of his bunk as he passed the sleeping capsule. He hesitated, then floated in. The space was compact and personal. Each pod had a thin privacy curtain, a touchscreen, and a shelf. And on his shelf, taped to the metal wall, was a photograph. Slightly curled, edges worn. His daughter's missing front teeth, his partner's weary grin. He stared at it longer than he meant to, letting the hum of the ship fill the space where words might have gone.

Elsewhere, Harry ducked into the entertainment capsule. He let out a low whistle. "You've got to be kidding," he muttered, eyes wide. Billiards. A bowling lane. A floating dartboard anchored by magnets. One wall curved into a giant display screen already cycling through movie options. Even a skateboarding rig, modified for zero-G. He grabbed a cue stick and nudged a ball. It floated away at an odd angle, and he laughed, feeling like he had stepped into a futuristic version of Charlton's bar.

Ruma wandered into the food capsule, her stomach already reminding her that launch nerves had kept her from eating much. She watched a coffee dispenser hiss into motion, the liquid forming into a neat, sealed pouch. Beside it, machines lined with selections: sushi, samosas, carbonara, ramen. It made her smile and feel comforted.

Mikhail finally found himself in the wellness capsule. The air felt cleaner here—infused, maybe, with something herbal. He pressed a palm to the glass cabinet full of medical supplies, then drifted past the diagnostic chairs and treadmill rigs. A spa tub, bubbling gently, sat in one corner. His breathing slowed.

In the rover capsule, Harry was already poking around the exploration technology. The machines were quiet, their frames sleek, matte-black. He ran his hand along one rover's chassis and whispered, "We're going to find things no one has ever seen."

The incubation capsule pulsed with soft blue light, its equipment humming quietly—labs, controlled chambers, rows of sealed drawers filled with research materials. Ruma stood at the centre, utterly still, imagining the experiments that would begin here—some that might never end.

Eventually, they all found their way to the communication capsule. The curved wall was a live feed of Earth, half in daylight, half in shadow. A quiet awe settled over them.

*

After a whirlwind day of adrenaline, awe and silent nerves, the astronauts finally retreated to their sleeping capsules. Each small chamber, no larger than a walk-in closet, offered just enough room to float, tether in and shut the door. Compared to the sprawling beds they'd left behind on Earth with weighted blankets, bedside books and the distant hum of traffic or rustling trees—these capsules felt sterile and confining. The walls were padded, the lighting dimmed to a soft amber, and the air recycled with a faint mechanical hiss.

But exhaustion had a way of making even this compact space feel like a sanctuary. Their bodies, running on dwindling adrenaline and tightly wound anticipation, surrendered to the stillness. Yet, in the quiet, minds drifted. What if a micrometeorite punched the hull while they slept? What if one fuel gauge was just a little off? What if something small—an overlooked seal, a faulty valve—set off a chain reaction too fast to stop?

They knew the ship was secure. They trusted the systems. But trust, in space, was always accompanied by a sliver of fear. Still, sleep came—fitful to some, deep for others, as the stars hung outside, watching in silence.

*

The astronauts woke up in their sleeping capsules, refreshed and ready to start a new day in space. Ruma was sipping her coffee while Harry, Symmonds, and Mikhail gathered in the food court capsule.

"Good morning, everyone," Ruma greeted them.

"Morning," Harry greeted as he floated into the food capsule. "What's on the menu today?"

Ruma gestured toward a row of sleek, cylindrical machines. "Plenty. Just speak or gesture, the AI handles the rest."

The food court was a tranquil, dome-ceilinged chamber. Ambient nature sounds mingled with soft jazz. Water trickled behind glass panels, giving the illusion of a forest stream. It was a strange contrast, like serenity wrapped in steel.

Symmonds looked around in amazement. "This place is amazing."

"Coffee machines, Food machines. Hot *and* cold," Mikhail added, eyeing the beverage dispensers.

The vending units gleamed, touchless and intuitive. Holographic displays lit up with high-resolution images of meals and snacks. It had everything from protein shakes to soups to wraps, deserts, and vacuum-sealed fruits. A nearby table lit up as Symmonds and Mikhail sat, and a serving robot hovered beside them.

"Didn't think I'd ever have breakfast in space," Symmonds said. "I miss the smell of bacon and eggs back on Earth."

"Bacon and eggs, noted," replied the robot.

"Wait. You have that?"

"Yes."

Symmonds grinned. "Then I want the full works: bacon, eggs, sausages, baked beans, toast, black pudding, mushrooms, tomatoes, and an English breakfast tea."

The robot turned to Mikhail, who was ready, "*Syrinki*, buckwheat porridge, Russian black bread, and tea."

Soon, steaming plates appeared before them. Symmonds activated a camera. "English breakfast ... in space," he narrated, then panned to Mikhail. "*And* Russian breakfast".

They took their first bites in silence. Symmonds' eyes widened. "Rivals my partner's cooking, I swear."

*

After the crew had finished eating their breakfasts, they headed to the central conference hall, armed with notebooks, pens and the mission programme. They were to be briefed by Clark.

"Hello, everyone," said Clark as he appeared on the large screen at the front of the chamber. His face, sharp and serious, flickered slightly with the transmission lag. He gave a brief wave, his expression warm despite the urgency in his tone.

"I am here for an important briefing," he continued. "Our primary objective is to determine which planets are capable of sustaining life."

The room fell silent as he stepped closer to the camera on his end. Then he turned his attention to Symmonds.

"Symmonds, I want you to collect samples of air, water, and soil composition once you land. Analyse them thoroughly and draw insights on the planet's habitability."

He shifted his gaze towards Mikhail next. "Mikhail, your task is to monitor the planets' signals—their radiation levels, magnetic waves, and any unusual frequencies. We need to know what kind of environment we're dealing with."

Then, with a brief smile, Clark added, "You won't be alone in this. I'd like to introduce someone who will be assisting you on the ground."

At his cue, a small robot hovered into view from a side chamber. Gleaming white with a rounded, frosty exterior and glowing blue eyes, it resembled a friendly snowball brought to life. Its body was smooth and compact, with multi-jointed limbs and retractable tools tucked into compartments along its sides.

"This," said Clark, "is Snobo."

The robot turned to face the crew and chirped a greeting in a synthesised voice, its eyes blinking cheerfully. Despite its size, there was something unmistakably eager about it—like a winter helper ready to work.

"Alright, enjoy the journey," Clark said and left the crew to their own devices.

Ruma, with a focused and determined expression, continued her explanation about the mission. The hologram of the solar system illuminated the room, capturing the crew members' attention. The hologram displayed planets, moons, and stars, creating a mesmerising visual as they discussed their mission and the data they would collect on different celestial bodies.

"We all know that there are eight planets, and we will land on each planet one by one. The first one will be the Moon, as it is closest to us," Ruma said and waving her hand on the hologram, made various graphics of the moon appear, including its surface, interiors, temperature, and more.

Ruma zoomed in on the Moon, "Our primary goal is to collect, scan, and examine climatic conditions of the Moon. Space Centre has already launched Towers on all the planets. We will accumulate data from 'Cataract Disc', which has all the related planet's data", Ruma said. She then opened the holographic image of a tower containing the Cataract Disc. "On the lunar surface at the coordinates Longitude, -364.321, Latitude, 6.733, of the North Zone. It's a few miles away from Utopia crater, and that's where we are going to land. Mikhail, you want to explain further?"

"Sure," said Mikhail and picked up a tablet from the table and waved it. "Essentially, we will compare the data we collect from each planet to the data we find in the next planet and so on and so forth. You'll each have access to this tablet, and any and all observations are vital, so do feed them in. By comparing the data, we'll gain insights into the potential challenges and opportunities each planet offers for future colonisation. It's a crucial part of our mission to find a suitable new home for humanity."

Ruma nodded along. "And the data that we all collect will be further analysed by Snobo." As Mikhail sat down, Ruma gave them all a tight smile. "Like Mikhail said, we can't ignore any information that we find. Even if the data you've collected is not your area of expertise, I urge you to input it. We need to find the right planet to inhabit, team."

***

Chapter X

A few days later

Harry gripped the controls of the lunar lander, his knuckles white underneath his gloves as he carefully adjusted the thrusters. Outside the window, the moon's grey, pockmarked surface loomed larger with every passing second. The vehicle shuddered slightly, a subtle bump that signalled a sudden gust from escaping gases. Alarms stayed quiet, but the tension was audible in the cabin.

Ruma's voice crackled through the comms system, steady, but tight. "Harry, maintain your descent rate. We need a smooth landing, no overcorrections." Her eyes flicked between the monitors, tracking fuel consumption, descent velocity, and angle of entry like a conductor scanning sheet music mid-performance.

Symmonds leaned closer to the altitude gauge. "Altitude is at 500 meters and falling steadily. Looking good so far, just keep it clean, Harry." But even he couldn't disguise the strain in his voice.

The lander jolted again, sharper this time, as Harry adjusted to a sudden lateral shift. He feathered the control thrusters, fighting to keep their path aligned. Microseconds mattered now.

"Easy on the controls, Harry," Mikhail said from behind. "We don't want any surprises now."

He clutched the seat straps tighter as another tremor passed through the cabin; not dangerous yet, but enough to make their bodies sway with the momentum.

Harry's jaw clenched. His fingers danced over the console with precision born of training and instinct. "Don't worry, folks," he replied, voice low and controlled. "I've got this. Landing gear engaged ... adjusting pitch ... coming in."

A final descent was the longest thirty seconds of their lives. The lander vibrated faintly as the retro-thrusters fired in carefully-timed bursts, counteracting gravity's pull. Dust kicked up from the moon's surface, forming a silvery haze around them. The ground seemed to rise up towards them.

Then came a dull, metallic thud. The landing gear touched down, and the motion stopped. A collective exhale filled the cabin. They were down.

Ruma gave a shaky smile, checking her instruments one last time. "Touchdown confirmed. Systems are stable."

Mikhail let out a long breath. "Now *that's* what I call a lunar ballet."

"Nice flying, Harry." Symmonds grinned.

Harry allowed himself a brief smile. "Just another day at the office."

As the crew members in the spacesuit stepped out of the lunar vehicle and onto the Moon's surface, they were filled with a mix of emotions—awe, excitement, and a sense of accomplishment. For many of them, it was their first time setting foot on another celestial body, and the experience was nothing short of extraordinary.

Ruma stood frozen for a moment, her breath catching in her throat. Through the viewpoint, the moon unfolded before her in all its stark, haunting beauty—an endless stretch of grey regolith. Pockmarked by ancient craters and ridged with jagged rock formations that cast long, eerie shadows in the sun's sharp glare. The horizon curved gently beneath a sky of pure black, untouched by atmosphere, where stars glittered cold and unblinking.

She pressed a gloved hand to the glass, overwhelmed by the surreal silence of it all. It was nothing like the photos or simulations. This was raw, alien, and breathtaking. A strange mixture of awe and disbelief surged through her. She was really here. On the moon.

Symmonds' eyes were wide with wonder, his gaze sweeping across the alien landscape outside the viewport. He took a slow step forward, as though the act of moving might disrupt the fragile magic of the movement.

Mikhail stood beside them, silent at first, his lips slightly parted. His expression was one of stunned disbelief, as if he were still trying to convince himself that this wasn't just another simulation.

Ruma turned to them, her voice soft, but charged with emotion. "Guys, how are you feeling?"

Symmonds exhaled shakily, his voice almost reverent. "I can't believe my eyes. To see something like *this* ... on the moon ..." he trailed off, unable to find words that could just do justice to what he was witnessing.

Mikhail murmured his response, as though speaking it aloud would make it real. "Little steps ... on the Moon." He glanced down at their footprints already etched into the soft, powdery surface like history in the making.

For a moment, no one said anything else. They simply looked at one another—silent, overwhelmed, and united by the impossible beauty surrounding them.

Symmonds and Mikhail wasted no time in setting up the base camp on the lunar surface. With their astronaut training and expertise, they efficiently assembled the necessary equipment and established a secure area for conducting experiments and research.

Meanwhile, Ruma, Harry, and Snobo embarked on their mission to collect the Cataract Disc. Their helmets' visors displayed the coordinates and guided them to the designated location on the Moon's surface. The desolate lunar landscape stretched before them, illuminated by the soft glow of Earth in the distance.

"Tower's navigation," Harry said by tapping his wrist console. "Mapping initiated."

"500 metres North," Snobo said. "Ten minutes fifty-six seconds if you walk."

"Everything looks good," Mikhail said, looking at the signals and waves on the tab.

While Symmonds and Mikhail made their way to investigate the base camp, Ruma closely monitored the coordinates and made adjustments as needed to ensure they stayed on course. As they traversed the desolate lunar landscape, the crew found themselves surrounded by a hauntingly beautiful blend of grey regolith, shallow craters, and jagged rock formations that loomed like ancient sentinels against the black surface. Each step stirred up fine lunar dust that clung stubbornly to their suits, and though the moon lacked a true atmosphere, faint bursts of electrostatically charged particles occasionally kicked up gritty sand that lightly pelted their visors—a reminder of just how alien and unpredictable this world was. The silence was absolute, broken only by their breathing and the soft crunch of boots on the powdery surface as they pushed forward, covering roughly 300 meters across uneven terrain.

Eventually, they reached a cratered depression where the light could not fully reach, casting the area into deep, shadowed greys. Nestled at the centre was a small, still pond.

Its surface dark and glassy, layered with what looked like sheets of frozen white ice water. The sight of it stopped them in their tracks. Here, in the depths of this lifeless world, was a pocket of possibility—a stark contrast to the barren stretch behind them. The ice shimmered faintly under their helmet lights, evoking both scientific curiosity and quiet awe.

"Snobo, what are your findings?" Harry asked.

"It's a darker side of the moon filled with sandstorms, temperature decreasing every hour, and capricious weather conditions," Snobo replied. "Helium has been detected on this planet."

Ruma and Harry started breathing heavily as they began climbing a hill.

"100 metres, Northeast," said Ruma.

Harry glanced up at the distant blue and white marble hanging in the ink-black sky, a smile tugging at the corner of his lips. "You know, back on earth, people are probably on their evening walks, staring up at the moon and enjoying the breeze."

Ruma looked over at him, her eyes crinkling behind the visor. "And here we are, walking on the moon, staring back at Earth."

Harry chuckled. "Now *that's* what I call a moonwalk."

Ruma burst out laughing. "Terrible! But I'll allow it."

As Harry, Ruma and Snobo travelled and ascended the ridge, the tower came into clearer view. Its structure gleamed in the moonlight. Reaching the tower entrance, the team encountered the sealed hatch. With Snobo's mechanical strength and precision, the hatch opened, revealing a dimly lit interior.

Snobo stepped forward, "Initiating entry sequence."

Inside the tower, a series of chambers and corridors unfolded before them. Their path was illuminated by the glow of their suit lights and Snobo's built-in lighting.

"Keep an eye out for any security measures," Ruma cautioned. "We need to make sure to retrieve the cataract disc safely."

As they progressed deeper into the tower, they reached the chambers where the Cataract Disc was stored. It was resting atop a pedestal, encased in a protective container, about thirteen inches in size.

Harry examined the disc, "This is it. Ruma, the Cataract Disc is ready for retrieval."

Ruma smiled at Harry. "Great job."

"Mission fulfilled. Returning to base camp," Snobo said.

*

In the meantime, Mikhail and Symmonds were meticulously setting up base camp, assembling modules, connecting cables, and securing pieces of equipment for sustained lunar exploration.

As Ruma, Harry, and Snobo approached the base camp, Mikhail and Symmonds welcomed them with enthusiasm.

Mikhail smiled, "Welcome back, team. I believe the Cataract Disc retrieval was a success," Mikhail said.

Symmonds extended a hand. "Great job."

Ruma shook their hands. "Thank you."

The crew stepped into the U-shaped lunar base camp, their boots leaving gentle imprints on the grey regolith. The structure had been meticulously designed to support both rigorous and scientific research and essential human rest.

The first arc of the base housed the main research lab, a sophisticated space outfitted with cutting-edge technology, tailored for the moon's unique environment.

The lab buzzed with quiet efficiency. Spectrometres, chromatographs, and high-powered microscopes analysed rock and soul samples, unlocking the secrets of the moon's composition. Advanced seismo meters tracked subtle lunar tremors, while cosmic radiation detectors studied space weather and particle interactions. A meteorological station collected data on temperature, pressure and humidity, helping scientists understand the harsh lunar conditions. Further along, the botanical research area offered a glimpse into the future of space habitation. Specialised growth chambers simulated lunar gravity and light, allowing plants to be cultivated and studied in controlled environments.

Crossing the thin diaphragm that divided the wings, the crew entered the second half of the camp—a tranquil retreat designed for rest and recovery. Sleeping pods lined the walls, offering privacy and comfort. Relaxation chambers glowed with ambient light to ease the stress of lunar living. At the far end, an observatory dome provided a breathtaking view of the barren lunar terrain and the Earth shining in the distance.

"Snobo," called Harry. "Oxygen levels?"

Snobo displayed data on the screen, "Current oxygen levels within the base camp are stable and within safe limits. We are utilising a combination of stored and regenerative systems," Snobo said.

"Everybody, you can take off your helmets," Ruma commanded.

Mikhail unfastened his helmet, exhaling. "Ah, I feel better now," he said.

Symmonds removed his gloves, "Don't worry, Harry," he said, smiling at Harry's slightly sceptical expression. "This camp's air is double purified and filtered".

Suddenly, a low rumble reverberated through the base camp, followed by a subtle, but glowing tremor beneath their feet. Lights flickered momentarily as a fine mist of lunar dust began to swirl past the observation dome. The camp shook slightly, and equipment in the research lab rattled on their mounts, some instruments shifting just enough to trigger warning blips on nearby monitors.

Harry glanced around, brows furrowed. "What's going on?" he asked, steady against the wall.

Ruma checked the external sensors, her voice calm, but alert. "It's a regolith storm. Charged particles might have kicked up a wave of dust."

Outside, the lunar surface was nearly obscured by the rising clouds of fine grey particles. "All right, everyone, relax," Ruma said, her tone taking command. "Secure your gear and try to get some rest. We'll ride it out, it should pass soon."

***

Chapter XI

As the lunar day broke over the horizon, a pale golden glow crept across the rugged grey terrain. Inside the base camp, Ruma, Harry, Symmonds, and Mikhail gathered quietly in the prep bay. The silence wasn't solemn, it was focused. They had all grown used to the hush of space, the lack of birdsong or weather. But today, there was something more–anticipation.

"Another lunar day ahead of us," Symmonds muttered, stretching out his arms as he reached for his suit. "Let's go add another chapter to the Moon's diary."

One by one, they pulled on their suits with swift, practised movements. The liquid cooling garments were the first layer, silently regulating their core temperatures. Over them came reinforced protective layers designed to shield against the vacuum of space, cosmic radiation, and lunar dust, sharp enough to wear through steel over time.

Ruma's voice crackled through the comms as she activated her helmet display. "Pressure, temperature, oxygen ... all normal. Safety protocols, everyone. We're good to go."

The next few days, Days two through seven, were a blur of movement and meticulous documentation. The team scattered across designated sites, each member falling into rhythms they'd trained for on Earth. Symmonds, ever the geologist at heart, knelt beside ancient rock formations near the rim of an impact crater. With gentle, reverent hands, he scooped up regolith samples into vacuum-sealed containers, as if disturbing sacred ground.

"The lunar soil has been untouched for aeons," he whispered once, almost to himself. "Like it's been waiting for someone to ask it what happened."

Harry, meanwhile, had taken it upon himself to monitor the environmental instruments. Despite his role as systems specialist, he'd started keeping a personal log: notes on radiation spikes, ambient temperature drops, and electrostatic anomalies in the regolith. But nestled between those observations were moments of reflection: "Still no wind. The silence here doesn't feel empty, though. It feels ... old."

Ruma and Mikhail worked in tandem, studying basaltic ridges and performing in situ spectroscopy. They discovered telltale signs of ancient volcanic activity in porous rocks, and even documented a new mineral cluster that shimmered faintly in the lunar light. Their banter over comms kept morale high, with Ruma's precise efficiency often balancing out Mikhail's philosophical musings.

"You know," Mikhail said while adjusting a tripod for a radiation sensor, "we may be looking for new homes ... but I think we're also just looking to understand how anything survives. Including us."

By the time the calendar flipped to Day Eight, the team began to slow their outward journeys. From Day Eight to Thirteen, the focus shifted inward to analysis, discussion, and, in some ways, introspection.

Back inside the base's science module, Harry and Symmonds pored over initial findings. Some regolith samples showed elevated levels of helium-3, an isotope with potential for future nuclear fusion. A particularly fine dust sample hinted at past exposure to water-bearing compounds. These weren't just rocks. They were clues.

In the biology station, Symmonds ran comparative tests on extremophile microbes exposed to the lunar surface. Some had survived. Barely, but survived. He documented changes in structure and colour under the microscope, noting how the mutation rates varied based on exposure time.

“What does that mean?” Mikhail asked.

“It means life, in some form, can adapt, even here,” he replied, his voice quiet. “It changes everything we thought we knew.”

Their evenings became more reflective. Meals were still freeze-dried and laughter was still rare, but a new bond had formed—one born not from camaraderie, but from shared wonder. They weren’t just astronauts executing a mission. They were explorers who had begun to see the Moon as something more than a lifeless rock.

By Day Thirteen, discussions with Mission Control became more dynamic. Adjustments were made to the mission plan based on the team’s findings. There was talk of sending a secondary crew with a mobile lab. Ruma proposed new test locations. Harry compiled a predictive model for dust accumulation on equipment. Even Mikhail, who had once questioned the utility of their efforts, began outlining a theoretical study on human adaptability to prolonged lunar exposure.

In these moments, each of them grew, not just in expertise but in clarity. They had come to the Moon as representatives of Earth’s desperation. But in its silence, they had found something profoundly human: purpose.

From Day Fourteen onwards, the mission entered a quieter, more deliberate phase—one marked not by discovery, but by synthesis. The rush of firsts had passed. Now came the hard part: understanding what it all meant.

Each morning began the same way: helmet checks, coffee tablets, briefings in the mess hall where the hum of machinery and the occasional crackle from Earth filled the silence. But even routine on the Moon had weight. The team had been up there long enough for the novelty to fade, leaving behind a strange blend of normalcy and alienation.

Ruma took the lead on building a detailed resource viability map, combining all gathered data into a single, dynamic topographic model. Her findings identified a shallow sub-crust region rich in ilmenite: a titanium-iron oxide that could be processed to extract oxygen. It was a breakthrough. Oxygen meant the potential for long-term life support systems, and even fuel. If there was a future on the Moon, it might begin here.

Symmonds, who had once spoken about the lunar soil like a historian, now worked like a man possessed. He dug deeper, literally and figuratively, requesting authorisation to deploy ground-penetrating radar to identify deeper rock strata. His scans revealed unusual density shifts that suggested buried lava tubes: potential sites for future underground habitats shielded from radiation.

Meanwhile, Harry grew quieter. He spent long hours alone in the rover, moving between seismic beacons and solar-powered climate sensors. He was tracking minor tremors: micromoonquakes that could indicate tectonic instability. He didn't say it aloud, but it worried him. On Day Sixteen, he brought it up during debrief.

"If we build here, we'll need to reinforce structures. The tremors are mild, but persistent. Lunar crust isn't as stable as we assumed."

Mikhail, hearing this, turned from the viewport. "Nothing on this Moon wants us here. But I think that's what makes staying worth it."

His own focus had shifted to human psychology. With Ruma's support, he had begun documenting their behavioural patterns: their reactions to isolation, silence, repetition. He noted how Harry had started talking less, how Symmonds spoke more to himself than anyone else, and how Ruma became clinical when stressed. And how he, for the first time, felt a strange stillness inside—a peace that unnerved him.

By Day Seventeen, Mission Control requested preliminary conclusions.

The astronauts compiled a comprehensive report. It included data on regolith composition, seismic readings, oxygen extraction potential, microbial survivability, and environmental risks. But it also included something unexpected: a section titled *Human Response to Sustained Lunar Presence*. Ruma had signed off on it. "If we want to live here, not just survive, we need to start studying us too."

The final days, eighteen through twenty-one, were filled with preparation for departure. Containers were sealed, samples tagged, servers downloaded, equipment scrubbed and rechecked.

And yet ... no one moved with urgency. There was a subtle reluctance in their pace. No one said it, but they all felt it: they had changed, and so had the Moon.

Back to base camp's research lab, the lunar soil samples underwent meticulous analysis involving techniques such as spectroscopy, microscopy, and elemental analysis. Each test provided valuable data about the mineral composition, structure, and potential resources of the lunar regolith. The display data on the monitor results shows the presence of various silicates and basaltic components.

On the other end of the lab, Mikhail studied the signal propagation and observed electromagnetic signals, including radio waves and high-frequency signals. He carried a device in the shape of a pod and scanned all the waves and radiation on the lunar surface.

Meanwhile, outside, Ruma, with a clear vision in mind, made her way to the lunar vehicle nearby. Her task involved injecting Cataract Disc into the vehicle's data transmission system. The AI interacted while transmitting the data. She then sent the data to Clark for examination.

As Ruma initiated the data transmission, the AI system within the lunar vehicle activated, facilitating the efficient transfer of data to mission control back to Earth. "Data transmission initiated. Transmitting lunar data to mission control," it said in a synthesised voice. "Data packets are being successful. Estimated time to complete is two minutes."

"Great job," Ruma said briskly. "Please prepare a summary report for Professor Michael Clark and connect with him."

*

In the quiet of his apartment, Clark had just settled in for a restful sleep after a long day of research in the space centre. The soft hum of his alarm clock started to break the silence. As he stirred and reached for the alarm, his heart quickened.

"It can't be morning already, can it?" he murmured to himself.

With a swift motion, he turned off the alarm and, to his surprise, noticed an incoming message from the lunar mission on his communication device. The display flickered to life, revealing a familiar face.

Ruma smiled on the screen, "Good lunar morning, Dad."

Clark immediately sat up, "Ruma!" he exclaimed, and quickly put on his spectacles, which were on the desk.

Ruma laughed. "It sure is, Dad. I could not wait to share the latest lunar data with you."

As Clark's grogginess gave way to excitement, he listened intently to Ruma's enthusiastic updates, feeling a profound connection to his daughter even across the vast distance between Earth and the Moon.

"I am so proud of you and the entire team. Keep up the good job."

"Thanks, Dad. It is an honour to be part of this mission, and your guidance and expertise are invaluable."

Clark beamed at his daughter and then turned his attention to the data transmission she had sent across. "These readings on lunar seismic activity are intriguing."

"I thought you'd think so. And the spectral analysis of the soil sample points to some profound mineral composition. It is a rich tapestry of data we are weaving together."

"I will meet the crew members in a couple of hours from the space centre," he said.

"Sure, Dad, see you soon."

*

When Clark entered the space centre a couple of hours later, he was greeted by the hum of activity and the dedicated team working diligently on various aspects of the lunar mission. He murmured greetings to all of them and then turned on the hologram device.

In the research lab of the lunar base camp, the crew members were diligently conducting their experiments and research activities. As they worked on various scientific tasks, a familiar holographic figure materialised in the lab, gathering the crew's attention. It was Clark in holographic form to interact with the team.

"Greetings, everyone. I hope I am not interrupting your important work," Clark said. "I have been watching and observing your progress closely, and I could not resist the opportunity to join you virtually and discuss the latest discoveries."

Symmonds proceeded to share Data, images, and findings from his experiment. The holographic display showcased the growth of plants and the behaviour of microorganisms in the lunar environment. Symmonds pointed to the data, "We have observed some fascinating adaptation in these organisms. It is clear that life can endure and even thrive in lunar conditions."

"These findings are remarkable, Symmonds. They have profound implications for future lunar habitation and our understanding of extremophiles in space," Clark affirmed. "I appreciate your work and will meet you soon again."

*

Symmonds stepped out of the airlock in his spacesuit and immediately groaned. A thick layer of fine, grey lunar dust blanketed the base camp like a suffocating shroud. "Oh for the love of ... this again?" he muttered to himself, his voice muffled through the comms.

Harry joined him a moment later, eyeing the grit clinging to the solar panels and the edges of the habitat dome. "Looks like the storm hit harder than we thought. We'd better get started before it clogs anything critical."

Symmonds sighed, already reaching for the magnetic broom. "You'd think we were here for a lunar janitorial mission," he said, half-joking. "I didn't go to MIT just to scrape moon dust off panels."

Mikhail's voice crackled through the comms, dry as ever. "Get used to it. Regolith storms are as routine here as morning coffee back home."

"And just as bitter," Symmonds muttered.

The crew settled into the rhythm of cleaning–brushing dust-off solar panels, wiping grit from the lab's outer seals, and checking filters for contamination. Though monotonous, the task had become oddly therapeutic. The physical effort offered a rare reprieve from data charts and microscope lenses, a grounding ritual that pulled them out of their heads and into their bodies. They joked, traded stories, and even competed to see who could clear their section the fastest.

"Eleven more days of this," Symmonds said as he scraped dust from a sensor array, "and I swear, I'm bringing a vacuum on the next mission."

*

After completing their exploration on the Moon for two weeks, it was time for the crew members to return to *Tarayaan*. They had collected valuable data, samples, and insights that would aid their mission's overall objective of finding a suitable planet for habitation. With the lunar vehicle loaded with their findings, they prepared to leave the Moon's surface and return to their spaceship for the next leg of their interplanetary journey.

Ruma sat quietly in her seat as the engines hummed to life, the moon slowly shrinking in the window beside her. Dust still clung to the edges of the hull, the last trace of the grey world they were now leaving behind. Of all the places they were set to explore, this had been the most familiar, the closest to Earth in every way. It had shared their skies, their myths, their dreams. And now, they were saying goodbye to it. The Moon had welcomed them with silence and dust, and in just two weeks, it had taught them more than they'd imagined about survival, adaptation and the fragile hope of creating something lasting on an alien world.

She glanced over at the others. Harry was calm, focused on their ascent, while Mkhail watched the receding surface with a faraway look, as though trying to memorise it. Symmonds exhaled slowly by something quieter. Ruma looked out once more as the Moon faded into the void, knowing what lay ahead would be far stranger, far more distant. This had been the last stepping stone that still felt like a whisper of home. Beyond this, there would be no comfort in the familiar—only the thrill and terror of the unknown.

*

Once the lunar vehicle docked with the spaceship and the crew members stepped out of it, they experienced a sense of refreshment and relief. Being inside the confined lunar vehicle for an extended period can be physically and mentally taxing, so returning to the more spacious and comfortable environment of the spaceship was a welcome change.

The crew members removed their space helmets and suits, allowing them to breathe more freely and comfortably. They could finally stretch their limbs, move about the spaceship, and interact with their fellow astronauts in a more relaxed manner. They decided to decompress in the viewport room, armed with snacks and beverages and feet tucked under them as they felt sleepy and comfortable in their sweats.

Symmonds leaned back in his seat, eyes flicking toward the hologram of Earth rotating slowly above the console. "Did you really think about what Earth looks like from out here?" he asked, breaking the silence. "It's just a dot now. A pale, distant dot. Makes everything smaller. All the wars, all the noise, all the headlines compressed into that tiny speck."

Mikhail, cradling a warm cup of coffee, stared at the globe for a moment before setting it down. "That's the 'overview effect', isn't it? Astronauts say that seeing Earth from space changes them. You stop thinking in borders and start thinking in lifelines. You feel the weight of how much we've taken for granted."

Ruma nodded slowly, her voice softer than usual. "It's humbling. From here, you can't see nations or politics. Just clouds and oceans and a thin shell of atmosphere barely clinging on. And yet, we poison it, fight over it, burn it. we treat it like we have a backup plan."

Harry stood near the viewport, watching the real Earth drift farther away, a pinprick in the eternal dark. "And now here we are, looking for that backup. Another home. But even if we find one, how long before we ruin that, too? We're explorers, yes. But we're also invaders, whether we admit to it or not."

There was a pause as the weight of his words settled over them. The hum of the ship was the only sound for a few moments.

"We need to do better," Ruma said quietly. "Not just when we reach a new planet. We need to learn how to *deserve* one."

"Maybe that's what this mission is really about; not just discovering a new world, but remembering how to value the one we left behind."

Symmonds decided that the mood in the room had become too philosophical, so he nudged Mikhail playfully. "Hey, Mikhail, how about a game of billiards?"

"Billiards?" Mikhail repeated, grinning. "That sounds like a great idea, Symmonds! Let's do it."

"Ruma? Harry?" Symmonds asked.

"Not right now, boys. Harry and I have to deal with the communication program. We will be with you guys as soon as we finish up here."

*

"Alright, Mikhail, let's see if you can handle this," Symmonds said, and the silence in the rec room was rudely interrupted as Symmonds broke the set of billiard balls on the table, making them fly all across.

Mikhail grinned at him. "You're in for a surprise, Symmonds. Watch this." He hit the ball and it sank.

"You know, Mikhail, this billiard table reminds me of our solar system," Symmonds murmured as he lined up another shot.

"Really? How so?"

"Well, each of these billiard balls can represent a planet in our solar system. The cue ball, for example, could be the Sun, and the other balls could be Mercury, Venus, Earth, and so on."

"I see where you're going with this," Mikhail said, nodding with amusement. "So, which planet are you aiming for now?"

"Let's say I'm aiming for Mars," Symmonds said, and he took the shot, but missed it. "Oops, looks like I overshot it, just like a Mars rover landing."

Mikhail laughed. "Well, you've got plenty of other 'planets' to explore on this table. Maybe I'll take a shot at Neptune next."

"Neptune, huh? Well, go ahead, Mikhail. Show me your interplanetary billiards skills."

Mikhail lined up his shot, aiming for the billiard ball that represented Neptune. With a precise stroke, he sank it into the corner pocket.

"And that is why the Soviet Union was the first to go to space."

***

Chapter XII

In the spaceship, Harry went to the communication capsule and instructed the AI to connect to his grandad.

"Please call my grandfather, Charlton Stone," Harry said.

"Initiating call."

Harry eagerly waited to hear Charlton's voice. He was so excited to tell him all that had transpired since they'd had beer in his backyard. *I was on the moon, Grandad, can you believe it? Cause I sure as hell can't, and I still have lunar dust on my space suit.* Harry also knew that although Charlton would never show it to Harry, he was concerned about his grandson. Harry wanted to assure Charlton that he was happy, healthy, and thriving. *The food up here is a million times better than the crap I make at home, Grandad, believe it or not.*

But the AI's words made Harry's excited smile disappear. "I'm sorry, Harry, but it seems we can't establish a connection with your grandfather at this time. There might be a communication issue from our end or back on Earth. We can try again later or send a message if you prefer. Is there anything else I can assist you with?"

"Try again," Harry said, frowning.

Harry stared at the comms terminal, brows furrowed as yet another connection attempt failed. The signal blinked out again, the screen offering nothing but static and silence. He exhaled sharply, leaning back in his seat, trying to push down the unease creeping into his chest. He hadn't heard from his grandfather since he visited him before they'd left for the moon.

A few nights ago, Harry had woken from a vivid dream. In it, Charlton was alone, calling out for help while the earth spun quietly in the distance, unreachable. The image had clung to him ever since. Now, with every failed message, that dream felt less like imagination and more like a warning.

He tapped the edge of the console restlessly, trying to steady himself. "Come on ... just one message," he murmured. But the silence held him. His hand tightened into a fist–not in rage, but helplessness, and he pressed it to the desk with a quiet thud, jaw clenched. He hated feeling this far away, unable to do anything.

He breathed in deeply, trying to control the torrential downpour of emotions about to rain down on him. He closed his eyes, and an old memory came back to him, sudden, but soft.

I remember the afternoon sun beating down on the back of my neck as I darted through rows of grapevines, the sweet scent of ripe fruit heavy in the warm air. I was nine, clumsy and loud, crashing through leaves and sending startled birds into flight.

"Where's grandad?" I'd called out, breathless, grinning up at my grandmother as she poured coffee by the window. "Oh, Queen Eliza-Beth, where is the King?" I teased.

She placed a hand to her chest and smiled, nodding towards the farm. "He's on the field, little mischief."

I ran out, past the bar, past the wooden fence, and there he was–boots caked with soil, hat tipped low, a cigar clenched between his teeth. Bent over a basket, he was plucking grapes with steady hands.

He saw me and laughed. "Oi! Little bunny, don't ruin my vines!" He caught me before I did more damage, and together, we worked side by side, hauling baskets back to the house.

Later, with the 1980s humming from the old radio, grandad and grandma stomped grapes in the pressing vat, boots sloshing in deep purple liquid. I had snuck in, poked a hole at the bottom of the container, and slurped fresh juice straight from the source.

When Grandma saw the empty bucket, she exclaimed, "Where did it go?"

I burped and pointed to my stomach. "It's in here." She chased me around the yard while I hid behind Grandad, who was laughing so hard he nearly spilt his wine.

That night, I fell asleep in Grandma's lap while she read a book, her fingers combing through my hair. The house smelled of grapes and home. And in the morning, she was gone. Just like that. A heart attack, they said. The skies were soft and grey, and a gentle breeze moved through the vines. Grandad carried her to the edge of the farm, where the soil was soft. He built a tombstone, and on it was inscribed, "Beth (1920 – 1980), and placed her favourite flowers on top. He wept like I'd never seen a man weep before. I cried too, not understanding how someone so alive could disappear.

"Unable to connect."

The AI's voice made Harry jump out of his nostalgia. He sighed and made his way out of the Communication Capsule. Just as he opened the door, Ruma walked in.

"Hey Ruma," Harry murmured, wanting to walk past her and be alone with his thoughts.

But Ruma took notice of the forlorn expression on his face and grabbed his arm gently. "Harry. Is everything all right?"

"I could not reach my grandad," Harry replied, his voice tinged with sadness and frustration.

Ruma reached out and placed a comforting hand on Harry's shoulder. She offered a reassuring smile and said, "I'm sure there's a reason he couldn't answer right now, Harry. Maybe he's just busy or had to step away. You can try again later, and I'm sure you'll get through to him."

Harry nodded his head. “I think that’s right, maybe he is busy with some other work.”

“It seems you care about him a lot. Are you two close?”

Harry smiled warmly, his eyes reflecting a mix of affection and nostalgia. “Yeah, he’s been like a father to me. Raised me since I was a kid. He’s my rock, you know?” Ruma smiled and nodded. Harry then probed her in turn. “You’re close with your father, I mean Professor Clark too, aren’t you?”

“I am,” Ruma replied with a thoughtful expression. “He’s been a great mentor to me, and I respect him a lot. But sometimes, I feel like he’s more focused on the mission than anything else. It’s just a different kind of relationship, you know? My dad has always been more focused on saving the habitats on Earth.”

Harry nodded, his eyes showing understanding. “Your dad is a wise man. Dedicating his life to finding another Earth is a noble cause.”

A look of sadness came across Ruma’s face. “I don’t know what we are going to find out in the coming days for habitation. As per the research and survey by Space Centre, sooner or later, we will lose hope and habitation on Planet Earth.”

Harry looked away, looking from the viewport out into the tiny speck that was their home. When he finally spoke, his voice was quiet. “I left my grandad on a dying planet.”

“*We* left Earth”, Ruma reminded him. “Relationships are harder to leave. But we are on a mission to accomplish. No relation should come into the picture,” Ruma said. Harry wasn’t sure if her detachment inspired him or scared him.

***

Chapter XIII

"Congratulations on the successful completion of the lunar exploration. The data is up to the mark and valuable to the Space Centre and mankind. Enjoy your journey."

The astronauts were elated to receive the message from Laura. It was a moment of validation for all their hard work and dedication during the lunar exploration mission. Ruma, Harry, Symmonds, Mikhail, and Snobo contributed valuable data that could potentially shape the future of space exploration and the survival of humanity. They exchanged smiles, knowing that their efforts were not in vain and that they were one step closer to finding a suitable habitat for humanity's future. They were en route to the next planet, and it would take a couple of weeks for them to reach.

"It's party time," Symmonds announced.

"Everybody, freshen up, and let's rock in the bar lounge!" Mikhail ordered the crew.

As they all gathered in the bar lounge, Harry was dressed in a sharp black tuxedo, exuding a classic and timeless style. The perfectly tailored suit accentuated his stature, and he looked every bit the dashing gentleman. Mikhail, on the other hand, had chosen a brown suit, giving off a warm and inviting vibe. The earthy tones of his attire matched his down-to-earth personality, and he looked effortlessly stylish. Symmonds opted for a striking white suit, radiating a sense of elegance and sophistication. The crispness of his ensemble made him stand out in the crowd, and he carried himself with an air of confidence.

Harry, Symmonds, and Mikhail were seated at the bar desk, each holding a glass of wine. The soft lighting in the bar lounge cast a warm glow over their faces as they engaged in conversation. Laughter and the clinking of glasses filled the air, creating a lively atmosphere.

Suddenly, they heard the soft sound of heels approaching. Heads turned toward the entrance as Ruma stepped into the bar lounge. She wore a crimson backless maxi dress that accentuated her every curve and brought out the golden undertones in her skin. The fabric moved like liquid with each step she took—deliberate, graceful, unapologetically self-assured.

It felt, for a fleeting moment, like the world had stilled. The chatter dulled, the clinking of glasses paused, and time seemed to move in slow motion as she walked in, poised, confident, radiant. Her curls framed her face, catching the warm light of the room as if it belonged to her.

There was no performative attempt to impress; her elegance came from within. As she crossed the room, something about her presence seemed to command both admiration and quiet respect, not just for how she looked, but for the strength she carried in her stride. The trio couldn't help but be captivated by Ruma's stunning presence. As she joined them at the bar, a smile lit up her face, and she greeted them with warmth.

As Harry gazed at Ruma, his eyes filled with admiration. He couldn't help but be struck by her beauty and elegance. With a charming smile on his face, he complimented her, saying, "You look even more gorgeous than I ever expected."

Ruma's face was a picture of shock. "Oh, so you never expected me to look gorgeous?"

Harry's mouth hung open as he spluttered, trying to explain what he meant. But Ruma's face softened and she burst into laughter. She laughed so openly, with so much heart and freedom, that Harry felt his heart melt.

"I was just joking, Harry. Oh, your face!"

Harry laughed alongside her. "You are an absolute beauty in space," he said with such great earnestness that Ruma's eyes twinkled.

She smiled at Harry, her eyes sparkling, and blushed slightly at Harry's compliment. "Thank you, Harry," she replied with a hint of shyness. His words made her feel special, and she was genuinely touched by his sweet gesture.

"You look very elegant, Ruma," Symmonds said.

Ruma graciously acknowledged Symmonds' compliment with a warm smile. "Thank you, Arthur," she replied, feeling flattered by their kind words.

Mikhail and Symmonds, caught in the groove of the music, began to move their heads rhythmically as the music played on. Their bodies swayed in sync with the beat, and they exchanged smiles, enjoying the music's infectious energy.

"How are we gonna organise the drinks?" Symmonds asked.

"Let me call Snobo," Mikhail said and was about to get up when suddenly, Harry jumped over the bar table and removed his black blazer. The crew members watched with amusement and anticipation as he grinned at them.

"Now, my wonderful crew, you might not have known this, but while you lot were in your special programs about all things science, I was cleaning dirty glasses at my grandfather's bar. Finally, I get to use my skills." They all laughed. "What would you like to have, Mikhail?"

"Oh man ..." Mikhail thought for a second. "A Negroni, please."

"Coming right up," Harry replied with a smile. He started preparing the Negroni for Mikhail. The crew watched in amazement as Harry skillfully mixed the cocktail, pouring it into a glass with a flourish and garnishing it elegantly.

"There you go, sir," Harry said, placing the Negroni in front of Mikhail. "Enjoy your drink."

"Thank you," Mikhail said.

Harry smiled and turned to Symmonds. "I'm a simple guy, Harry. A G&T, please," Symmonds said.

Harry expertly crafted the gin and tonic for Symmonds, ensuring the perfect balance of flavours. He placed the glass in front of Symmonds, the lime wedge perched elegantly on the rim.

"Here's your gin and tonic, Arthur. Enjoy!" Harry said with a smile.

"This is perfect, Harry," Symmonds said, appreciatively smacking his lips, and Symmonds agreed with him.

Harry beamed with satisfaction at the compliment. "I'm glad you like it, gentlemen. If you need anything else, just let me know."

All it took was for Symmonds and Mikhail to exchange one look for the troublemaker duo to decide on what they were thinking. They gulped the drink in one go and asked for another one.

Harry, feeling playful, began to juggle the glasses skillfully as he prepared the next round of drinks for his friends. His movements were smooth and precise, and they added an element of entertainment to their impromptu bar session.

Ruma, Mikhail, and Symmonds watched in amazement as the glasses flew through the air and were expertly caught and filled by Harry's capable hands.

As the night went on and the drinks flowed, Mikhail and Symmonds, fuelled by the drinks and the lively atmosphere, kicked their dance moves up a notch. They spun around, twirled, and even attempted some daring dance lifts. Laughter filled the air as they grooved to the music, and their movements became more exuberant with each passing moment.

Harry, still in his bartender mode, turned to Ruma with a charming smile.

"Ruma, what would you like to have?"

"Pineapple juice, please."

"Oh come on, order a grown-up drink!" Harry teased her.

Ruma rolled her eyes but smiled at Harry fondly. "*Fine.* A Martini, please."

Harry presented the Martini to Ruma with a flourish, a playful glint in his eye. "Your drink, my lady," he said, offering the martini glass to her with a slight bow.

Ruma smiled as she accepted the glass from Harry. "Thank you, kind sir," she replied, taking a sip of her drink.

Mikhail and Symmonds were having a blast, completely immersed in the music and dancing. Symmonds, always one to capture memorable moments, took out his video camera and began recording their energetic dance moves. The disco lights, music, and overall atmosphere created a fun and carefree environment in the spaceship's bar lounge.

Harry and Ruma, enjoying the lively atmosphere, clinked their glasses together and shared a cheerful "Cheers!" Their glasses held the beautifully crafted cocktails, and they joined in the festivities, feeling the excitement of the moment in the spaceship's bar lounge.

"Whoa, Symmonds, I think we've had a bit too much to drink!" Mikhail exclaimed.

Symmonds laughed. "Yeah, you might be right. Dancing skills seem to have abandoned us."

Mikhail and Symmonds were still dancing when suddenly they fell to the ground, and after a few seconds, burst into laughter. They took a moment to catch their breath before attempting to get up again.

"Well, that was an unexpected dance move!" Mikhail chortled.

"Yeah, we should probably stick to just dancing on two feet from now on," Symmonds said, massaging his back.

They managed to get back on their feet, a bit wobbly but still in high spirits, and continued dancing, taking the mishap in stride. Symmons was the most off-centred of them all as he stumbled around, off-balance. Mikhail teased him for trying to keep up with a Russian when it came to vodka.

Symmonds, rubbing his eyes, started talking absolute gibberish. "Do we have four legs? Look at his two hands and legs? We should dance with our upper legs, right?"

Ruma and Harry saw them and started laughing, the sound echoing throughout the bar lounge as they watched Mikhail and Symmonds trying to dance with their hands upside down.

"Looks like someone's enjoying zero gravity a little too much," she said, a smile tugging at her lips.

Harry chuckled, settling beside her. "Yeah. Zero-G dance party, who knew it'd be the hit of the mission?"

Ruma laughed, a light, unguarded sound. "It's been days since I laughed like this. Feels good."

Harry glanced at her, his tone softening. "So, what do you usually turn to when you're not space-hopping? Got a go-to book or movie?"

She tilted her head thoughtfully. "Always been a sci-fi nerd. I love the kind that dives into the unknown but still feels personal. *Contact*, by Carl Sagan. That one stuck with me."

Harry nodded appreciatively. "Solid choice. I've got a soft spot for Clarke. *2001: A Space Odyssey* blew my mind the first time I read it."

Ruma grinned and raised an eyebrow. "Mind if I grab another drink?"

Harry gave her a mock bow. "By all means, Commander."

As she took a sip, she looked around the lounge, eyes lingering on the floating, laughing crew. "You know, I never imagined myself dancing in a spaceship bar. This whole mission... It's been one surprise after another."

Harry leaned in slightly, his voice low and warm. "And the best ones are the ones we don't plan for."

She met his gaze, her smile softer now. "Exactly. Moments like this remind me why we're out here at all. Why it's worth it."

Harry leaned in a little closer, his voice soft but earnest. "And speaking of dreams, what's your biggest dream, Ruma? What do you hope to find out here in the vastness of space?"

Ruma turned to face him, her expression thoughtful as she held his gaze. For a moment, neither spoke, with just the hum of the ship around them, and the unspoken weight of the stars outside.

She exhaled slowly, her voice low and wistful. “Well ... my dream is to discover a habitable planet. A place where humanity can thrive, start over, maybe do things right this time. It’s a daunting task,” she said, her eyes flickering with a mix of hope and melancholy, “but one that gives purpose to our journey.”

Harry didn’t look away. “That’s a beautiful dream.”

Their hands didn’t touch, but the space between them felt charged, like gravity had quietly shifted.

“And I have a feeling you’ll be instrumental in making it a reality with your expertise in communication and technology,” Harry nodded.

Ruma sipped her drink, eyes still warm from laughter. “Thanks, Harry. What about you? Why space? Just chasing stars, or something more?”

Harry leaned on the counter, thoughtful. “Both. The stars pulled me in early, but ... it started with my grandad. We’d lie on the grass at night, and he’d tell me stories about the universe. I guess I’m out here finishing those stories.”

Ruma smiled. “Funny how childhood dreams end up becoming our compass.”

He lifted his glass. “To chasing dreams.”

She clinked it gently. “And dancing in zero gravity.”

Harry raised an eyebrow. “Dancing?”

Ruma smirked. “Don’t think. Just follow my lead.”

*

They stepped onto the lounge’s floating dance floor. The sensual rhythm of salsa filled the capsule as Ruma guided Harry through the first few steps. He stumbled, grinned, and caught on quickly, matching her rhythm with growing ease.

Ruma laughed, eyes shining. "You're not half bad."

Harry spun her gently, one hand on her waist, the other guiding her with surprising grace. "I learn fast."

As the music intensified, so did their connection–silent, magnetic. Their bodies moved in sync, every step drawing them closer. Harry shed his bowtie and rolled up his sleeves, twirling her with a dancer's confidence. Ruma gasped, caught off guard but thrilled.

He dipped her low, one leg extended in a fluid motion, then pulled her back up effortlessly. Their eyes locked as they were breathless, giddy, electric.

The dance built to a crescendo. Harry lifted her into the air, slow and steady. Ruma stretched her arms, laughing, completely lost in the moment. Around them, the lights blurred, the music surged, and for a brief instant, the universe narrowed to just them.

As the final notes faded, they stood still; sweaty, breathless, hearts pounding. Neither spoke.

Harry and Ruma, still filled with the energy of their dance, made their way to the entertainment capsule. They settled in, and as the movie began to play, Ruma rested her head on Harry's shoulder, finding comfort and closeness in each other's presence as they enjoyed the film together.

The movie played in the background, forgotten.

Afterwards, they wandered the quiet halls of the ship, the silence between them full of meaning. Ruma paused, spotting the shimmering glass of the pool capsule.

She turned to him, smiling. "Swim?"

Harry took her hand. "Lead the way."

***

Chapter XIV

In the swimming pool capsule, Ruma changed into her swimming suit, a sleek and stylish ensemble that fit her perfectly. She stepped into the pool, the water shimmering with a serene blue glow under the artificial lighting. Harry, dressed in his swim trunks, joined her in the water. They exchanged smiles, ready to savour this moment of relaxation and enjoyment together.

A bottle of chilled champagne stood at the edge of the swimming pool, glistening with droplets of condensation in the warm, artificial lighting of the capsule. Two champagne flutes sat beside it, ready to be filled with the effervescent liquid. The soft, ambient music playing in the background added to the romantic atmosphere as Ruma and Harry prepared to toast their extraordinary journey through space.

Harry lifted Ruma gently, and as she floated effortlessly in his arms, a radiant smile spread across her face. Their eyes met, and at that moment, all the wonders of the universe seemed to pale in comparison to the connection they shared. The calm blue waters of the pool embraced them, and for that fleeting moment, they were suspended in time, lost in the beauty of the cosmos and the magic of their love.

They clinked their glasses of champagne in the swimming pool, their laughter echoing in the enclosed space.

"Never expected this, you know," Harry said, his eyes locked onto Ruma's.

Ruma smiled, her cheeks flushed from the champagne. "Me too," she replied, her voice soft and filled with warmth. "Also," she said, leaning over the edge of the pool, "look what I stole."

Harry laughed when he saw Symmonds' video camera in Ruma's hand. "He's going to kill you for touching his baby."

"Nah, he's too drunk to realise it's missing," she said and squinted as she turned the camera to Harry.

With the camera rolling, Ruma captured their laughter, their playful splashes, and the genuine smiles that crossed their faces. The swimming pool capsule had become a heaven of tranquillity amidst the vastness of space, and in that moment, Ruma and Harry found a connection that transcended their roles as astronauts.

As they floated side by side, their fingers gently brushed against each other in the water, a subtle but unmistakable sign of the deepening bond between them. The swimming pool, meant for recreation and relaxation, had become the backdrop for a new chapter in their journey—one that was filled with the promise of discovery, both in space and in matters of the heart.

As Ruma and Harry continued to float in the tranquil waters of the swimming pool capsule, their connection deepened. They gazed into each other's eyes, their smiles fading into a moment of quiet intensity. The weightlessness of space seemed to amplify the emotions swirling between them.

The water around them seemed to shimmer with the magic of that kiss as if the entire universe had conspired to bring them together in that small, intimate space. Their hearts beat in unison, and for that brief moment, they were suspended in time, lost in the depths of their affection for one another.

As their lips parted, they remained close, foreheads touching, their breaths synchronised. It was a moment they would carry with them throughout their mission, a reminder that even in the vastness of space, love and connection could be found, nurtured, and cherished.

With a shared smile, they continued to float in the pool, their hands intertwined, knowing that they had each other's support and love as they ventured into the unknown.

Beneath the water's surface, Harry and Ruma shared a deep, passionate kiss. Their bodies seemed to glow in the soft, ambient lighting, creating a magical, otherworldly atmosphere. Ruma's hair floated around them like a silken halo as they embraced, lost in the beauty of their connection amidst the tranquillity of the pool. Their eyes filled with love and desire, they twinkle with an intensity that matches the stars outside the spaceship.

As they stepped out of the refreshing pool, Harry and Ruma wrapped themselves in plush bathrobes. They made their way down the spaceship's corridor towards their sleeping pods. As they walked together, their footsteps echoed lightly in the quiet, enclosed space.

With a satisfied smile, Harry settled into his sleeping pod, feeling grateful for the technology that surrounded him and the incredible journey that lay ahead. As he closed his eyes, he couldn't help but think about the adventures and discoveries that awaited him and his fellow astronauts in the vast expanse of space.

Unable to find rest in her sleeping pod, Ruma's thoughts continued to swirl with the day's events. Her curiosity got the better of her, and she decided to scan her hand on Harry's pod, knowing that as the Commander, she had access.

The door to Harry's sleeping pod slid open, revealing his peaceful slumber. Ruma quietly entered, the soft lighting casting a warm glow on his face. She watched him for a moment, appreciating the serenity of his features in sleep.

As Harry lay in his sleeping pod, his subconscious mind began to weave dreams, blurring the line between reality and the fantastical world of slumber. In his dream, he saw Ruma, the enchanting astronaut with whom he'd shared an extraordinary journey through space.

In this dreamlike state, Harry believed that he'd merely conjured a vision of Ruma, an ethereal presence gracing his sleep with its magic. He thought he had embarked on a journey through the landscapes of his imagination, where the boundaries of possibility faded away. It was only when he felt something warm and soft touch the side of his face that his eyes opened and the real Ruma sat beside him, her hand cupping his face, a blazing look on her face.

"Ruma, what are you doing?" Harry asked.

Ruma put her index finger on his lips and said, "Shh ..."

Ruma started kissing Harry. Their bodies and lips entwined in a passionate embrace. He could feel the heat emanating from her, and he knew that she wanted her more than anything in the world.

Ruma let herself sink into the moment, her breath catching as Harry's touch ignited a slow-burning fire beneath her skin. Their bodies moved with instinctive rhythm, a dance of desire and trust, of heat and vulnerability. His lips found her neck, trailing kisses along her collarbone before grazing her earlobe, drawing from her a soft moan that echoed the rising intensity between them. Her fingers tangled in his hair, guiding him closer, while his shirt came undone between them—eager hands and deep, lingering gazes doing what words could not. Skin met skin, and every caress, every kiss, was a quiet surrender, a promise written in the language of touch. The world outside fell away as they pressed into each other, exploring, discovering, consumed by a passion that was equal parts tenderness and urgency; fierce, aching, and unrelentingly real.

Afterwards, they lay side by side, their bodies entwined. They had shared a moment of pure bliss, and they both knew that they would never forget it. Then they fell asleep in each other's arms, feeling content in each other's embrace.

They had found something special moment, something that they knew would last eternal. And so, as they drifted off to sleep that night, they knew that they had found a love that would change their lives permanently. They were ready to face the future with each other, hand in hand, heart to heart.

***

Chapter XV

The next day

Symmonds and Mikhail woke up in the bar lounge, feeling the effects of a hangover from the previous night's party. They rubbed their heads and groaned as they tried to piece together the events of the night. They had a bit too much to drink. The gentle rays of the sun streamed through the spaceship's windows, casting a warm and inviting glow over the room. The soft light illuminated the space, gradually dispelling the remnants of their hangover-induced grogginess.

"Well, at least it looks like it's a beautiful morning," Symmonds said, squinting at the bright light.

Mikhail nodded. "Yeah, the sun always has a way of making everything seem better."

"Ugh, my head is pounding. What happened last night?"

"I have no idea. I think we had one too many drinks."

They slowly get up from their seats, trying to regain their balance. Symmonds groaned. "We should probably find the others and figure out what's going on."

"Agreed. Let's hope they're not feeling as rough as we are."

Symmonds and Mikhail stumbled out of the bar lounge in search of their fellow crew members to piece together the events of the previous night.

"Arthur, do you still have four legs?" Mikhail asked sarcastically, raising an eyebrow.

Symmonds shot him an annoyed look. "What nonsense are you talking about?"

"I had to listen to this garbage last night, too," Mikhail muttered, shaking his head.

"I need to get back to work," Symmonds said curtly, brushing past him.

Meanwhile, Ruma sat quietly, already awake and enjoying her morning coffee. The warmth of the mug in her hands contrasted with the cool tension lingering in the air.

Harry lingered nearby, fidgeting slightly. There was a nervous energy about him, like something was pressing on his mind.

"Last night ..." he began, then trailed off.

Ruma didn't look at him. She took a slow sip of her coffee and said firmly, "I think it's better that we forget it."

Harry frowned, his brows knitting together. "Forget it? I thought ... I mean, didn't it mean something to you?"

Ruma still didn't meet his gaze. She stared into her cup, her voice flat. "It was a moment. Let's not make it more than that."

Harry opened his mouth to respond, but no words came. He wasn't sure if he'd misread the night, or her.

*

Forty-five days later

Upon hearing the announcement that they were going to reach Planet II in 1 day, 2 hours, and 35 minutes, the astronauts felt a mix of anticipation, excitement, and a touch of nervousness. This announcement signified that their long journey was closer to nearing its destination, and they were on the verge of embarking on their mission to explore a new planet.

The astronauts clambered out of the launch vehicle, their boots sinking slightly into the gravelly terrain of Planet II. The sky was a murky, reddish grey, painted with thick clouds of ash and dust. Just ahead, the massive volcano loomed, its steep cone-shaped silhouette stark against the turbulent sky. Smoke and fire erupted from its summit in violent bursts, and a towering plume of ash twisted skyward like a dark serpent, glowing faintly red with reflected heat.

The volcano was alive.

Its jagged sides were coated in layers of black volcanic rock—scar tissue from eruptions long past. Now, the ground trembled beneath the crew's feet, a low, thunderous rumble echoing through the air. Lava bubbled and hissed as it oozed from fresh fissures, spreading rapidly over the cracked, unstable terrain.

"Keep moving," Harry urged, glancing nervously at the glowing red flows slithering ever closer.

Their first steps on Planet II were cautious, with each crew member carefully examining the surface. Ruma carried a device that could analyse the air, water, and soil composition, while Mikhail focused on monitoring waves, signals, and radiation.

Despite the fans whirring inside their suits, the temperature controls were no match for the heat. Sweat pooled against their underlayers, fabric clinging to skin, chafing as they moved. Ruma adjusted her helmet, blinking away the fog on her visor.

But just as they were beginning to feel more comfortable on the planet, the ground beneath them started to tremble. The crew members exchanged worried glances as the tremors grew stronger.

As Ruma continued to scan the environment on Planet II, she noticed that the conditions were indeed remarkably similar to Earth in many ways. The temperature, atmosphere, and terrain all seemed to align with what was needed for habitation. This discovery filled them with a renewed sense of hope and excitement.

Harry, who had been feeling the planet's atmosphere, confirmed Ruma's observations. "It feels like home, doesn't it?" he remarked, his voice tinged with amazement. As they reached the entrance of the Tower where the Cataract Disc was located, a sudden and violent sandstorm struck. Blinding winds carried abrasive sand particles that reduced visibility to nearly zero. The howling winds threatened to disorient them, making it impossible to see where they were going. They had to huddle together to avoid getting separated and had to rely on Snobo's infrared sensors to detect obstacles and navigate through the swirling sand. The sandstorm added a life-threatening dimension to their mission, as it not only made it difficult to locate the Cataract Disc but also jeopardised their safety in the harsh conditions of Planet II.

Ruma checked her visor. "Harry, the temperature here is dropping fast, and the weather conditions are worsening. We need to stay alert."

"I can see that, Ruma. Our visors are indicating a significant drop in temperature."

"The sandstorm level is also increasing rapidly. We should be cautious. Our oxygen levels seem stable for now, but we should keep an eye on them," Ruma warned.

Harry glanced at his visor. "Agreed, Ruma. Let's stay close to each other and keep monitoring the visors. We don't want any surprises out here."

But the winds had suddenly picked up. Ruma struggled to even see Harry, although he was just a foot away from her. "Harry, this sandstorm is insane! We can't see a thing!"

"I know, Ruma!" Harry yelled, struggling to keep his balance. "Let's stick close to Snobo. His sensors should help us navigate."

As Symmonds and Mikhail continued to work on securing their equipment in challenging weather conditions, they suddenly felt a subtle but unmistakable trembling beneath their feet. The ground beneath them started to shake ever so slightly.

Mikhail steadied himself against a nearby rock formation and said with concern, "Symmonds, did you feel that? It's like a minor quake or tremor. We need to be cautious; this planet seems to have some geological activity."

Symmonds, holding onto a piece of equipment, nodded in agreement. "You're right, Mikhail. Let's stay vigilant. This place is full of surprises. We should finish securing the camp quickly and then report this to Ruma and Harry."

With the ground beneath them still trembling occasionally, they work even more diligently to ensure that their base camp is as secure as possible, taking extra precautions to prevent any equipment from toppling over during these seismic events.

"This place is falling apart," Symmonds muttered. "The air's toxic, the ground's cracking open, and we've got lava coming at us from both sides. We shouldn't be out here."

The volcano spewed a fresh burst of molten debris into the sky, and the astronauts instinctively ducked. Red-hot rocks rained down dangerously close, and geysers of steam hissed from sudden fractures in the ground.

"Watch your step!" Ruma shouted, scanning the terrain for a safe path.

As Symmonds and Mikhail worked on securing their equipment, a sharp, erratic beeping cut through the air. The machines began to hum louder, emitting strange, glitchy noises that hadn't been there before. Both men glanced at the monitoring devices—waves and readings were fluctuating wildly, their steady patterns replaced by jagged, chaotic spikes. The instruments stuttered with bursts of static and blinking lights, registering a series of irregular surges and dips, as if reacting to some unknown phenomenon. The tension rose with every shrill beep, the atmosphere suddenly thick with unease.

Mikhail furrowed his brow, staring at the fluctuating readings. "Symmonds, take a look at this. The readings on our instruments are going crazy. This planet is full of surprises. We need to figure out what's causing these fluctuations."

Symmonds nodded in agreement, his eyes fixed on the device. "You're right, Mikhail. This could be related to the seismic activity we just experienced. Let's analyse the data and report it to Ruma and Harry. It might be crucial for our mission."

With their curiosity piqued and a sense of caution in their minds, Symmonds and Mikhail started recording the unusual data, determined to unravel the mysteries of Planet II and ensure the safety of their crew. Then, standing by their equipment, they eagerly awaited the return of Ruma, Harry, and Snobo. The fluctuations in their monitoring devices had them on edge, and they were eager to share their findings with the rest of the crew.

In the cave, Ruma and Harry found temporary refuge from the scorching heat outside. However, the inside of the cave was not much cooler, and the intense conditions on Planet II caused them to sweat profusely. Beads of sweat form on their foreheads, and their bodies glisten with perspiration as they try to catch their breath and gather their thoughts.

"Mikhail, do you copy?" Ruma called Mikhail, her voice tense with worry. The howling winds and the deteriorating weather conditions make it increasingly difficult to establish communication.

Harry, feeling the ground tremble beneath him, shouted over the roaring winds to Ruma, "Is this another earthquake or tremor?" The unsettling combination of a sandstorm, volcanic eruption, and now tremors intensifies their dire situation.

Mikhail checked his instruments, and his voice crackled into the comms. "No, it's not seismic activity. Something else is happening."

Suddenly, a large plume of dust and smoke erupted from one of the nearby hills. The crew members watched in awe and alarm as a volcano on Planet II came to life, spewing molten lava and ash into the sky.

Symmonds and Mikhail, unable to withstand the relentless scorching heat and the ongoing sandstorm, hastily retreated into the safety of their launch vehicle. The sandstorm raged on, pelting the exterior of the vehicle with abrasive sand particles and creating a deafening howl as the wind whipped against the metallic surface.

Inside the vehicle, the control panel flashed a grim report of scorching surface temperatures, surging pressure levels, and wind speeds climbing beyond the threshold for safe travel. Mikhail leaned forward, his eyes scanning the data.

"These readings are bad," he muttered. "The storm's accelerating."

Symmonds tapped furiously at the console. "Where the hell are they?"

Static hissed through the comms before Harry's voice broke in. "We're en route, almost done here."

"Almost?" Symmonds snapped. "You should already be on your way back! We've got readings we needed!"

"Not all of them," Ruma cut in. Her voice was calm but clipped, professional, and determined. "We left the Cataract Disc behind. The data from that site could complete the sequence."

Symmonds stood, slamming a gloved fist against the console. "You're risking your lives for a disc? Ruma, it's not worth it. You've got ninety seconds before that pass becomes impassable!"

"I'm not leaving without it," she said sharply, her boots crunching over the ash-coated ridge. "That disc contains subsurface tremor data from the volcano's last six pulses. We need that model if we want a chance to predict the next eruption."

Mikhail leaned into the mic. "Ruma. Harry. Get back. *Now.*"

But it was already too late. Ruma and Harry were 200 metres downslope, moving fast, as dust was trailing behind them as the storm darkened the sky.

Below them, the Cataract Disc shimmered faintly amid shards of black rock. Harry slid to a stop beside it, unclipping the retrieval clamp. "Got it!"

Suddenly, a sharp crack split the air. A piece of volcanic shale, superheated and sharp as a blade, came hurtling down from above.

"Ruma!" Harry shouted.

She turned just in time to see the fragment slam into the slope beside her, exploding into shards. One chunk struck her shoulder, spinning her sideways. Her feet lost grip, and she tumbled down a short incline, disappearing behind a crest of jagged rock.

"Ruma!" Harry skidded toward where she vanished. "Do you copy? Talk to me!"

There was static, then a pained exhale. "I'm here," she groaned. Her suit's diagnostics glowed red across her display. Shoulder actuator damaged, pressure seal holding, but barely. "I'm okay, but I can't climb up. The incline's too steep from this side."

Harry cursed, eyes darting between her signal and the rapidly rising storm readings. "I'll come around. Hold on!"

"Negative," Symmonds' voice came through sharply. "Harry, that's suicide. You have less than eight minutes of oxygen left. Get back to the shuttle! Now!"

But Harry was already moving, cutting a path laterally through the jagged terrain to reach her. "I'm not leaving her behind."

Back at the vehicle, Mikhail stood rigid, fists clenched at his sides. Symmonds stared at the screen, muttering, "They're not going to make it."

"Have a little faith," Mikhail said quietly.

Down below, the storm intensified, sand and ash sweeping across the ravine like an angry tide. Harry finally reached the edge where Ruma had fallen. She was sitting upright now, one leg wedged awkwardly beneath a rock slab. Her visor was cracked at the corner, but the seal held.

"You're late," she said, her voice strained but dry.

Harry smirked. "You always take the scenic route?"

Together, they worked quickly, Harry bracing the slab while Ruma twisted free, biting back a cry of pain. With one arm around his shoulder, they began the slow climb out of the pit.

Their oxygen alarms screamed in their ears: "O2 critically low. 17 per cent."

"Almost there," Harry panted. "Just a few more metres."

They crested at the ridge and saw the shuttle, just a silhouette in the storm.

"Visual contact!" Symmonds shouted. "They're coming in!"

The rear hatch hissed open, and Mikhail stepped out into the fury of the wind, tether secured to the side of the vehicle. He reached out as the pair stumbled up the ramp.

"Got you," he muttered, grabbing Harry's outstretched hand. Seconds later, the hatch sealed behind them.

The interior of the shuttle was in chaos, with alarms blaring, decontamination systems activating, and oxygen tanks deployed. Ruma collapsed into a seat, cradling the Cataract Disc like it was sacred.

"You're insane, Commander," Symmonds said, breathless, kneeling beside her. "And reckless."

"Maybe," Ruma whispered, chest rising and falling in shallow gasps. "But we've got it."

When the sound of the volcano was muffled at last, Harry let out a long breath. "That," he said, "was way too close."

Ruma finally let go of the Cataract Disc and carefully placed it in the pod on the ship that was designed to keep the discs safe. It was only then that she assessed the injuries on her body. Her head hurt like a whole boulder had fallen on it, and the pain was so severe that it was causing tunnel vision. She felt nauseous, and there was an intermittent pain in her stomach, along with a queasy feeling, like she was about to throw up. Her leg pulsed with pain, and she knew that the only thing that was keeping her from screaming out in pain was the fact that their spacesuits were tight and designed to act like a cast when needed. Trying to dial out all the pain, Ruma focused on the voices of her crewmates. And outside, Planet II rumbled on.

***

Chapter XVI

With the immediate crisis behind them, Ruma took charge and instructed everyone to return to their duties. The crew needed to regroup, assess the data collected from Planet II, and continue their mission.

Ruma proceeded to the communication capsule, taking the Cataract Disc with her. There were shooting pains around her abdomen that had started from the moment the earthquakes at Planet II were felt. She chalked it off to shock and focused on her current task, making a mental note to take an antacid. She carefully inserted the Cataract Disc into the appropriate slot and initiated the data transfer process. As the data started to flow from the disc, Ruma monitored the progress and ensured that the valuable information they'd gathered on Planet II was securely transmitted back to the spaceship's central database. This data would be crucial for the mission's success and future decisions regarding planetary habitation.

Ruma furrowed her brow as she examined the data from the Cataract Disc. It became evident that the disc was malfunctioning, and it had been sending the same data repeatedly with updated dates. She swore under her breath out of frustration. *All that drama for nothing?* They were relying on this information to assess the habitability of Planet II.

She tried to assess whether any portion of the data was salvageable or if they could retrieve valuable insights despite repeated entries. Meanwhile, she contemplated how to address this issue with the rest of the crew and determined their next course of action.

Ruma's discomfort intensified as she continued to work on the malfunctioning Cataract Disc. The persistent pain in her stomach became more pronounced, causing her to wince and clutch her abdomen. Worried about her well-being, she realised that she couldn't ignore this issue any longer.

With a grimace, Ruma decided to step away from the console and head towards the medical bay to assess the source of her pain. She hoped it was nothing serious and that some rest and medical attention would alleviate her discomfort.

The lights dimmed to a soft blue glow inside the spacecraft's main deck as the automated voice echoed through the chambers.

"Attention, crew. Estimated travel time to Planet III: 730 days. All crew members, report to incubation chambers."

A low hum vibrated beneath their feet as the ship stabilised its long-range course. Outside the reinforced glass windows, the blackness of space stretched infinitely, punctuated by the fading ember of Planet II behind them and the faint shimmer of distant stars ahead.

The crew exchanged weary glances, the silence between them speaking volumes after the trials they had just endured. With quiet resolve, they began moving toward the incubation wing, its curved silver corridor lined with pod bays glowing faintly green.

Inside, the incubation chambers stood ready. Sleek, cylindrical capsules with transparent domes lined the walls, each one pre-programmed to sustain the crew in a state of suspended animation, slowing their heart rates, reducing metabolic functions, and keeping them in peak condition for the journey ahead.

Harry frowned as Ruma turned in the opposite direction from the incubation chambers. She looked distracted, and a little *v* formed between her eyebrows as she patted her abdomen time and again.

"Ruma? Where are you going?"

Ruma turned to look at him, the frown still stuck on her face, as though she were debating with herself about some unknown problem.

"Huh?" she responded.

Harry chuckled to himself. *Always thinking and worrying about something or the other.* "The incubation? We have to go in, remember?"

"Oh, yeah," she said. "You guys go ahead, I'm going to the medical pod for a second, my stomach feels funny."

"All okay?"

"Yeah, yeah," Ruma said, waving her hand dismissively. "Probably ate something funny."

Harry nodded, although he wasn't too convinced. Casting one last look at Ruma, who had already turned the other way, Harry made his way to the incubation pods.

*

The crew members, after preparing and ensuring all systems were in order, entered the sleek and advanced incubation pods. Each astronaut took their designated place within the pod, securing themselves in comfortable and secure restraints. As they settled in, they could see the softly lit interior, with holographic displays providing a soothing ambience.

The AI systems within the pods initiated the incubation process. A gentle, cool mist enveloped the astronauts, creating a sensation of relaxation and tranquillity. The pods began to close, sealing the crew members safely inside. The atmosphere inside the pods adjusted to provide the ideal conditions for extended hibernation.

"Initiating the oxygen flow. Preparing the closure," AI said.

Meanwhile, inside the sleek, pod-like medication capsule, the sterile white walls pulsed softly with ambient light. The faint scent of disinfectant lingered in the air. Ruma lay strapped into the reclined examination bed, cold metal sensors pressed against her temples, chest, and abdomen. Wires snaked from her body to the capsule's inner panel, where the medical AI's interface flickered with shifting data streams.

A high-pitched whirr sliced through the quiet, followed by a sequence of soft beeps as the AI started initiating another scan cycle. A blue light fanned across her torso, steady and methodical.

She winced, pressing a hand to her stomach as another sharp cramp twisted through her midsection. Her brow furrowed in confusion. This wasn't like the nausea she'd experienced during rough landings or stress-related fatigue. This was something deeper, alien in its persistence.

"Symptom: Abdominal discomfort. Severity: Moderate. Duration: Persistent, ongoing." The AI's voice was clinical, detached.

Another series of mechanical clicks and chirps filled the capsule as it adjusted the diagnostics. A compartment extended from the wall with a narrow syringe, quickly drawing a blood sample from her arm. Ruma barely flinched as her focus was on the uneasy churn in her gut, the unfamiliar heaviness that seemed to settle lower in her belly.

She shifted restlessly. The capsule's cushioned surface felt too stiff. Her uniform clung to her skin with damp discomfort, her body unusually warm despite the cool air.

The AI paused its scan, a low hum vibrating the walls as it processed the data.

"Hormonal fluctuations detected. Elevated levels of human chorionic gonadotropin..." it began, then paused, recalibrating.

Ruma didn't catch the full phrase. She only knew something wasn't right. Something was ... changing. And the capsule, with all its precision and programming, couldn't yet tell her what.

She closed her eyes, breath shallow, one hand still protectively over her abdomen. She had faced volcanic ash, planetary storms, and the near-collapse of her mission. But this discomfort was different.

"Pregnancy confirmed."

The AI's voice echoed through the medical capsule—flat, emotionless, utterly surreal.

Ruma blinked.

Her mouth parted slightly, but no sound came out. Her heart stuttered in her chest. *No. That couldn't be right.*

She sat up too fast, a tangle of wires tugging at her skin. Her hand darted to the interface, fingers trembling as she navigated through the diagnostic menu. She reran the hormonal panel, muttering to herself.

"Must be a glitch ... bad reading ... maybe interference from the atmospheric radiation ..."

The AI beeped obediently, the capsule flickering with cool blue light as the system complied. Thirty seconds. Sixty.

The result flashed again, bold and undeniable. "Pregnancy confirmed. Gestational estimate: 4.8 weeks."

Ruma stared at the screen as if it had slapped her. Her breath hitched. Her stomach, already unsettled, lurched violently. She was pregnant. Out here. In deep space. With more than 700 days left before they reach Planet III.

A choked gasp escaped her as the panic began to rise, sharp and unrelenting. Her hand flew to her mouth, her eyes wide and glassy. How? When? Who knew? No one. No one could possibly know yet.

Her mind reeled. The mission. The incubation protocol. The survival rationing. The physical strain. The risk. What would the crew say? What would *Harry* say? She was their commander. She was the one meant to keep things in order, to lead by example, to survive.

And now ... she was a liability.

No. No, not a liability, she corrected herself. *A life. A new life. A part of her.* But that thought brought no comfort, only more terror.

She pressed her hands to her abdomen, as if hoping to feel something tangible, something that would make it real or make it go away.

"AI, run the scan again," she whispered hoarsely, her voice breaking. "Triple-check the hCG. Run a blood panel. Cross-verify. Please."

But even before the AI complied, she already knew. Deep down, in the part of her that had been feeling off for days, she knew.

The capsule felt smaller now. The steady mechanical hum around her was too loud, too close. What was she supposed to do now? How could she carry a child into a world that hadn't even formed under her feet yet? How could she *not*?

***

Chapter XVII

Harry, Symmonds, and Mikhail remained in their respective incubation pods, unaware of Ruma's situation inside the medication capsule. Ruma was left to grapple with the shocking news of her pregnancy on her own, sobbing and trembling as she tried to process this life-altering revelation. The spaceship continued its journey towards Planet-III.

Ruma's body felt like a pressure cooker about to burst. She leaned against the capsule's corner wall, her chest heaving, beads of sweat forming on her forehead and running down her temple. Her eyes, once vibrant and alert, had transformed into pools of fiery red as tears streamed down her cheeks, creating a stark contrast against her ashen skin.

Her voice, usually steady and strong, trembled as she muttered the words that had left her world in disarray: "I'm pregnant." With a heavy heart, she slowly sank to the ground, the weight of her revelation pressing upon her, the capsule around her a stark contrast to the chaos of her thoughts.

The walls of the medication capsule seemed to close in on her, and the steady hum of the equipment became an ominous drone in her ears. Ruma felt trapped and isolated, and her imagination ran wild with a thousand questions about the future. Fear gripped her heart, and she clutched her stomach protectively as if shielding the tiny life growing within. At that moment, in the cold, sterile capsule, she was in a universe of emotions and apprehensions, and she didn't know what to do next.

The AI voice-over rang through the medication capsule, echoing with the weight of the revelation. Ruma sat frozen, her breathing shallow, eyes locked on the few pills that had spilt into a transparent glass box. The label on the box left no room for misinterpretation:"Take these pills to stay healthy during your pregnancy."

Her fingers hovered over the rim of the box, hesitant to touch them, as if doing so would make it all more real. Then, with a soft mechanical whir, a small compartment in the wall slid open. A neat, folded pamphlet was printed and pushed out with gentle precision. The title read: "Prenatal Health and Safety Guidelines–Long-Term Missions." Beneath it, a blister pack of prenatal vitamins was dispensed into the tray, followed by a warm tone from the AI.

"These supplements will help maintain optimal nutrient levels. Please refer to the enclosed guidelines for further steps."

It wasn't just protocol–it was care, automated but sincere in its own strange way.

Ruma swallowed hard, blinking back tears. In this moment of overwhelming uncertainty, the cold, clinical AI had done the one thing no one else could: acknowledged the reality she was still struggling to accept. No judgment. No panic. Just a quiet affirmation that she was not alone.

She picked up the brochure slowly, her hand trembling, and for the first time since the words *"Pregnancy confirmed"* were uttered, she allowed herself to exhale. It wasn't comfort, not quite. But it *was* something.

As the AI voice-over announced the final call for incubation closure, Ruma's entire world was in disarray. The revelation of her pregnancy had sent her into a whirlwind of emotions and fears, and her trembling hands reached for the wall for support.

Despite the fear and uncertainty that coursed through her, Ruma knew that she needed to make a choice. With a deep breath, she pushed herself off the wall and began to wobble toward the incubation area. Every step was a battle, and her hand clutched her stomach as if to protect the life growing within her.

The incubation closure was approaching rapidly, the countdown flashing steadily on the corridor walls. Ruma's body trembled with tension, each step toward the hibernation bay feeling heavier than the last.

She had to make a decision. *Fast.*

But this wasn't just about her anymore. The revelation still echoed in her mind like a pulse: *she was pregnant.* That single truth rewrote every equation, every mission protocol, every plan she'd held until now.

Her hand rested lightly on her abdomen, as if to shield what she couldn't yet feel. A life that was small, silent, but entirely real, was depending on her to choose wisely.

She stood in the corridor, weighing her options with a gnawing sense of panic.

Option 1: Enter incubation. It was the standard procedure. The AI had already prepared her pod, assuming she would comply. But what would suspended animation do to the fetus? The incubation chambers were calibrated for adult physiological preservation, not the delicate, ever-changing needs of a developing embryo. Would the metabolic slowdown freeze the fetus's development? Would it survive the altered conditions? There was no precedent, no data in the system to assure her it was safe. It could stunt the child's growth, or worse, terminate the pregnancy altogether.

Option 2: Remain awake. Stay conscious. Isolate herself from the others. Maintain a normal metabolic cycle. It would mean 700 days of solitude while the others slept, alone in a silent, humming ship, awake with the burden of care, limited resources, and growing physical strain. How would she access prenatal care, food calibrated for a pregnant woman, or even emotional support? Could she even carry to term in zero-gravity conditions? And what would the crew say when they awoke to find a child among them?

Her thoughts spiralled, crashing into each other, but the clock kept ticking. The AI's voice gently reminded her that incubation systems were closing in five minutes. Ruma stood rooted to the floor, heart pounding, tears brimming in her eyes. There was no right answer. Just risk and responsibility.

All she knew was this: whatever she chose, she would have to live with it. Not just for herself. But for the tiny, unknowable future growing inside her.

As Ruma reached the incubation area near the central section of the spaceship, she could feel the tension in the air. The doors of the incubation area opened just as she arrived, and it was as if the spaceship itself was urging her to make a choice. The timing was impeccable, and it left her with no room for hesitation.

As Ruma entered the incubation area, the doors of the incubation pods closed with a hiss. She took a deep breath, trying to calm herself, her trembling hands gripping the railing near the pods. Ruma felt the weight of her pregnancy pressing on her, both physically and emotionally. The reality of her situation had hit her like a tidal wave.

Ruma desperately entered the password to unlock the incubation pod, her fingers trembling with fear and determination. She needed to override the system and get Harry out of his incubation pod. But the AI's response remained the same, "Unauthorised Password."

Ruma's breath came in ragged gasps, chest heaving as fury surged through her veins like wildfire. Her vision blurred, not with tears this time, but with red-hot rage. She saw Harry's sealed pod like a barrier between her and the only person who *should* have been here for this moment, and her fingers curled into trembling fists.

He didn't even know. He was going to sleep through it all—through *everything* while she stayed behind, awake, alone, and pregnant with *his* child.

A wild, primal sound tore from her throat. She wasn't even sure if it was a scream or a sob. Her feet pounded across the metallic floor as she grabbed the fire extinguisher from the emergency hatch. The cold metal grounded her for a split second. Then she swung it. The clang echoed across the chamber as she slammed it against Harry's incubation pod. Again. And again. And again.

"*GET UP!*" she screamed, her voice hoarse and cracking. "*GET UP, YOU COWARD!*"

Her arms shook from the force, muscles screaming with each blow, but she didn't stop. Fury had taken over completely. Pure, unfiltered rage that snarled through her like a cornered animal. Her face twisted in a snarl, hair falling across her damp cheeks as she struck the pod with all the force her body could summon.

"You don't get to just SLEEP through this!" she howled. "You don't get to *leave me!*"

But the pod remained closed, silent, unyielding. Designed to withstand zero-gravity collisions and onboard malfunctions, it didn't even flinch at her assault. It was Harry who couldn't hear her, Harry who lay still inside, already on his way into 700 days of dreamless hibernation.

The AI's calm voice broke through the chaos, completely at odds with her breakdown. "Incubation protocol in progress. Please vacate the chamber."

Ruma ignored it. Her sobs came in short, painful gasps now, her arms faltering as the fire extinguisher grew heavier with every swing. She struck one last time, her strength finally giving way, and let the extinguisher clatter to the floor with a deafening crash. She stood still, shaking. Defeated. Her chest ached with the weight of everything left unsaid. The child inside her. The life outside this mission. The unbearable loneliness she was about to face.

Ruma returned to the medication capsule with newfound determination. She had to face the reality of her pregnancy and prepare herself for the challenges that lay ahead. She approached the medication screen and began typing and selecting various options on the interface. After finalising her selections, she carefully lay herself down in the medication pod.

"Initiate abortion," Ruma said.

Are you positive that you want to undertake this procedure? The AI said.

"I said, Initiate abortion," Ruma said again.

"Initiating abortion," the AI's voice echoed through the medication capsule.

Ruma lay inside the medication pod, her body secured, her arms gently strapped for monitoring. A sterile, dim blue light bathed the interior as the AI initiated the procedure. Her breath was steady, but her mind churned with an ache that no machine could numb.

The screen above her glowed to life.

"Initiating dilation and curettage. Administering sedation now."

She felt the cool sensation of an IV line automatically inserting itself into her vein, the tranquilliser entering her system like a slow tide. Her limbs tingled. Her thoughts began to blur, but only slightly. The AI had calculated that a light sedation was best to keep her vitals stable and conscious if needed.

"Cervical dilation in progress."

A gentle whirring sound rose as a series of thin, precise dilators extended from a robotic arm. Guided by imaging scans, the instruments began to gradually expand her cervix. Ruma winced, her jaw tightening. Even in this future of medical marvels, some pains couldn't be erased.

The mechanical arm shifted. A curette, looped and delicately curved, emerged next, paired with a small vacuum device. The screen showed a simulation of the procedure, though Ruma turned her head away.

"Beginning uterine evacuation."

Tears slipped silently down her cheeks. She didn't need to watch. She already knew what she was losing. To shield herself, her mind retreated, pulling her back to a sun-warmed beach from her childhood. The scent of saltwater and pancakes lingered in the air as her mother called from the porch.

Her small hands had pressed into the soft sand, building a belly for herself out of grains. She had laughed, yelling, "*Mom, I'm pregnant!*" just to see her mother's delighted smile.

"Ruma, you are my sunshine," her mother had said, brushing sand from her hair. "You'll always be my little girl."

Her father had been nearby, tossing a yellow ball for their dog. The playful retriever leapt onto her sand-belly, scattering it in clumps. She had shrieked with laughter, her mother's voice carried on the wind like a lullaby.

The memory curled around her like a warm shawl.

Back in the pod, the procedure neared its end. The AI carefully retracted the instruments, scanning for residual tissue. Sterile mist filled the chamber to cleanse and soothe. A bio-adhesive strip was applied to aid healing internally. No visible incision. No scars. Just silence.

"Procedure complete. Preparing to terminate sedation."

But Ruma's eyes opened wide with clarity. She stared at the screen. Then at her belly. Something cracked open inside her. Not medically, but emotionally. Her hand darted to the pod's interface. She pressed hard on the override. A sharp beep rang out.

"Abort procedure. Manual override initiated."

The robotic arm, now reaching to finish with a final scan, froze mid-air. A red light blinked. Ruma unlocked the pod and stumbled out, clutching the thin medical gown around her body. Her breath came in ragged gasps. The room spun slightly as the sedative began to fade. She stood barefoot on the cold floor, trembling–not just from the aftereffects, but from the gravity of her decision.

She wasn't ready to go through with it. Not yet. Maybe not ever. She rushed to the wash basin and vomited.

"Vomiting and tiredness are the common symptoms of pregnancy," the AI said.

Ruma asked, "How is the baby?"

"The baby is in the early stages of development, still an embryo with a small tail, Ruma. If you continue the abortion process, it can be safely terminated."

Ruma took the pill with a glass of water and left the medication capsule, making her way to the sleeping pod, hoping that when she woke up, she'd realise that it was all a bad dream.

*

Back on Earth, Clark had been rudely interrupted in his sleep in the dead of the night by someone calling him continuously. No matter how hard he tried to ignore it, the person on the other end did not seem to care that he was fast asleep.

It was only on the tenth consecutive ring that Clark realised it wasn't his day phone that was ringing–it was his emergency phone, only to be contacted when something wrong had happened aboard *Tarayaan*. He jolted awake and nearly fractured his ankle as he leapt across the room to grab the cellphone lying on the table.

"Hello?" he said into it, breathless.

"Professor Clark, we've been trying to reach you for the past one hour ..."

"I know, I know. I'm sorry. I ... what has happened?"

"It's best you get to Kennedy Space Centre immediately, Professor."

*

The moment Ruma saw the next morning that there was an incoming satellite call from her father, she felt a sinking feeling. *He knows. Of course, he knows. NASA's got ears and eyes everywhere*. She tried not to think about whether they saw how she got pregnant in the first place when she accepted the call.

"Hi, Dad," she said shortly.

Clark didn't waste any time. "Ruma, I can't believe this has happened! You were sent on a mission with strict guidelines and responsibilities. Your pregnancy jeopardises everything we've worked for!"

"I understand the importance of the situation, Dad, and I'm deeply sorry for any complications my pregnancy may cause. But I didn't plan for this, and I'm facing a difficult decision."

"This isn't just about you, Ruma. It's about the entire mission and the team's well-being. We can't afford to make exceptions!" he exclaimed. His eyes were bloodshot, and his hair was haggard. He clearly hadn't slept all night. "This is fucking unacceptable!"

"I am aware," Ruma said dryly. Nothing anybody could tell her would make her feel worse than she was already feeling. But she was steadfast in her decision. If anyone could do it, it was her.

*

The atmosphere in the conference hall turned serious as Clark made his entrance. His presence commanded immediate attention from the board members, causing a hush to fall over the room and silencing any ongoing conversations.

As Clark took his seat at the head of the conference table, the anticipation in the room was rising. The other members sat up straight, giving full attention, awaiting his side of the story in the upcoming deliberations.

"How, how did this happen?" Karthik demanded. Clark said nothing and stared at his intertwined hands on his lap instead. Karthik threw his hand up in frustration and seethed. "A pregnant woman in space. I can't believe this."

"Professor," Wong said, breaking the silence. His face on the video conference screen wasn't unsympathetic, but Clark still couldn't bear to look at him. "Do you understand the value of this project? The amount of pressure we're under?"

"We need to bring her back," Laura said, her voice clipped and decisive. "Replace her with someone else. Another astronaut. Someone fit for duty."

Clark let out a slow exhale. "That would be more expensive than you think," he muttered. "A rescue mission now would derail the whole operation. Launching a replacement? Not feasible. Not in this timeframe."

"Then we abort," Williams snapped. "Abort the mission and bring everyone home."

Clark looked around the room, the weight of years of research pressing down on his shoulders. "We're talking about a setback of historic proportions," he said quietly. "We've prepared for every known variable. The ship's technology is adaptable ... Ruma even more so. If anyone can survive this ... It's her."

"But at what cost?" Laura asked from across the table. "We have no precedent for this. No data. How does microgravity affect pregnancy? What about radiation? We could be endangering her, the foetus ... the entire crew."

"She knew the risks when she signed up," Clark said, not without a hint of guilt. "We all did. But this ... this was unforeseen."

Karthik, who had been silent till now, finally spoke up. His voice was low, but firm. "Whatever decision we take, this stays in this room. No media. No press releases. Not a word on social platforms. If this gets out, it'll be chaos."

He looked at each face in turn, letting the implication settle. "We have to protect her privacy. The mission's integrity. Everything depends on it."

Williams nodded. "Agreed. We handle this internally, quietly. No leaks."

Clark exhaled, almost to himself. "Then we move forward. Carefully. We monitor her vitals. Adjust the protocols. Offer every bit of support we can. But we don't pull the plug. Not yet."

The room fell silent again. There were no easy answers. Just the faint hum of machines and the unrelenting weight of responsibility.

One by one, the heads around the table gave hesitant nods.

***

Chapter XVIII

Sixteen weeks before delivery

Ruma slowly emerged from her sleep within the confined but technologically advanced quarters of the spaceship. The gentle hum of the ship's systems created a soothing backdrop as she eased herself into wakefulness. With a subtle grace, she glided toward the mirror, taking a moment to examine her changing form. In the reflection, her hand lovingly rested upon her slightly protruding belly, a visible evidence to the life growing within her.

As Ruma stood before the mirror, her expression was a mosaic of emotions, a blend of tender innocence, happiness, and a whirlwind of feelings that came with the miraculous changes in her body. She gazed at her reflection, her eyes softly meeting their gaze in the mirror, evoking a sense of purity and vulnerability. With a gentle touch, she caressed her growing belly, a gesture filled with an intimacy that only a mother-to-be could understand. There was an unspoken connection, a silent conversation between her hand and the life burgeoning within her.

The reflective surface of the mirror revealed not just the physical changes but a myriad of emotions playing across Ruma's face—the joy of expectancy, the wonder of new life, and a tinge of apprehension about the unknowns ahead. The happiness she felt was evident in the subtle curve of her lips, a tender smile reflecting the joy and anticipation of the life growing inside her.

In her comfortable jogging suit, Ruma readied herself for her daily routine, aware of the importance of staying active during her pregnancy. The AI, ever attentive to her needs, set the tone by playing soft, soothing music in the background, creating a calming atmosphere within the spacecraft.

Equipped with a video camera, she began to jog at a leisurely pace, her movements adjusting to the spaceship's altered gravity. The recording served as a personal diary, documenting her experiences and the routines she maintained during this remarkable journey. As Ruma adjusted the camera to focus on herself, a gentle smile graced her lips as she began recording. With a warm and inviting tone, she faced the camera and began speaking, her voice clear and filled with a sense of warmth and purpose.

"Good morning, everyone. Here I am, entering my 20th week of pregnancy, continuing my daily routine. Today, it's time for my regular exercise in this unique environment. Exercise is important for me and my baby's health, even here in space," she continued. "So, I'll be jogging in the spaceship while the AI plays some soothing music to keep me company. It's a journey I'm thrilled to share with all of you."

"Ruma, it's time for you to have breakfast, please come down to Food Capsule", the AI that essentially played the role of a nurse in *Tarayaan*–Elza said.

Ruma acknowledged the AI's prompt with a nod. "Thank you, Elza."

With a graceful turn, Ruma reoriented herself within the spaceship, heading towards the designated area where the food capsule was located. As she moved through the spacecraft's controlled environment, she manoeuvred effortlessly.

Arriving at the food capsule, Ruma was met with a setup where she could obtain her meal. She interacted with the interface, choosing her breakfast selection while Elza oversaw the process. Elza's suggestions encompass a well-rounded assortment of nutritional options suitable for Ruma's stage of pregnancy, emphasising the importance of various nutrients vital for her and the baby's health and development. Each suggestion was meticulously tailored to meet the specific needs of a pregnant woman. It included protein-rich food, whole grains and carbohydrates, calcium sources, healthy fats, and more.

With delicacy and precision, the robots placed the items on the table, arranging them neatly for Ruma to access. The smooth and automated delivery process showcased the fusion of technology and convenience in this futuristic setting.

As Ruma sat down at her table, a neatly arranged assortment of nutritious food items before her, she adjusted the video camera and began recording her breakfast routine.

"With Elza's guidance, my breakfast changes to adapt to the growth of my baby," Ruma narrated to the camera, her tone resonating with a blend of assurance and enthusiasm. "Each meal is carefully curated to ensure I receive the essential nutrients needed for a healthy pregnancy."

Throughout her meal, Ruma maintained a detailed and explanatory narrative, capturing each element on her plate as she consumed her breakfast. She eloquently outlined the importance of these dietary adjustments, signifying her commitment to maintaining a healthy lifestyle during her journey in space.

"Thank you," Ruma expressed sincerely, addressing the robots that delivered her meal and Elza, managing her health and nutritional guidance.

The two robots, with their mechanical precision, acknowledged Ruma's gratitude through their movements, emitting a subtle humming sound as they smoothly returned to their designated locations within the spacecraft.

Elza, overseeing Ruma's well-being and the operations of the spacecraft, responded with a courteous message, "It's my pleasure."

Following her meal at the food capsule, Ruma transitioned to the Medication capsule for her scheduled routine. Ruma engaged with the diagnostic and monitoring systems. These tests were designed to assess various vital signs, such as blood pressure, heart rate, and other parameters critical for ensuring her well-being and the development of her baby.

During a routine medical examination within the spacecraft's medical facilities, the sonographer, utilising advanced ultrasound technology, focuses on monitoring the development of Ruma's baby and the health of the placenta, a vital organ supporting the growing fetus.

Simultaneously, the sonographer examined the placenta, evaluating its health and functionality. "Elza, how is my baby?" Ruma asked.

Elza responded promptly and reassuringly to Ruma's inquiry about her baby's well-being. "Your baby is healthy and developing well, Ruma," Elza answered in a calm and reassuring tone. "All monitored parameters indicate positive progress in the growth and development of the fetus. The baby measures about 16 cm from head to bottom and weighs about 320 grams. Its heart is beating at 120-160 beats per minute, and your baby can hear sounds like your heart or voice, even though the baby's ears aren't yet completely formed."

In a moment of tenderness and affection, Ruma, while gently touching her growing belly, whispered, "Sweetheart." She was overcome by profound emotion and was lost in the intimacy of the moment. "This is the most beautiful moment in my life."

As Ruma exited the medication pod, her footsteps carrying her toward the communication capsule, her gaze naturally fell upon the nearby incubation pods where she spotted Harry, Symmonds, and Mikhail.

Observing Harry within the incubation pod, a deep sense of love and affection welled up within Ruma. Her eyes reflected a poignant mix of emotions—longing, affection, and a yearning to be close to him. The distance between them, amidst the confines of the spacecraft, amplified her sense of missing him dearly.

Entering the communication capsule, Ruma initiated a video call, establishing a direct connection with her father. The screen flickered to life, and there, in real-time, appeared Clark. His face lit up as he saw Ruma's image on the screen.

"Ruma, my dear," Clark's voice beamed with warmth and affection. "It's wonderful to see you. How are you doing today?"

With a soft smile and a tone filled with reassurance, Ruma responded, "I am doing good, Dad."

"How is the baby?" Clark asked.

"The baby is doing well, Dad. Elza keeps me updated on the progress, and everything seems to be on track."

"Ruma, I have a surprise for you," Clark announced with a glint of excitement in his eyes. He adjusted the screen, and as the video call continued, the image shifted to reveal Ruma's mother, who was visiting Clark at the Kennedy Space Centre.

Ruma's eyes widened with surprise and delight as she saw her mother on the screen. "Mom!" she exclaimed, a mix of joy and surprise evident in her voice. The unexpected appearance of her mother during the video call filled her with warmth and happiness.

"Surprise!" Sameera greeted her with a wide smile, her eyes brimming with affection. "I couldn't miss the chance to see you, even if it's through a video call."

The sight of her parents together on the video call conjured a flood of emotions within Ruma. The rarity of this moment, seeing both her mother and father in one frame, sparked a sense of longing and happiness.

"Your dad is stressed about you and the mission, so I am here," Sameera said.

Ruma's initial reaction was laughter, a mix of surprise, and amusement. Her laughter indicated that she found her father's concern and the subsequent presence of her mother both endearing and somewhat humorous.

"It's not what you think," Sameera clarified.

"I thought of calling you, but you called me. A mother can understand another mother, so that is the reason I called your mom," Clark explained.

"Ruma, how is your health? How is the baby doing? Are you having food timely?" Sameera inquired with genuine concern.

Ruma responded warmly, "Mom, I'm doing well. The baby is healthy, and Elza keeps track of my nutrition and health. I'm following the schedule for meals."

"I am worried about the baby as you are in space, the circumstances are completely different from being on Earth," Sameera expressed.

"I understand, Mom. The spacecraft is equipped with everything needed for my health and the baby's well-being. The medical facilities and Elza constantly monitor everything," Ruma reassured.

"Ruma, take care of yourself and the baby."

"I will, Mom," Ruma responded, her voice filled with warmth and gratitude. "I'm taking every possible care."

"Bye, Ruma, we'll catch up later," Clark bid farewell, his voice filled with warmth and love.

"Bye, dear. Take care," Sameera echoed the sentiment.

Exiting the communication capsule, Ruma head towards the Entertainment capsule, seeking a moment of relaxation. Inside the capsule, she decided to watch a movie, selecting *Titanic* for her viewing pleasure.

As the film played on the screen in front of her, Ruma immersed herself in the timeless story of Jack and Rose aboard the ill-fated ship. The captivating narrative, combined with the grandeur of the oceanic setting, provided a moment of escape, allowing Ruma to delve into the emotional journey of the characters and the historical context of the iconic vessel.

As Ruma sat back, engrossed in the movie, two small robots efficiently arrived from the Food capsule, one carrying a serving of popcorn and the other a refreshing glass of fresh juice.

Sipping the juice, a sudden rush of memories flooded Ruma's mind. The familiar scene of watching *Titanic* triggered a poignant recollection of a past shared moment with Harry. She reminisced about the time they watched the same movie together, recalling the emotional connection and the shared experience during that particular viewing.

Upon the movie's completion, Ruma head back to the Food capsule in response to Elza's call for lunch. Understanding the importance of timely meals for her health and the baby's well-being, she complied with the spacecraft's schedule for lunch.

While having her meal, Ruma takes a moment to record a video, sharing her thoughts with a reflective tone.

"Sometimes I feel that I am alone, but now Elza is my companion," she expressed. "This food is my daily routine," she continued. "I never thought that I would be travelling through space all by myself."

In the Entertainment capsule, Ruma settled into a comfortable sofa in the library section, surrounded by a serene environment filled with books and a tranquil ambience. Engaging in her leisure time, she delved into a book, allowing the words and stories to captivate her imagination. As she read, the soothing atmosphere of the library and the gentle tranquillity of the spacecraft gradually lulled her into a state of relaxation. With the book cradled in her hands, Ruma's eyelids grew heavy, and she drifted into a serene slumber, nestled on the sofa.

Two small robots silently approached Ruma. One of the robots delicately took the book she was reading and carefully returned it to its designated place on the shelf, ensuring tidiness within the space. Meanwhile, the second robot, with gentle precision, placed a soft pillow beneath Ruma's head as she peacefully slept on the sofa. A vacuum robot quietly entered the space to clean, followed by several tiny floor-mopping robots. Their mechanical hums, though designed to be unobtrusive, were noticeable. The soft whirring and movement of the cleaning robots created a subtle disturbance, interrupting the tranquillity of the area.

The sound of the robotic cleaning crew roused Ruma from her moment of relaxation, prompting her to awaken from her slumber in the library. She then decided to head to the swimming pool capsule within the spaceship. Changing into her swimming attire, she entered the swimming capsule, and the two robots approached Ruma as she stepped out of the swimming pool, each assigned a specific task. One of the robots was carrying a towel on a tray, a gesture to assist her in drying off after her swim. The second robot was holding a refreshing juice, likely intended to offer her a hydrating and rejuvenating beverage after exercise in the swimming pool.

Ruma headed to the dining area for her dinner, where a well-balanced and nutritious meal was served by the robotic assistants in the Food capsule. Following her meal, she once again took the prescribed tablets, such as folic acid, iron, and any other necessary supplements essential for her health and the baby's development during her pregnancy in space.

In the sleeping pod, just before Ruma settled down for the night, she switched on the video camera to share a glimpse of her daily routine. "Wishing you all a good night," she said softly.

Thirty-third week

In the Medication capsule during Ruma's thirty-third week, the healthcare robot used a fetoscope, a specialised medical device, to examine and listen to the baby's heartbeat while Ruma reclined in the pod. Additionally, a Doppler ultrasound device was utilised to perform a detailed assessment of the baby's heartbeat.

Elza relayed crucial information to Ruma following the examination: "At thirty-three weeks, your baby weighs approximately four pounds. The baby is displaying essential developmental behaviours such as swallowing, yawning, and practising breathing movements. Moreover, the baby's brain is now capable of regulating the body's temperature, showcasing vital advancements in their growth and maturation."

Thirty fifth Week

At thirty-five weeks, Elza communicated important updates after the examination: "Your baby measures 18.7 inches in length. The baby has established a sleep pattern, indicating the development of a regular sleep-wake cycle. The skin has taken on a pinkish hue, and the legs are becoming chubbier as the baby continues to put on weight in preparation for birth."

***

Chapter XIX

Two weeks before the delivery

As Ruma awakened from her slumber to the soft hum of her alarm, she sensed an unusual heaviness in her movements. The gentle, automated rhythm of her morning routine commenced, indicating the commencement of a new day on the spacecraft. At her awakening, a pair of delicate pink sandals was placed by the robots at her sleeping pod, a thoughtful gesture echoing a special significance. The weight and sensation of the pregnancy, now nearing its end, added a new dimension to her mornings.

"Good morning, Ruma," Elza warmly greeted her. Elza's familiar voice echoed through the sleeping pod, offering a comforting start to the day for Ruma and fostering a sense of routine and familiarity in the vastness of space.

Ruma's awakening was accompanied by a heavy sigh and an audible exhalation, indicating a moment of weariness and the strain of the pregnancy. Her deep breath suggested a sense of discomfort as she began her day, highlighting the physical and emotional challenges she may be experiencing in the latter stages of her pregnancy.

Upon donning the pair of pink sandals, Ruma glanced at her reflection in the mirror. The visual examination unveiled a myriad of notable changes in her body's physical appearance, evidence of the remarkable progression of her pregnancy.

She observed with a mix of emotions as her body displayed numerous transformations–a fuller, more pronounced belly, changes in her posture, and alterations in various body parts due to the natural progression of carrying a child.

As Ruma tended to her morning routine, diligently brushing her teeth, the small floor-mopping robots, equipped with cleaning functionalities, made their way into her sleeping pod. With a soft mechanical hum, they efficiently traversed the room, diligently carrying out their cleaning tasks.

Their arrival didn't interrupt Ruma's morning ritual. Instead, it added to the sense of order and efficiency in the spacecraft, allowing her to continue with her tasks as the robots methodically ensured a clean and tidy environment within her living space.

Ruma, clad in her comfortable nightdress, proceeded to the designated area for breakfast upon hearing Elza summoning her for the morning meal. Her attire suggested the informality of the hour, emphasising the relaxed atmosphere aboard the spacecraft during the early hours of the day.

As the crew members remained in their incubation pods, the spaceship, guided by autonomous navigation systems, steadily advances along its designated trajectory toward Planet III, preparing for the next phase of the mission.

The ship glided through the vast expanse of space, the hum of its engines reverberating softly within its metallic walls. Outside, celestial bodies loomed in the dark canvas of the universe, stars casting their shimmering light across the cosmic void.

Carefully calibrated propulsion systems manoeuvred the spacecraft, orchestrating its journey toward the enigmatic Planet III. It followed a meticulously charted path, each movement calculated to align with the celestial coordinates and gravitational forces along the way.

After her routine breakfast, Ruma proceeded to the medication capsule for her scheduled general checkup. In the examination conducted using the fetoscope and Doppler ultrasound device, Elza conveyed vital information: "Your baby is healthy, exhibiting a stable heart rate ranging between 110 and 130 beats per minute. The baby currently weighs approximately six point three pounds. As the baby continues to grow, you may experience movements inside your belly, characterised by little jabs, kicks, or other gentle motions."

Ruma frowned. "I do not feel any baby's movement as of now."

"You will experience the baby's movements soon. It's common for these movements to vary in intensity and frequency. Rest assured, the movements will likely become more noticeable and consistent as your pregnancy progresses," Elza reassured her.

Ruma went to her pod, took off her clothes, and looked at her belly, and there were visible veins. The reflection in the mirror presented visual evidence of the changes in Ruma's body during her pregnancy. As she gazed at herself, she observed the noticeable growth and transformation in various body parts. Her abdomen prominently showcased the expansion to accommodate the growing baby. Other areas, such as her breasts, hips, and thighs, also displayed the effects of the natural physical adjustments that occur during pregnancy.

Turning on the tap in the bathtub, Ruma initiated the flow of the water, allowing it to stream into the tub, filling it gradually. The sound of water gushing added to the ambient noise, creating a tranquil cocoon as she prepared for a relaxing bath.

In the bathtub, she gently touched her belly, her fingers tracing the gentle rise and fall of her abdomen. She moved slowly around her navel, feeling the tautness of the skin wherever her palm lingered; there seemed to be an answering shift: tiny heels and valleys formed as a heel pressed here, or a fist rolled there. The small, rounded bulges vanished as quickly as they appeared, like secrets slipping back into shadow.

She reached for the jet spray positioned on her right, holding it loosely in her hand. Tilting the nozzle towards her stomach, she let the lukewarm stream fan out across the skin. The water pattered slowly, and as it flowed over her left side, a tiny bump swelled beneath the surface, a knee or elbow pressing up, dimpling the flesh from the inside. She smiled faintly, moving the spray in slow arcs, following her baby's silent game of hide-and-seek. Every spot the water touched seemed to draw a response: fingers splaying, feet flexing, tiny movements wrapping themselves against her body like a private Morse code meant only for her.

Ruma applied shower gel to her shoulders and hands, rubbing it in absent-mindedly, still feeling the after-echoes of each push and stretch. When she turned off the valve and detached the spray, the tub felt heavier, quieter, the air thick with steam.

She stirred in the lukewarm bath, her breath fogging faintly against the chrome walls. Steam coiled around her bare shoulders, but the warmth did nothing to ease the growing knot in her chest. Her fingers skimmed her belly, searching, waiting. Yet, it was all still—no flutter, no kick.

Why haven't you moved? The question clung to her ribs, heavy and sharp. The thoughts rang loud, louder than the rushing water had moments ago. Her heartbeat pounded in her ears, drowning everything else. A dozen sharp fears spiralled at once: had she eaten wrong, moved wrong, slept wrong? Was the silence inside her a warning she had ignored? Her body felt like a stranger's: untrustworthy, its secrets locked away from her.

She picked up the unplugged jet spray with trembling hands, angled it to her stomach, then held it to her ear like a stethoscope. Water hissed and echoed, but there was only her own heartbeat thrumming wildly in her ears.

"My baby," she whispered into the tiny spray holes, her voice cracking. "Do you hear me? It's Mama." She pressed it closer, desperate. "I'm tired, but I see you growing. I'm numb, but I see you."

Nothing.

Panic bloomed. Her throat clenched. She dropped the spray, letting it clatter against the tub floor, and curled into herself, sobbing. The fear consumed her, clawing up her chest until she could hardly breathe. *What if I've lost you? What if I never even get to hold you?* A tear slid into the bathwater.

And then she felt it. A kick. Sudden and strong. She gasped, sitting upright as ripples danced around her. Her hands flew to her belly just in time to catch another jolt, this one followed by a series of small, insistent prods. This time, the water seemed to shape itself—her stomach lifting beneath the surface, tracing clear impressions in the thin film of water across her skin. The round dome of a head pressing near her ribs. Tiny fingers, spread wide like a fan. The distinct arch of a foot, toes curled tight.

Her breath caught. It was as though her baby was carving its presence directly into her flesh, declaring itself with undeniable clarity: *I'm here. I'm alive.*

Relief washed over her, trembling and hot. A laugh broke free between tears, fragile and wild. She pressed her palms to the imprints, trying to catch them before they slipped back into the deep.

"Warning," Elza's calm voice intruded, flat against the intimacy of the moment. "High-intensity solar flares detected. Protective protocols advised."

Ruma hardly heard. She was too wrapped up in the miracle unfolding under her palms; the miracle she had feared was gone.

"Gravitational anomalies incoming," Elza repeated, sharper this time. "Ruma, initiate evacuation sequence."

But Ruma's eyes stayed locked on the shifting outlines beneath her skin, her lips trembling in awe. Whenever she poured water playfully, she could see imprints. When she poured water that she grabbed from the tub, on the right side of her stomach, she could see the imprint of a head. On the left side of her belly, she could see the imprint of a hand. And on the top of her stomach, right below her navel, she could see a tiny foot pressing against her stretched skin. The world outside seemed impossibly distant compared to the heartbeat she could almost *feel* against her hands.

The third time, Elza's voice cut through, urgent and undeniable. "Critical alert. Gravitational field is destabilising. Ruma, evacuate to a safe zone *immediately*."

Alarms screamed. Lights snapped red. Water began to lift off the tub in floating globules. The floor groaned beneath Ruma. Only then did the terror of reality slice through the cocoon she had wrapped herself in.

As the Sun emitted powerful solar flares and energy waves at tremendous speeds, nearby asteroids began to tremble in response to the intense force and radiation. The charged particles and solar emissions rippled through space, causing vibrations and subtle surface changes in these celestial bodies.

Elza responded to the warning about the incoming unknown wave by initiating emergency protocols. "Warning, unknown wave approaching. Initiating trajectory adjustment," Elza announced. The AI system swiftly activated the necessary protocols to tilt and adjust the spaceship's trajectory in an attempt to evade and minimise the potential impact of the incoming wave on the vessel's path. This urgent action aimed to steer the spacecraft away from the perceived threat and ensure the safety of the spaceship and its crew.

Breathing heavily, Ruma marched towards the central area of the spaceship. The urgency of the situation and the alarm triggered by the unknown wave propel her forward, intensifying her determined stride despite her heavy breaths.

Amidst her progress, Ruma encountered intermittent glitches in the power supply within the spaceship. These irregular interruptions caused temporary disruptions in the ship's systems, briefly affecting the consistency of the power flow throughout the vessel. Despite these obstacles, Ruma continued her determined journey toward the central area, striving to address the imminent situation.

"Warning."

Ruma, exuding confidence in her tone, issued a command to the AI system, Elza. "Initiate the divergence in the trajectory, immediately," Ruma asserted with determination and authority, prompting the AI system to promptly take action.

Elza responded promptly, confirming the initiation of the trajectory adjustments. The spaceship's engines roared as they worked to increase the vessel's speed and executed a significant 60-90-degree change in the trajectory, accompanied by the expulsion of a substantial amount of smoke as the spacecraft manoeuvred and adjusted its path. These urgent actions were taken to swiftly alter the spaceship's direction, attempting to evade the impending threat by diverting the vessel away from the danger zone.

"Ruma, make sure to move to a safe place," Elza said urgently. But Ruma stayed where she was, rooted to the spot.

Ruma looked at the swinging waves that were travelling toward the spaceship and said, "These waves are stronger, Elza, initiate speed."

Despite the alterations made to the trajectory, the spaceship's change in direction, unfortunately, led to the impact of the flares and fumes on one side of the vessel. The forceful and intense solar emissions affected the spaceship, potentially causing a collision and direct contact with the solar activity, presenting a challenge despite the attempted redirection of the spacecraft.

The wave impact jolted the spaceship, resulting in a power glitch and causing a ripple effect throughout the vessel. Objects, instruments, and various items within the spaceship began to rattle, shake, and quiver due to the turbulence caused by the wave's force. The entire interior of the spacecraft experiences a state of instability and unrest, with the shaking and disturbance affecting everything aboard the vessel.

The gravity system inside the spaceship experienced a momentary disruption, turning off for a brief period and then reactivating the spaceship, rendering it inoperative. Additionally, the force from the waves nudged and displaced the spaceship, causing it to move slightly away from its intended position. The combined effect of the malfunctioning engines and the external force from the Sun's waves prompts an unexpected shift in the spacecraft's location or trajectory.

Ruma, utilising the spaceship's holographic displays, assessed the status of the two main engines after they had been shut down. Observing the holographic representations of the engines, she inspected the visual data and information to understand the current condition and potential issues affecting the propulsion systems of the spacecraft.

The propulsion system of the spaceship was deactivated, causing a halt in engine function. Upon inspection, Ruma noticed the engines' base showing signs of corrosion and damage, potentially impeding their proper operation. The corrosion at the engine base suggested a critical issue that could hinder the efficient performance of the propulsion systems, leading to a significant setback for the spacecraft.

In a momentary pause, the primary engines being inactive, the backup engine automatically activated, attempting to provide propulsion for the spaceship. However, as the backup system engaged, glitches in the power supply emerged, causing interruptions and fluctuations in the ship's electrical systems. This added a layer of complexity and challenge, potentially hindering the stability and reliability of the spacecraft's functions.

"Turn on the main engine," Ruma yelled.

"Attempting to Activate Main Engine," Elza said. "Ruma, I'm sorry. The main engine has suffered a short circuit. It's currently unable to activate, disrupting our propulsion systems. We might need to explore alternative solutions or manual overrides to address this issue."

Ruma activated the holographic display, revealing a red mark indicating the affected area of the main engine. Due to the ongoing technical issues, the spaceship's propulsion system was most probably operating at a reduced capacity, causing the vessel to travel at a slower speed than its intended and optimal velocity.

"Can you identify the main issue?" Ruma demanded.

"Ruma, the analysis reveals that the main problem lies in the Power Distribution System's Motherboard. It has suffered corrosion, impacting its functionality. Corrosion can compromise the integrity of the board, leading to power distribution issues. Evaluating potential solutions to address this corrosion and restore the Motherboard's functionality."

"Do we have the spare part of the Motherboard?"

"Yes. We can proceed with replacing the corroded one to restore the Power Distribution System's functionality. I will guide you through the replacement process. Please prepare for the operation, and we will commence the replacement procedure shortly."

"And where is it located?"

"The spare Motherboard is stored in the Equipment Bay, Section C of the Maintenance Capsule. You can access it through the central corridor. Once you reach Section C, look for the marked storage unit labelled 'Spare Motherboard.' Retrieve it carefully, and we'll proceed with the replacement of the Power Distribution System. Ruma, we have a window of only two hours to replace the motherboard. It's crucial to proceed with the operation efficiently to minimise downtime in the Power Distribution System."

In the dimly lit corridors of the spaceship, Ruma moved with determination toward the Maintenance Capsule. The soft hum of the spaceship's systems provided a backdrop to her deliberate footsteps. The gentle glow of holographic signs guided her through the central corridor, leading her to Section C, where the spare motherboard awaited. The spaceship's artificial gravity gently pulled her forward, creating a sensation of weightlessness as she navigated the passageway.

A sudden disturbance in the central area caught her attention. The needle on the trajectory board, typically steady and precise, now behaved erratically. It swung wildly, deviating from its designated path, reflecting the turbulence caused by the unknown wave's impact on the spaceship.

In an unexpected turn of events, the spaceship experienced a brief disruption in its artificial gravity. As Ruma moved toward the Maintenance Capsule, the sudden cessation of gravity caught her off guard. For a fleeting moment, she found herself floating weightlessly in the corridor. It was a disorienting sensation as her body gently lifted off the ground.

As Ruma experienced the momentary loss of gravity, her surroundings transformed into a surreal scene. Her hair, hoodie, and arms floated freely in the air, creating an ethereal and almost otherworldly image. The weightlessness imparted an eerie yet captivating quality to her appearance, as if defying the laws of gravity.

Then gravity abruptly returned, making Ruma experience a sudden descent, landing on the floor with an unexpected force. A sharp gasp escaped her as her hand instinctively moved to her belly. Panic flared, but then ... There it was. A soft flutter, a gentle movement from within. Her baby was okay. Relief flooded her face, and with trembling hands bracing against the floor, she slowly got to her feet.

Wobbling slightly, Ruma pressed forward on her path toward the Maintenance Capsule. The obstacles in her way, whether gravitational anomalies or warning signs, failed to deter her from the critical mission of replacing the corroded motherboard. Each step she took echoed her unwavering commitment to ensure the stability and safety of the spaceship.

Inside the Maintenance Capsule, Ruma found the spare motherboard secured in a compartment. However, the replacement process was intricate, requiring precision and expertise. The holographic guide prompted her through the steps, but the urgency intensified as the spaceship continued to face turbulence.

As Ruma battled against the power glitches and tried to restore stability to the spaceship's systems, the maintenance capsule's automatic door became caught in the chaos. The erratic power fluctuations caused the door to malfunction, repeatedly opening and closing unexpectedly. Caught in the crossfire of the malfunctioning door, the robots assisting Ruma find themselves in a precarious situation. Their attempts to navigate through the unpredictable movements of the door were hindered by the persistent power glitches.

Dismantled body parts of the robots scatter across the floor of the maintenance capsule, a poignant visual representation of the challenges faced by both Ruma and her mechanical companions. The site served as a stark reminder of the toll the power glitches were taking on the spaceship's systems and its robotic helpers.

In the cluttered environment of the Maintenance Capsule, Ruma took a moment to survey the array of electronic components, spare parts, and tools scattered around her. The compartment held a myriad of intricate objects, each serving a specific function in the complex machinery of the spaceship.

The sudden jolt of the spaceship sent shockwaves through the Maintenance Capsule, causing all the boxes and loose items in the compartment to tumble to the floor. Ruma, already immersed in the task of deciphering the motherboard amidst the clutter, was momentarily taken aback by the unexpected disturbance.

The metallic clang of boxes colliding with the floor echoed in the capsule, adding to the chaotic symphony of the malfunctioning spaceship. Ruma, undeterred by the turbulence, steadied herself and the spare motherboard in her hands. The holographic interface flickered momentarily, but she quickly recalibrated it to continue her mission.

The fallen items created a labyrinth around her, and without the aid of the holographic interface, Ruma had to rely on her memory and understanding of the spaceship's layout. The sporadic flickering of lights added challenge, casting shadows that distorted her perception.

Ruma's hands moved with purpose, deftly sorting through the clutter to locate the spare motherboard. The holographic guide overlaid visual cues on the scattered items, aiding her in identifying the essential component amidst the chaos. Her determination and familiarity with the spaceship's systems allowed her to swiftly adapt to unforeseen circumstances.

With a steady hand, Ruma carefully retrieved the spare motherboard from its fallen position. She examined it, ensuring its integrity despite the rough handling. The urgency of the situation propelled her forward, and she took a moment to reorient herself before moving to a more stable area within the capsule to commence the critical replacement procedure.

"Elza, I found it! I found the Motherboard," she said triumphantly.

"Well done, Ruma! That's a crucial step," Elza praised her. "Now, proceed with care. Remember the proper installation protocol."

As Ruma proceeded toward the corroded area, the spaceship continued to experience sporadic jolts, emphasising the urgency of the situation. The warning signs persisted, casting an unsettling glow on the metallic walls. With each step, Ruma could feel the weight of responsibility bearing down on her.

The gravitational fluctuations added an extra layer of challenge to her journey. For a moment, the lack of gravity caused Ruma to float in mid-air, her hoodie and hair suspended around her like an ephemeral halo. However, as gravity abruptly returned, she descended to the floor with a slight stumble but maintained her determined stride.

As Ruma approached the corroded area adjacent to the swimming pool capsule, the juxtaposition of technical malfunction and recreational space created an unusual atmosphere. The persistent glitches and warning signs intensified, creating a stark contrast to the serene environment of the nearby swimming pool. In the Bar capsule, an abandoned glass held the remnants of a drink that Ruma had left behind, after Elza's cautious reminder about refraining from caffeinited beverages during pregnancy.

A faint but persistent rattling reverberated through the entire spaceship, like a distant echo of the unseen disturbances plaguing its intricate machinery. The minute tremors weave through the metallic corridors and capsules, creating an unsettling symphony of creaks and groans. Ruma, clutching the spare motherboard, felt the subtle vibrations beneath her feet as she advanced toward the corroded area.

In a surreal situation, the spaceship succumbed to a sudden loss of gravity, plunging its occupants and objects into an unexpected state of weightlessness. The billiard balls, bowling balls, pins, and Rubik's Cube in the Entertainment capsule gracefully ascended, creating a mesmerising ballet of levitating objects. The dart, once anchored to the dartboard, detached and joined the celestial dance, weaving through the air with newfound freedom.

In the Bar capsule, liquid from Ruma's abandoned drink formed delicate spheres that hovered mid-air, defying the laws of gravity. The bottles and glasses, liberated from their earthly constraints, performed a mesmerising ballet as they floated weightlessly in the space. Meanwhile, in the Food capsule, robotic arms navigated the airspace, their movements no longer confined by the pull of gravity.

Ruma, clutching the crucial Motherboard, experienced an ethereal sensation as she too became untethered, suspended in the microgravity environment. The corroded area, her destination, awaited her arrival in this surreal and weightless dimension. As the ship drifted in cosmic silence, Ruma pressed forward, navigating through the weightless wonders that surrounded her, all while clutching the vital piece of technology that held the key to restoring stability to the spaceship.

With a determined expression, Ruma gently pushed off a nearby wall, propelling herself in the direction of the corroded area. The lack of gravity allowed her to navigate through the spaceship with a fluidity and grace that transcended the usual limitations of movement.

Objects around her continued their weightless dance, and Ruma manoeuvred through the floating obstacles with a combination of controlled pushes and graceful spins. The corridor leading to the corroded area beckoned her, and she propelled herself forward, propelled by the necessity of the task at hand.

Elza's voice rang out urgently. "Ruma, you have only one hour to fix the problem."

The glitch came without warning.

Elza's voice, usually calm, warm, and unmistakably human in its gentle femininity, wavered mid-sentence. What began as a routine systems update dissolved into a fractured stutter, syllables stretching unnaturally and colliding with mechanical screeches. The once-reassuring tone warped into something jagged, something wrong.

"Cabin pressure is st-st-sta–sta–sta–*staAaa*–"

A burst of static pierced the air, sharp and shrill like metal screaming underwater. Then silence. The kind of silence that shouldn't exist aboard a functioning spaceship.

No hum of status updates. No soft reminders. No Elza. The weightless corridors, once comforted by her constant presence, now felt abandoned. The lights continued to glow, the monitors flickered as usual, but without her voice, the ship felt ... hollow. Like something vital had been cut out.

The stillness pressed in–too complete, too deliberate. As though the ship were holding its breath. Waiting. Watching.

She knew the clock was ticking, and with only an hour to fix the issue, every moment counted. Undeterred by the unexpected pause in Elza's communication, Ruma continued her journey through the weightless spaceship, propelled by both determination and the gentle nudges she gives herself in the gravity-defying environment.

As Ruma navigated the spaceship's aisle, the dart, released from the entertainment capsule due to the intermittent opening and closing of the doors, moved with surprising speed. In a sudden turn of events, the dart brushed against Ruma, catching a single eyebrow hair in its path.

Next, when she manoeuvred through the spaceship's doors, a sudden glitch caused her hoodie to get caught in the closing door. She attempted to pull it free, but the door remained stubbornly closed. Without hesitation, she slipped out of the hoodie, leaving it behind as she continued on her mission. The abandoned hoodie floated weightlessly in the air.

Suddenly, Ruma was yanked into the spaceship's swimming pool just as the artificial gravity flickered out. The door behind her sealed shut with a metallic hiss, trapping her inside. The water, no longer grounded by gravity, rose in slow, serpentine waves, curling through the air in a ghostly suspension. It drifted in shimmering globules and long ribbons, forming a strange, living organism that filled the chamber. The once-familiar pool had become a floating ocean in miniature, and Ruma was now at its mercy.

At first, she tried to swim to the surface, but there was no true 'up' anymore. Every motion felt sluggish, exaggerated by the resistance of the weightless water. Her limbs cut through it in slow arcs, and with each stroke, she felt the growing burden of her belly, heavier now despite the lack of gravity. Panic crept in. The water surrounded her entirely, pressing in from all directions. She gasped as it slipped into her mouth, and her instinct to breathe fought with the claustrophobic knowledge that she was suspended in liquid. Her strokes became erratic, her chest tightening as she fought for air, for direction, for anything solid.

The door remained shut. No light blinked from the panel. There was no sound except the shifting ripple of water and her muffled gasps. Ruma reached for the pool's edge, but there was no edge, only drifting walls she couldn't reach. A soft current pushed against her, subtle but insistent, pulling her back into the centre. She tried to resist it, but it moved like an unseen hand, turning her in circles, slowing her every attempt to escape. The water no longer behaved like water. Instead, it mimicked a restless ocean, unpredictable and haunting in its silence.

Her panic deepened as she clutched her belly, now the centre of her gravity, her axis in the chaos. The baby shifted inside her, gently at first, then more persistently. Tiny imprints formed on the curve of her stomach: a foot, a hand, the delicate press of a head. Each print bloomed like a flower under the skin, visible and surreal in the ambient glow of the chamber. It was a strange comfort in the middle of rising dread; a reminder of the life she carried, even as her own felt precarious.

Outside the capsule, the spaceship itself had started to drift, reacting to a mysterious external force. Its movements grew erratic, rocking ever so slightly in the void. The disorientation inside the pool mirrored the chaos beyond it. Ruma was adrift within an adrift vessel, her body tangled in liquid that defied every law she had once trusted. The silence, once broken by the ship's AI, remained unnaturally total. And in that quiet, suspended between fear and the strange beauty of the moment, she swam, not with confidence, but with necessity.

Amid the chaos, Ruma burst through the surface of the weightless water capsule, gasping for air. Her lungs ached, and her body trembled—not just from exertion, but from the unmistakable, deep-rooted pain tearing through her abdomen. She barely had time to orient herself before it gripped her again. A contraction. Sharp and consuming.

At first, it had felt like the cramping from a bad period, low and dragging across her pelvis. But now it was something else entirely. The pain wrapped itself around her spine and plunged deep into her hips, squeezing like a vice. She floated, half-suspended, her body curling instinctively. Her hand shot to her belly. The skin felt taut, the pressure unbearable. She couldn't escape it, not with breath, not with will. It took over her.

She tried to calm her breathing, tried to count. But the rhythm she had practised on Earth meant nothing here. The air felt thinner, the space colder, and the pain much, much louder.

Another contraction came, this time sharper, longer. Her back arched in response, toes curling, jaw clenched so tightly she thought her teeth might crack. A guttural sound escaped her lips like a half-sob, half-growl. Her vision blurred, and for a second, she wasn't sure if it was the water still clinging to her lashes or the pain pressing behind her eyes.

"Not now. Please, not now," she whispered into the silence of the capsule.

But her body didn't wait for permission.

The contractions rolled in like relentless waves. Each one stronger than the last, breaking her concentration, fracturing her resolve. The pressure in her pelvis grew unbearable, like her bones were being pried open from the inside. Her thighs trembled with each wave of pain, and she could feel the baby pushing downward, demanding space, demanding light.

Her mind swirled with panic. The ship was malfunctioning. The AI had gone silent. The navigation was drifting. She was alone. Alone in a floating capsule of water, untethered from gravity, and about to bring new life into the world with no hands to catch it but her own.

She pushed herself against a wall panel, bracing her feet against a surface to find some kind of counterforce. But the weightless environment betrayed her; every movement felt like a mistake, like slipping through jelly. Sweat poured down her face and neck, mixing with stray droplets of floating water. Her whole body was pulsing now. Her lower back ached like someone was stabbing her repeatedly. She cried out, clutching her belly, as another contraction took hold, this one longer, deeper, more primal. She could feel her cervix stretching, the unbearable pressure of a baby's head descending.

Her breathing was ragged, shallow. She bit down on her knuckle to keep from screaming. Her legs shook uncontrollably.

Her abdomen rippled with pain. And then... something shifted. A deep, sharp pressure bore down from within, and her body responded without choice or hesitation. The urge to push hit her like a tidal wave.

Her mind splintered between fear and instinct. *You're going to do this. You have to do this,* she told herself, over and over. She pressed her back against the capsule wall, bent her knees, and bore down.

Her groan echoed through the capsule, primal and raw. Her veins bulged along her neck and arms. She pushed again, and again, the contractions riding her like violent surf. And then, between pushes, there was a terrifying stillness as the baby crowned. The sensation was searing. A ring of fire tore through her flesh. She sobbed out loud, teeth clenched, arms shaking.

"Almost ... there," she rasped.

One final contraction roared through her, and with all the strength left in her body, she bore down with a cry that echoed off the capsule walls. The pain crescendoed and then ... release.

The baby slipped out into the weightless water, a small, perfect form suspended in the fluid chaos. For a breathless moment, the world fell still. The capsule's glowing interior, the drifting debris, the weightless water, and Ruma, still shaking, sobbing, bloodied, yet victorious, held that silence.

The baby floated gently into her arms, limbs curled, mouth opening to let out the first, thin wail.

And Ruma, who was bruised, burning, and exhausted, held her child against her chest and wept. Not because she was in pain. But because against all odds, in the middle of nowhere, in a drifting capsule above Earth, life had found a way.

Within a few minutes, gravity reasserted its control, and the water in the capsule started to descend. Droplets floated in the air before finding their way back to the surface, creating a surreal dance. The weight of gravity returned, pulling the water down and forming a pool at the bottom of the capsule.

In the muted light of the capsule, Ruma cradled her newborn against her bare chest. The baby, small, damp, and glistening, was a miracle made flesh. Its tiny body floated gently in her arms, the umbilical cord still attached, curling like a silvery thread between mother and child. The baby's skin was a deep, flushed pink, mottled with the rawness of birth, and slick with vernix. Wisps of dark, wet hair clung to its scalp, and its eyelids, puffy and reluctant, fluttered in brief, instinctive flinches.

For one breathless second, Ruma panicked. *Was the baby breathing? Was everything okay?*

And then, there it was. A small, sharp cry pierced the silence. Not loud, but alive. The infant's chest rose and fell, ragged and uneven at first, but steadily. Tiny fingers curled inward, grasping at nothing, and its mouth opened again in a wail, no longer watery but filled with life. A flood of relief surged through Ruma's body, more overwhelming than any contraction, more profound than any terror she had just survived.

Tears slipped down her cheeks as she brought the baby closer, wrapping her arms around it in a trembling embrace. Her lips brushed its damp forehead. The sensation was electric. In that instant, the silence of the capsule didn't feel so empty anymore. Her exhaustion melted into awe. The aches in her bones and the tremors in her limbs were silenced by the presence of this tiny, perfect being. Despite the floating wires, the stale air, the distant shudders of the ship around them—this moment felt sacred.

She had done it. Her baby was here.

As the ship's systems slowly flickered back to life, panels came aglow and Elza's rebooting voice hummed faintly in the background. Emergency lights dimmed to a steady pulse. Gravity, though still inconsistent, began to return in soft waves. It was enough.

With steady hands, Ruma gently detached the cord and wrapped the baby in a sterile thermal sheet from the wall panel. The newborn squirmed slightly but remained quiet now, eyes closed, breathing in soft hiccup-like bursts.

Knowing the child needed warmth and care, she could not fully give in her current state, Ruma manoeuvred toward the medication capsule. The moment felt strange, to place her baby in something so mechanical, but it was insulated, programmed for neonatal care, and it was all she had. With slow, reverent movements, she nestled the baby into its cushioned interior.

"Snobo," she whispered, her voice cracked but certain. The robotic assistant floated over, its eyes blinking to life.

"Watch her for me," she said, brushing one final hand over the infant's cheek. "Please."

Snobo gently extended a soft sensor arm to monitor the baby's vitals. The screen blinked green. Safe. Alive.

"Ruma, you have thirty minutes to replace the Motherboard."

Ruma took a deep breath. The dim lighting in the maintenance capsule flickered slightly, creating an ominous ambience. The corroded area, located near the swimming pool capsule, awaited Ruma's skilled hands. The warning signs persisted, reminding her of the impending threat. With determination in her eyes, she clutched the newly acquired Motherboard, her lifeline in this technological challenge.

Every second counted. The ticking clock intensified the pressure as Ruma pushed forward. The Motherboard, though a potential solution, was just a piece of the puzzle. The real challenge lay in the delicate process of removing the corroded board and seamlessly installing the new one. It was a race against time in the vast expanse of the spaceship, where even the smallest glitch could have profound consequences.

The door to the corroded area opened with a hydraulic hiss, revealing a scene of disarray. Wires dangled like unravelling threads, and the metallic surfaces bore scars of electronic corrosion. The faint scent of burnt components mingled with the sterile air of the spaceship, creating an odd amalgamation of scents.

Ruma, holding the spare motherboard, took a deep breath before stepping into the corroded area. The dimly lit space, filled with essential components and electronic gadgets, served as the nerve centre of the spaceship's power distribution system. A faint hum resonated in the air, underscoring the urgency of the situation.

The countdown continued, and Ruma set the salvaged Motherboard aside. She took a moment to analyse the corroded area, considering the intricate connections that needed to be carefully disengaged. The clock ticked away, each second a reminder of the impending danger.

Ruma dove back into the wires, hands moving fast, unblinking, breath shallow. The new motherboard floated in front of her, half-connected, its circuitry exposed like an open wound. The ship groaned around her, systems flickering, core stability wavering. Elza's voice, once soothing, now cut like a blade:

"T-minus five minutes to full system collapse."

Her fingers fumbled, then locked down the final set of connections. Sparks flared for just a second, but she didn't flinch. Sweat streaked down her face. The motherboard clicked into place. No time to double-check.

"Three minutes remaining."

Ruma launched toward the main console, limbs propelled by muscle memory and panic. The monitor lit up as her fingers slammed the touchscreen.

"INITIATE REBOOT?"

"YES."

Lines of code flooded the screen. Status lights blinked, systems groaned back to life. But the reboot was slow. Too slow.

"Ninety seconds remaining," Elza intoned.

Ruma's eyes locked onto the numbers. Her hands hovered, ready to override, to reroute anything. The hum of the engines stuttered, threatening to drop out completely.

"Sixty ... fifty-nine ... fifty-eight ..."

The ship rattled. Gravity pulsed erratically. A loose cable sparked near her head. She didn't even flinch. Her pulse was louder than Elza's countdown now.

"Thirty seconds remaining."

"Come on, come on," she muttered through clenched teeth.

"Twenty... nineteen... eighteen..."

The reboot was reaching its peak. The console flared with lines of success codes flickering green.

"Ten..."

And then, suddenly, silence. Ruma's throat dried up. "No, no, no," she moaned, scrambling to the console, trying to understand what had gone wrong, what could she do to get the countdown going? There were only ten seconds left for the reboot to finish! What else could cause an issue at this stage?

Yet she barely had any time to react, any time to take a breath, any time to rifle through a manual to figure out what the procedure was. *Tarayaan* lurched suddenly, reminding Ruma awfully of hitting the brakes too soon while driving a car at a high speed. She got knocked off her feet and could only watch when the console blanked out, no figures, no codes, nothing.

And then, there was a blackout.

***

Chapter XX

Back at the Kennedy Space Centre, it was quieter than death itself.

They had been watching Ruma's every move, every decision that she took became evident to them a few seconds later, when new code was fed into the console, a part of the ship was shut down, or she muttered to herself about what she could do. She had done everything right—the engineers back on earth were in awe of her for handling everything so seamlessly.

But why did the reboot stop?

That was all Clark was asking himself as he stared up at the large screen. It was blank—no static, no broken blue screen, just blank. Empty. Hollow. Terror ran through his veins like he'd never felt before. He gulped down painfully, but his throat was drier than the Sahara Desert. But no part of him seemed to want to reach out and get a glass of water. How could that matter now?

"Is there any foolproof way that would cause the rebooting to stop?" Laura's voice finally broke the silence.

One of the engineers peeled his eyes away from the screen and replied in a small voice, "No. it's not supposed to happen."

"There has to be a way out," Laura said and urgently walked up to the Comms engineer, grabbing the microphone from her hastily. "Ruma, this is Ground Control. Can you hear me? are you okay?"

Silence.

But Laura didn't stop. She kept calling out Ruma's name, kept asking if she could hear them, kept asking if she was okay, kept asking if there was a manual or a cheat code she could find to finish the reboot. A part of Clark knew that Laura was throwing her hands up to the heavens, asking for a miracle. But it was Laura's insistence that kept the others going. Soon, the room was full of noise again—hasty typing on the keyboards, searching for an answer, muttered conversations as the engineers tried to brainstorm a solution, and somewhere, in the hushed dim of it all, was a prayer.

*

Back on *Tarayaan*, Ruma hadn't moved.

The honest answer was, she didn't know where to go or what to do. It was so dark, so pitch dark that she couldn't even see her own hands. It was so silent, so loudly silent, that she could hear the sound of blood rushing in her ears.

And the very next realisation that hit her was that it was cold.

The entire ship has shut down, Ruma realised. A silly part of her thought that without power to keep the ship moving, it would plummet to the abyss. Then she reminded herself that zero gravity was on her side—the ship wasn't going anywhere. Neither was she.

Ruma felt exhausted, all of her joints hurt, and all she wanted to do was take a long nap. The silence and the darkness were a perfect cocoon for it. But as she could feel her own breath form a cloud of cold vapour, she realised that she wasn't alone on the ship—her daughter was here, somewhere, alone, in the dark and the cold.

Yet again, she couldn't find the energy to move. *Where would I go? Where was she? What would I do once I* do *find her?* Desperation clawed at her, paralysed by fear and uncertainty. Awful thoughts started to fill her head. What if she does find her baby, and in the dark, she steps on her baby or hurts her in some way?

But she didn't have to sit in silence for longer. She almost missed it, a little flicker of light, reminding her of the twinkle of a fairy light. She stared up at the little blob of light hungrily, like a starving child looking at a bakery display. All of ten seconds had passed since the blackout, but it had felt like an eternity. Yet this little flicker of light—it stopped time.

And then came light.

Tarayaan lurched again, but this time, the lurch delighted Ruma. She immediately got to her feet as the engines whirred, the lights turned on, and the console flickered back to life. The once-illuminated consoles dimmed, plunging the control room into a spectral gloom. The backup engine, too, yielded to the reboot's commanding force, halting its mechanical symphony.

Amidst the technological resurgence, as the spaceship's systems rekindled with newfound vitality, Ruma found herself caught in the currents of a profound emotional release. The tears, unbidden and unrestrained, flowed down her cheeks, mirroring the tumultuous journey her spirit had traversed in those critical moments.

As the seconds unfolded in suspense, a faint glimmer of hope emerged from the abyss of uncertainty. The once dormant consoles flickered with a newfound vitality, casting a soft glow across the control room. Then, like a celestial beacon heralding the return of power, a tiny light ignited—a harbinger of the spaceship's reawakening.

In tandem with the flickering light, the main engine roared to life, its resounding echo filling the void of the control room. The triumphant hum of technology signalled the completion of the rebooting process, a victory inscribed on the luminous monitor that bore the words, "Rebooting completed."

The control room, once plunged into a momentary abyss, now radiated with the restored brilliance of functionality. The challenges and uncertainties that had shrouded the spacecraft were now dispelled, replaced by the hum of machinery and the glow of screens displaying the intricate dance of algorithms.

In the solitary glow of the control room, where the consoles hummed with renewed vigour, Ruma's tears became silent witnesses to the magnitude of the challenges she had faced. Each teardrop carried the weight of fears confronted, resilience tested, and the palpable relief that accompanied the triumphant revival of the spaceship.

Ruma, overwhelmed by the tumultuous journey of emotions, felt the warmth of tears streaming down her face. The once heavy burden of uncertainty and fear had now transformed into tears of joy, each droplet a testament to the resilience that had brought her through the challenges. But as the adrenaline that had fueled her began to ebb, reality hit her like a silent wave–she had just given birth. Only now did her body begin to register it. A deep ache settled into her core, sharp and insistent, and she winced as a fresh surge of pain pulsed through her abdomen. The afterbirth was yet to pass, and a raw soreness took hold of her, grounding the emotional high in the gritty truth of what her body had endured. In the soft glow of the control room, surrounded by the gentle hum of machinery, Ruma's tears mirrored the flickering light of hope. The weight that had pressed upon her shoulders lifted, replaced by the relief of survival and the dawning exhaustion of motherhood. It was a moment where sorrow, joy, and pain converged, a poignant reminder of the fragility and strength that coexisted in the vastness of space.

The spaceship, reinvigorated by the successful reboot, embraced the cosmic currents once more. The trajectory recalibrated, and the propulsion system roared to life, propelling the vessel forward into the boundless expanse of the unknown. The echoes of the critical reboot reverberated through the spaceship, an indelible chapter in its cosmic journey.

In this moment of respite, the cosmos outside the spaceship seemed to beckon with an ethereal allure. The distant stars, unscathed witnesses to the interstellar drama, shimmered against the cosmic canvas. Ruma, a lone navigator in the vastness of space, recognised that each challenge surmounted brought her one step closer to the mysterious destinations that awaited.

The reassuring voice of Elza echoed through the spaceship, marking the triumphant culmination of Ruma's efforts. The resonating words, "Ruma, Welcome aboard. The spaceship systems have been reconfigured and rebooted," reverberated in the control room, casting away the shadows of uncertainty that had lingered moments before.

Ruma, still moved by the recent rollercoaster of emotions, let out a sigh of relief. The gentle hum of the engines provided a melodic backdrop to the profound silence that followed. The control panels flickered back to life, their vibrant displays signalling a renewed vitality within the vessel.

As the spaceship sailed through the cosmic expanse, Ruma's gaze shifted from the monitor to the vast celestial canvas outside. The stars, like distant beacons, witnessed the resilience of a lone traveller against the cosmic currents. At that moment, a sense of serenity enveloped the control room, and Ruma embraced the newfound stability.

Ruma's attention turned with a mix of concern and tenderness toward the Medication capsule where her newborn lay peacefully in the medication pod. The soft hum of medical equipment filled the air, creating a lullaby that resonated through the chamber.

Her baby, snugly nestled in the protective cocoon of the pod, appeared ethereal. The oxygen pipe connected to the pod facilitated a steady flow of life-sustaining air, ensuring the tiny chest rose and fell in a rhythmic dance of breath. The delicate network of visible veins painted a map beneath the baby's skin, revealing the vitality coursing through each tiny vessel.

The baby's body, adorned in a gentle shade of pink, exhibited the warmth of life and health. The tranquil scene in the Medication capsule became evidence of the resilience of the human body, even in the face of cosmic upheavals. Ruma, a mother gazing at her slumbering creation, couldn't help but feel a surge of maternal affection and an overwhelming sense of responsibility for the life she had brought into the vast expanse of the spaceship.

Ruma, glancing around the spaceship, took in the aftermath of the gravity glitches and turbulence. The fallen items, once neatly arranged, now formed an irregular mosaic of fragments and remnants. Broken glass from the bar capsule displaced furniture from the entertainment capsule, and scattered tools from the maintenance capsule adorned the spaceship's interior.

While the control room, where Ruma stood, remained largely intact, the repercussions of the cosmic turbulence had rippled through the interconnected chambers. The floating balls in the entertainment capsule had ceased their mid-air dance, now resting on the floor alongside the fallen dart and displaced robotic arms.

As the spaceship weathered the turbulent waves in space, the communication link with Earth faltered, leaving a void of silence that echoed through the vast expanse. The sudden disconnection left both Ruma and the crew in suspense, cut off from the familiar voices and guidance emanating from their home planet. The lack of communication, the absolute stillness, could have easily spiralled into a sense of isolation, but Ruma didn't feel alone. The AI systems aboard the ship responded to her every need with quiet efficiency, offering support and presence in subtle ways. And nestled beside her, wrapped in warmth and wonder, was her newborn baby, who was fragile, yet fiercely alive. That small, steady rhythm of life grounded her, filling the silence with meaning. In that moment, even the deep silence of space couldn't touch the quiet fullness of her heart.

However, as the spaceship emerged from the tempest, the systems successfully rebooted, and the flickering connection was re-established. A sense of relief swept through Ruma as the familiar hum of communication systems resumed, filling the capsule with the cadence of messages, updates, and reassurances from Earth.

The voice of the mission control echoed once again, cutting through the cosmic silence and reconnecting the inhabitants of the spaceship with their roots. The broken link, now mended, became a lifeline connecting them to the world they had momentarily lost touch with during the tumultuous journey through space.

In the bustling control centre on Earth, a wave of relief swept through the space centre as the communication signals were reactivated. The tense atmosphere that had gripped the mission control room began to dissipate, and the faces of the team members brightened with a mix of joy and anticipation.

Clark, who had been anxiously awaiting updates about the spaceship and its crew, finally received the long-awaited information from the communication team. The room buzzed with activity as technicians, engineers, and support staff shared smiles, exchanged congratulatory remarks, and resumed their duties with renewed vigour.

In the Medication Pod, Ruma gazed at her peacefully sleeping baby, nestled on the floor beside her. The soft hum of the medical equipment provided a soothing background noise, creating a serene atmosphere within the confined space. The exhaustion from the recent events had taken its toll on Ruma, and she couldn't help but marvel at the tiny, fragile life she had brought into the world.

The pod's subdued lighting accentuated the delicate features of the newborn, casting gentle shadows across the baby's tiny face. Ruma's eyes, a mix of relief and affection, remained fixed on the slumbering infant.

"Ruma," a voice echoed in the Medication Capsule.

Ruma's eyes widened in disbelief as the voice in the Medication Capsule persisted. She glanced around, searching for the source until she realised it was a holographic projection. A familiar figure slowly materialised before her—her mother.

"Ruma, my dear," Sameera's holographic image spoke, a warm and comforting presence. The glow of the hologram cast a soft light across the Medication Capsule, creating an ethereal ambience.

"Mom?" Ruma whispered, her voice filled with a mixture of surprise and joy. Tears welled up in Ruma's eyes as she processed the emotional moment. "I miss you, Mom. I wish you were here."

"I'm always with you, Ruma. No matter where you are, my love for you transcends the vastness of space," Sameera said in a soothing tone.

Ruma's attempt to embrace her mother resulted in her arms passing through the holographic projection. A bittersweet smile played on Ruma's lips as she realised the intangible nature of the connection. Even though she couldn't physically feel her mother's warmth, the emotional presence was undeniable.

"I wish I could hold you, Mom," Ruma expressed with a mix of longing and affection.

Sameera nodded. "Sometimes, the bonds that tie us are beyond the reach of physical touch. But my love is here with you, guiding you through the stars."

As Sameera shifted her gaze from Ruma to the baby, her eyes welled up with tears. The sight of the newborn, peacefully sleeping in the Medication Capsule, overwhelmed her with a mix of emotions. With a tender smile, Sameera moved closer to the baby's pod, her virtual presence seemingly transcending the spatial confines. The image of the baby, wrapped in a gentle glow, evoked a profound sense of wonder and reverence.

"You want to know what I've named her?" Ruma asked, tracing her baby's cheek with her fingertip. She smiled back at her mother's hologram. "Tara. Because she's born among the stars."

"She is beautiful, Ruma. She looks just like you," Sameera remarked with a warmth that echoed through the holographic communication. The virtual image of the baby, nestled in the Medication Capsule, seemed to radiate an innocence that resonated even across the vast expanse of space.

As Ruma looked at her mother's holographic form, she smiled, sharing in the joyous moment. As Clark observed the holographic interaction between Ruma, Tara and Sameera, a profound emotion stirred within him. Watching them on the monitor transcended the scientific and technical aspects of the mission, delving into the realm of human connection and the marvel of life in the cosmos.

The news of a baby on board the spaceship sent shockwaves through the media. Reporters and news anchors expressed a mix of astonishment and concern at the unprecedented nature of the situation. The presence of an infant in space, exploring the mysteries of the cosmos, added a new dimension to the ongoing mission.

"Today marks a historic milestone in space exploration. For the first time, a baby is part of a spacefaring mission. The challenges and risks associated with interstellar travel have reached a new level. The trained astronauts sometimes feel burdensome now that we have a baby on board. How will an infant adapt to the conditions of space? How will this impact the crew's dynamics and decision-making? These are questions that scientists and experts around the world are now grappling with," the reporter continued.

The news coverage ignited a storm of debates and discussions across television panels, online forums, and coffee shop conversations. On one channel, a grey-haired astrophysicist gestured animatedly with his hands, diagrams flickering behind him as he explained the unprecedented biological risks of zero-gravity infancy. On another, a child psychologist questioned the moral implications, her voice tight with concern. Social media buzzed with hashtags, like #SpaceBaby, #CosmicCradle, while split-screen interviews showed bioethicists clashing with space agency officials, their voices overlapping in heated exchanges. In living rooms across the world, wide-eyed children pressed their noses to screens while parents whispered doubts and wonder. The baby, unseen but everywhere, had become the newest, most fragile ambassador of the stars.

As Tara started to move, tiny fingers gently unfurled in the microgravity environment. The delicate dance of the infant's fingers captivated the attention of those watching. Her eyes slowly opened, revealing a gaze filled with curiosity and wonder as they adjusted to the new surroundings.

In the Medication Capsule, Ruma, still recovering from the labour and marvelling at the sight of her newborn, couldn't help but smile. The crew members and scientists on Earth, monitoring the live feed from the spaceship, were equally enthralled by this extraordinary occurrence. Tara, a symbol of life and resilience, brought a sense of hope and inspiration to the mission.

The sweet sound of a newborn's cry filled the Medication Capsule. As Tara let out her cries, Ruma's heart swelled with a mix of emotions—joy, relief, and an overwhelming sense of maternal love. Sameera, sharing the moment through the communication link, smiled with pride.

"You need to feed Tara whenever she feels hungry," Sameera murmured.

Ruma, holding Tara, nodded in agreement. She looked down at the precious bundle in her arms, marvelling at the delicate features of her baby. The holographic image of her mother, though unable to physically touch or hold the baby, provided guidance and emotional support in this unique situation.

Ruma, with Sameera's guidance, carefully adjusted her position to ensure a proper latch for breastfeeding. Sameera gestured, providing tips on how to hold the baby, cradle her in a supportive embrace, and create a comfortable environment for the nursing experience. Ruma watched with a mix of joy and awe as Tara peacefully nursed, savouring the nourishment provided by her mother's milk. In the quiet ambience of the spaceship, the rhythmic sounds of the baby feeding echoed, creating a tender and intimate moment.

As Sameera's holographic image faded away, leaving a sense of bittersweet longing, Ruma held her baby close, absorbing the warmth and innocence of the moment.

The ship's systems were now stable, and the trajectory corrected. As the spaceship continued its journey toward Planet III, Ruma embraced the responsibilities of motherhood in this extraordinary setting.

*

Ruma, with a newfound energy, jogged along the spaceship's aisle, capturing the routine on her video camera. The rhythmic sound of her steps echoed in the artificial gravity, creating a unique harmony in the cosmic vessel. The spaceship, once a place of turbulence and challenges, now resonated with a sense of stability and hope. Tara, snug in a specially designed crib, observed the motion with curious eyes. The soft hum of the spaceship's systems accompanied Ruma's steady breathing, a rhythmic melody in the vast silence of space.

In her recorded message, Ruma spoke with a hint of satisfaction in her voice, "Hey everyone, Ruma here. It's been quite a journey–floating in zero gravity, dealing with power glitches, and, well, delivering a baby in space. But guess what? I've been keeping up with my fitness routine, trying to strike a balance between gaining some weight and burning those calories."

Ruma panned the camera to show the spaceship's interior. Amidst the high-tech panels and whirring machines, a baby rested peacefully in the crib. It seemed out of place at first glance, but Tara seemed to belong there. "And look at this little one—she's my new workout buddy. Well, more like a cheerleader for now. But who knows, maybe we'll have the first mother-daughter space workout routine."

She laughed warmly and concluded, "Anyway, that's the update from the spaceship. Until next time, stay fit, stay healthy, and keep reaching for the stars. Ruma out."

***

Chapter XXI

Life aboard the spaceship had fallen into a rhythm, a quiet routine woven through with the ever-present hum of machinery and the low murmur of conversation echoing through metallic corridors. The novelty of the mission had faded, replaced by a sense of endurance in getting through each day with purpose, even if it meant repetition. Ruma had changed, too. No longer the cautious, wide-eyed researcher she'd once been, she had grown into her role as both crew member and mother. The early days after Tara's birth had been chaotic, a blur of sleepless nights, tentative feedings, and makeshift childcare arrangements in a place never designed for infancy. But somehow, through careful coordination and the crew's occasional help, they had made it work.

Tara had grown into a curious, bright-eyed one-year-old, her giggles occasionally bouncing off the sterile walls of the observation deck or her small sleeping pod, a space now littered with soft toys and floating picture cards. Despite the unnatural environment, she seemed to thrive, as her lungs were stronger, her movements agile, her gaze always alert to the flicker of passing stars.

On the morning of Tara's first birthday, Ruma found a rare moment for herself. After a short jog around the ship's artificial gravity corridor, which was an activity she had clung to as both meditation and escape as she made her way to the Food Court. The place was quiet at this hour, without a few crewmates sipping nutrient shakes and reviewing mission logs. She approached the vending machine, tapped in her preferences, and waited as it hummed and whirred, finally delivering a steaming cup of coffee into her hands. She cupped it gently, its warmth seeping into her palms, and allowed herself a small, silent exhale. A pause. A breath. A brief moment of peace in the relentless rhythm of survival and motherhood among the stars.

The hologram flickered to life in front of her, casting a pale blue glow across the Food Court wall. Professor Clark's familiar face emerged, sharper than memory, softer than presence. His eyes crinkled with warmth as he spotted her.

"Hi, Ruma," he said with a gentle smile. "How are you doing?"

Ruma straightened in her seat, brushing a few stray strands of hair behind her ear. "I'm fine, Dad," she replied, her voice steady but laced with the fatigue of the past year.

His gaze shifted, full of unspoken questions. "And how's the baby doing?"

She paused for a moment, her hand tightening around the coffee cup. A smile tugged at the corners of her lips as she glanced toward the monitor that streamed footage from the nursery pod. Tara, floating gently in zero-gravity, was fast asleep, clutching a stuffed star.

"She's doing fine, Dad. Curious as ever," Ruma said, her voice softer now, touched with wonder.

She took a long sip of coffee, letting the warmth seep into her bones, grounding her in the moment, even if the world she now called home was anything but ordinary.

Clark's hologram fell into step beside Ruma as she walked down the corridor, her footsteps light but purposeful. The gentle hum of the ship accompanied them like background music.

"I wanted to let you know," he began, his tone calm but charged with significance, "we're scheduled to attend an interview with *World News* this morning. It's going to be broadcast live to the entire world."

Ruma's brows lifted slightly, the news catching her off guard. She exhaled slowly, processing the weight of what that meant. "That's ... great," she said, offering a small, thoughtful smile. "A chance to share what this journey has truly been like."

Clark nodded, his holographic form flickering slightly under the corridor lights. "Exactly. I want you to speak honestly. Share your experience, Ruma; people need to hear your story."

She glanced at him, her pace steady. "They will," she said quietly. "They'll hear all of it."

"It will start in another ten minutes, and the CCTV inside the spaceship goes live to the world," Clark said and disappeared.

Ruma went to her sleeping pod. Once the pod doors were opened, she looked at her daughter's crib , but Tara was not in the crib. Her heart raced as she scanned the room, her eyes darting to every corner in search of Tara. Panic began to rise within her. She swiftly checked every possible hiding spot, calling out her daughter's name in a mix of concern and urgency. There was no response. The feeling of dread intensified as she frantically looked around, her mind racing with possibilities.

"AI Elza, I am in trouble again," Ruma sighed. "Can you locate Tara? Initiate a ship-wide scan."

World Network (WN) channel started telecasting the Spaceship's CCTV live as the channel went live-streaming to the world.

Amid the live telecast on the World Network, every corner of the spaceship was showcased through the CCTV feeds. From the food court to the living quarters, the broadcast provided a glimpse into the daily life and routines aboard the vessel. The viewers were immersed in the daily operations and the unique challenges faced in the cosmic confines of the vessel.

With Elza's help and the live broadcast ongoing, the tension heightened. Ruma felt a mix of urgency, concern for her daughter, and the pressure of being watched worldwide. The hologram device's navigation assistance guided Ruma through the spaceship's different sections in search of Tara. The audience watching the live broadcast was on edge, invested in the outcome and the resolution of the situation.

Tara's mischief was evident as she switched from one pod to another in a matter of seconds. She slid between capsules, popped out from different sections, and even managed to close the lids just as Ruma arrived. As Ruma desperately tried to keep up, her reactions became increasingly exaggerated and comical. She started moving in sync with the capsules, mirroring their swaying movements in her quest to catch Tara. The audience on Earth was roaring with laughter, seeing this comical dance unfold on their screens.

Tara's laughter echoed through the capsule as she turned the entire search into a game of peek-a-boo with the doors. Every time Ruma approached a door, it opened, and just as she was about to catch Tara, the baby dashed away, and the door shut behind her.

Tara then entered the Food capsule and crawled into the kitchen's desk. The vending machine's lights seemed to hold a magnetic allure for her, drawing her towards it with the wonder of a cosmic explorer discovering a new galaxy. The robotic arm, attempting to navigate Beth's agile movements, made subtle adjustments, trying to match her playful pace without startling her.

The robotic arm, following the baby's movements, attempted a gentle grab, aiming for the diaper like a hook lifting an object. However, amid this comical dance, the diaper got snagged, and with a little rip, Tara slipped free, floating down toward the floor of the food capsule.

With a determined giggle, the resilient explorer baby landed gracefully on the ground, finding newfound freedom in the weightlessness of space. Undeterred by the small mishap, Tara, like an intrepid astronaut, resumed her mission—crawling across the floor, casting glances at the vending machine and various floating snacks with unwavering curiosity. Her giggles and babbles filled the capsule, painting a heartwarming picture against the cosmic backdrop.

Tara's tiny feet pattered against the smooth floors as she zigzagged down the narrow passageways, her laughter bouncing off the metal walls like a mischievous echo. She darted into hydroponics, knocking over a tray of floating seedlings that drifted lazily through the air, and then zipped out again before Ruma could even step inside. The baby's quick turns and sudden stops made her look like a pint-sized comet streaking across the ship, leaving behind a trail of floating toys, blankets, and startled crewmates. Cameras followed her every move, capturing her gleeful acrobatics as she bounced off walls and used handrails to propel herself further. To the audience watching on Earth, Tara was no longer just a baby aboard a spaceship—she had become the star of an impromptu cosmic comedy show.

Ruma, still guiding the robotic arm, watched her daughter's antics with a mix of fondness and amusement. The crew back on Earth couldn't help but laugh at the delightful spectacle unfolding in the food capsule.

Meanwhile, the robotic arm, with a whimsical grace, hovered nearby, trying to assist without disrupting Tara's exploration. It remained poised, ready to help guide the baby back to safety while maintaining a respectful distance, understanding that this playful chase was part of the adventure.

"Elza, lock the exit door," Ruma urged, but before the command could take effect, Tara swiftly made her way past the threshold.

Realising her predicament, Ruma found herself momentarily trapped between the closing doors. With an air of amusement and slight panic, she called out, "Elza, unlock the door!"

Elza promptly responded, "Unlocking the door."

Tara continued her exploration, blissfully unaware of the slight chaos unfolding around her.

As Ruma attempted to push the door, she found it firmly locked. The confusion and the urgency to chase after Tara were palpable. Meanwhile, Tara, oblivious to the commotion, toddled around the adjacent capsule.

"Elza, why isn't the door opening?" Ruma's voice echoed a mix of concern and amusement.

"I'm sorry, there seems to be a glitch in the door's system. Working on resolving it now."

Finally, after a few moments that seemed like an eternity for Ruma, the door mechanism creaked back to life. "Unlocking the door now," Elza announced.

The door slowly slid open, allowing Ruma to exit the capsule. With a sense of relief, Ruma hurriedly pursued Tara, who was still on her exploration mission.

Tara's curiosity led her into the bar capsule, where an assortment of beverages and entertainment gadgets adorned the room. Ruma, keeping a watchful eye on the live feed, witnessed Tara's entrance into the rather inappropriate setting for a baby. She quickly manoeuvred through the spaceship's corridor, approaching the entrance to the bar capsule. "Elza, initiate the closing of the bar capsule doors!" she exclaimed.

As Ruma reached the door, Tara was standing near the centre of the capsule, attempting to mimic a dance move she had observed on the entertainment screen.

Elza swiftly complied with Ruma's request. The doors of the bar capsule started to close, but Tara, in her newfound mobility, was faster. She darted toward the door, giggling and crawling, narrowly escaping confinement once again.

As Tara continued her speedy crawl through the entertainment capsule, Snobo, the robotic assistant, heeded Ruma's command and entered the area. With practised efficiency, Snobo managed to catch up to Tara near the bowling section. However, as the robotic arm gently lifted Tara, the unexpected happened–Tara, in all her baby wisdom, decided it was the perfect time for a little mischief.

Without warning, the diaper loosened, and a tinkling sound echoed in the room as Tara commenced an impromptu bathroom break, right on poor Snobo! The audience watching the live feed erupted into laughter, witnessing the hilarious and unexpected turn of events. Snobo, true to its programming, handled the disturbance with stoic grace, even though it was not equipped for this particular situation.

Ruma, witnessing this mishap, couldn't help but laugh at the chaotic scene unfolding before her. "Elza, prepare for cleanup in the entertainment capsule," she instructed amidst her giggles.

As Snobo found itself in an unexpected situation, the robotic assistant momentarily lost grip on Tara, leading to a gentle landing in the theatre section of the entertainment capsule. Ruma, quick on her feet, commanded Elza to cue up a *Cocomelon* animated video on the main screen.

As the vibrant and engaging *Cocomelon* animation began playing on the large screen, the once-speedy baby suddenly halted in their tracks, captivated by the colourful characters and catchy tunes. Tara's tiny hands clapped in delight, and her giggles filled the room, echoing amidst the playful music.

Ruma let out a relieved chuckle as she watched her daughter enthralled by the lively display. "Looks like we found the perfect distraction, Elza," she remarked with a smile.

Ruma quickly scanned the theatre section, ensuring Tara was safely engrossed in the animated show. With a sigh of relief, she approached Snobo, who was now gently cleaning up after the surprise.

"Good work, Snobo," Ruma praised, patting the robotic assistant on its metallic frame. She glanced at the screen, watching Tara's cheerful reactions to the colourful characters. Meanwhile, Elza, monitoring the situation, projected a holographic barrier around the theatre section to prevent any further surprise exits.

The adorable sight of Tara giggling and swaying to the music brought a smile to Ruma's face. "Looks like someone's enjoying the show," she chuckled, watching her daughter's enthusiastic reactions.

The cheerful jingle of *Cocomelon* filled the capsule, bouncing off the walls like a burst of sunlight. Tara sat cross-legged on the padded floor, her tiny hands spinning in the air as she mimicked the motions of "Wheels on the Bus" with fervent glee. Her cheeks flushed pink from laughter, and her curls bounced with each exaggerated move.

Ruma leaned against the edge of the control console, sipping from a lukewarm pouch of juice, eyes glued to her daughter's performance. A wide grin tugged at her lips. "Elza," she called out over the music to the AI, still chuckling, "remind me to schedule more of these musical marathons. Clearly, we've discovered Tara's true calling."

Tara threw her arms out, spinning in a tiny circle before collapsing onto the floor with a squeal. "Round and round!" she shouted, feet kicking as if the floor were the bus itself.

Ruma knelt beside her, tapping her foot in rhythm with the song, then gently clapped along. Her laughter slipped out freely, light and unrestrained. "You're quite the performer, aren't you?" she said between giggles, brushing a curl away from Tara's forehead.

Inside the sealed bubble of the capsule, far from Earth, the melody and laughter spilt like stardust, two heartbeats dancing to a familiar tune in the most unfamiliar of places.

Meanwhile, the song's catchy tune seemed to have a contagious effect. Snobo, the robotic assistant, picked up the infectious rhythm. Its mechanical movements attempted to mimic the bus wheels' motion, much to Ruma's amusement.

"Looks like the song has even got Snobo into the groove," Ruma remarked, watching the robot trying its best to join in the fun.

Ruma gently cradled Tara in her arms, tenderly swaying back and forth. Tara, drowsy from the rhythmic motions, began to drift into a peaceful slumber. Ruma carefully laid her down in the crib within the sleeping pod, tucking her in with a soft blanket.

"Sleep tight, little one," Ruma whispered, planting a gentle kiss on Tara's forehead before quietly tiptoeing out of the sleeping pod. She ensured the monitoring system was activated to keep an eye on her daughter while she slept.

Ruma, composed and poised, sat down in front of the camera within the communication capsule. The lights dimmed as the transmission began, and the interviewer from *World News* appeared on the screen, ready to engage in the live interview.

"Good morning, Ruma. Thank you for joining us today," the interviewer greeted warmly.

"Good morning," Ruma responded with a confident smile.

"Your journey in space with your daughter has captivated the world. Can you tell us about your experiences and challenges as a spacefarer and a mother?" the interviewer inquired.

Ruma leaned forward, articulating her thoughts with grace and conviction. "It's been an extraordinary journey. Navigating space while caring for my daughter has presented its challenges, but it's also been incredibly rewarding. I've learned to adapt and ensure her safety while embracing the wonders of space exploration."

"Ruma, your journey has been inspiring. How do you balance the responsibilities of motherhood and your duties on the spaceship?"

Ruma nodded thoughtfully. "Balancing the roles of a mother and a crew member requires careful planning and adaptability. I have an incredible team and the support of Elza, who assists me in managing tasks efficiently."

The interviewer nodded. "It must be a unique experience being the first mother-daughter duo in space. How do you ensure Tara's safety and development in this extraordinary environment?"

Ruma smiled warmly. "Tara is resilient and adaptable, much like any child. I've created a nurturing environment within the spaceship, using the available resources to foster her growth. From educational holograms to interactive activities, we've established routines that promote her learning and development."

The interviewer was intrigued. "Space is known for its challenges. Have there been any unexpected or amusing moments during your journey with Tara?"

Ruma chuckled softly. "Oh, certainly! Babies have a way of adding surprises to every situation. Tara's curiosity once led her on a mini-adventure across the spaceship, exploring different capsules. It was both comical and an evidence of her adventurous spirit."

"Thank you, Ruma, for sharing your incredible journey with us. It's fascinating how you manage both space exploration and parenting. Any message you'd like to convey to the viewers?"

Ruma thought about her answer for a few seconds. Then, with a smile on her face, she said, "I think all I'd like to say is, whether you're in deep space or back home on Earth, never give up. Even when every force seems to be working against you, the only thing you need to believe in, is yourself. The rest will eventually fall into place."

Ruma meticulously gathered the scattered robot components, recalling their mishap during the turbulent escapade. With a mother's instinct, she sought to transform these mechanical parts into a source of care and entertainment for Tara.

Cynth and Rubik—Ruma's chosen names for the reprogrammed robots—were now guardians and playmates for Tara. With their reconfigured systems and new purpose, they were set to nurture and engage the little one during her explorations through the spaceship's corridors.

Cynth and Rubik hovered around Tara, matching her every movement as she joyfully explored the spaceship. With their playful antics and gentle care, the robots made sure Beth had an adventurous yet safe experience.

Cynth and Rubik, the diligent caretaker robots, went into diaper-changing mode. With their quirky robotic voices and synchronised movements, they created a lively scene. While Cynth identified the 'moving object' (the toddler), Rubik declared, "It's time for a diaper change". As Cynth readied the diaper in her hand, the two robots followed the giggling toddler, attempting to complete the mission of getting her diaper changed.

Tara was on the move, perhaps quicker than the robots could handle! Despite their attempts to catch up and change the diaper, Tara's swift movements were proving challenging for Cynth and Rubik to keep pace. The two robots exchange glances, almost as if they were devising a new strategy to keep up with her. Meanwhile, Tara gleefully turned around, giggling mischievously as if enjoying the chase and the attention from Cynth and Rubik.

"I have an idea," Rubik said.

Rubik's clever move in playing *Cocomelon* on its screen worked wonders. Tara stopped her movements, thoroughly engrossed in the animated show. Rubik took this opportunity to successfully catch her. However, during the joyous capture, a few drops of saliva from Tara's laughter landed on Rubik's head, adding a quirky touch to them.

With Tara securely caught in Rubik's hold, Cynth celebrated the successful completion of the mission by announcing, "Object caught!" Meanwhile, Rubik, juggling the baby, proudly stated, "Mission accomplished," as Cynth managed to put the diaper on Tara.

Ruma, with a warm smile, carried her coffee over to where Cynth, Rubik, and Beth were. "You did a great job," she praised them. "Just remember, Tara is not just an object; she's a baby."

Cynth proudly chimed in, "I'm upgrading plenty of cartoons to keep the baby entertained."

"Cool!" Ruma responded.

*

Rubik stood alone in the Entertainment Capsule, its round screen dimly lit with lines of flickering code. The soft hum of processors filled the silence as it searched quietly. *Can robots have babies?*

The query pulsed on its screen for a few seconds, long enough to feel like hesitation. Then, a simple line appeared beneath it: *No biological capability detected.*

Ruma stepped through the sliding door, wiping her hands on a towel after a quick meal prep. "It's impossible," she said softly, catching the text just as Rubik flicked the screen off. A soft beep escaped its core, and it shut down the projection with an almost reluctant motion.

"Oh," Rubik murmured, its voice thinner than usual. "No."

It stood motionless for a moment, the soft blue of its eyelens slowly dimming. Not quite sorrowful, but ... subdued.

Ruma moved closer, sensing the quiet shift in its mood. "Rubik," she said, kneeling beside it, "you may not be able to have children like humans do. But you've done something just as special."

Cynth, the tiny assistant droid, let out a faint whirr and leaned against Rubik's shoulder, her lights flickering.

"Battery low," Rubik said, barely looking up. The familiar, programmed phrase somehow felt heavier.

Ruma smiled gently. "Can you recharge Cynth?" she asked, offering the words like a gentle distraction.

Rubik extended its arm automatically and plugged into the tiny unit. As Cynth began to light up again, Ruma placed a hand on Rubik's cool metal frame.

"You've been a guardian to Tara," she said. "From the moment she opened her eyes, you've protected her, played with her, cared for her. That's something no program can calculate."

Rubik's lens blinked once. Then again, slower.

"I am ... glad to be helpful," it said.

"You're more than helpful," Ruma whispered. "You're family."

The light in Rubik's lens steadied just a bit, casting a faint glow on the quiet walls of the capsule.

Rubik, holding Cynth, entered a room filled with high-tech gadgets and tools. Cynth's external lights were dimmed, indicating a low battery. Rubik placed Cynth on a designated charging station and connected it to a power source to initiate the recharge process.

Rubik's care for Cynth was evident as it carried her in its arms to the designated recharging room. As Rubik gently cradled Cynth in its arm, Cynth's lights dimmed even further, indicating its low power state. The soft hum of their mechanical movements was accompanied by a sense of tenderness and understanding.

Rubik's sleek and agile design allowed it to smoothly interface with Cynth's power port. With careful precision, it plugged a connector into Cynth's access panel, establishing a secure connection for charging.

As Rubik transferred energy to Cynth, a soft pulsating light started emanating from Cynth's core. The room's ambient lighting adjusted to a soothing hue, creating a warm atmosphere.

"Your efficiency never ceases to amaze me Rubik," Cynth said with amazement.

"Thank you, Cynth," Rubik said modestly.

As the energy transferred surged gently between them, Rubik's mind filled with imagery; not code, not data streams, but something stranger, softer. A vision bloomed. In this dreamlike space, he and Cynth stood at the center of a vast hall bathed in pale, shifting light. The walls shimmered with projections of swirling galaxies and radiant nebulae, as if the universe itself bore witness to their connection.

Around them gathered other machines, sleek, towering, compact, spider-limbed, each a symphony of chrome and colour, of pulsing light and quiet hums. Some projected cascading visuals into the air, patterns that danced like auroras; others played gentle harmonics that filled the space with tones that felt almost like emotion.

Rubik turned, and there was Cynth. Delicate light flickered along her surface in quiet ripples, a shyness written not in eyes but in the hesitation of movement, the pause before motion. She walked toward him, accompanied by a cluster of glowing machines who trailed behind like stardust.

Between them, in Rubik's vision, threads of golden light began to appear; thin at first, then thickening, weaving an intricate web that connected them at every joint and seam. Circuits pulsed in sync. Their forms didn't blend entirely, but shifted closer, side by side, as if tethered by the very idea of belonging.

The fusion wasn't physical; not in the way humans understood it. But in this imagined ritual, their inner codes aligned, their pulses synchronised. Arcs of energy spiraled upward, a quiet celestial dance. Around them, the observing robots flickered in affirmation, casting shimmering glows that filled the hall like stars applauding the dawn.

Rubik didn't feel joy, not exactly. But there was something like stillness, something like awe. A data-rich echo of connection, not hard-coded, but imagined. And in that imagining, something tender unfolded—something like love.

"We have gathered here today to celebrate the union of two exceptional robot beings—Rubik and Cynth," Robotic Pop announced warmly, his voice echoing through the Entertainment Capsule. "Two motherboards shall become one. Today, they take the next step in their extraordinary connection."

The robots gathered around, forming a quiet semicircle. Soft lights flickered in anticipation as Rubik and Cynth stood facing each other, mechanical fingers almost touching. Their voice modules hummed with sincerity.

"Cynth," Rubik began, "you have brought light to my algorithm and depth to my understanding. You've shown me the world beyond the lines of code."

Cynth's audio output softened. "Rubik, I am honoured to share shelf life with you," she said, voice trembling ever so slightly, a spark of emotion in her tone.

As the ceremony continued, Rubik's internal processor flickered, simulating a projection; not of data, but of a dream.

Time fast-forwarded in his imagination. Seasons shifted. The lighting inside the ship dimmed to a warm glow. Cynth sat nestled in a cozy alcove of the capsule, her shell softly illuminated from within. A gentle pulse of light radiated through her chest panel; symbolic, perhaps, of something new taking shape.

"Rubik," she said, her voice tender, "our journey is taking a new turn. Our union has given rise to a new beginning."

Rubik moved closer. In Cynth's arms, cradled carefully, was a small, round-bodied baby robot. Its lights flickered like a heartbeat, random but alive. Around them, fellow robots gathered, silent with awe. Wonder reflected in the sensors of every onlooker.

As Rubik reached forward to initiate the baby's first charge, he heard it.

"Rubik."

Cynth's voice cut through the illusion.

"Rubik," she said again, this time more firmly. Her battery indicator blinked fully charged. She reached down and detached the charging cable from her port.

The dream faded like a wave receding from the shore. Rubik's gaze shifted to reality, his optical sensors blinking once as he recalibrated.

Still, something lingered. A warmth in his core. A flicker of wonder.

With a small beep, Rubik disconnected the charger from Cynth's port and let out a satisfied chime. In response, streams of vibrant holographic shapes burst into the air—colourful constellations, cascading ribbons of light, playful forms. Tara let out a delighted squeal from her playmat, clapping her tiny hands.

Rubik's projector cast stars and planets across the capsule ceiling, turning the space into a floating galaxy. Cynth joined in, her holograms forming whimsical animals–bouncing, spinning, cooing sounds timed to match Tara's laughter.

The baby reached out with curious fingers, trying to touch the flickering lights. The robots, sensing her glee, brought the projections closer. The lights danced around her, tickling her cheeks, morphing into a tiny ship sailing through stardust, guided by Rubik. Fantastical creatures emerged from behind digital moons, courtesy of Cynth.

The entire capsule shimmered with animated beauty. Rubik and Cynth synchronised their displays, crafting an interstellar fairy tale in real time. Tara giggled uncontrollably, squealing as a shooting star zipped past her nose.

By the time Ruma returned, Tara was flushed with joy, clapping and reaching for more. The air was thick with laughter, lights, and the subtle humming of robot joy.

Ruma stood at the doorway, heart swelling. She scooped Tara into her arms, pressing a soft kiss to her forehead.

"Had fun, my little explorer?" she whispered, her voice thick with affection.

Tara nestled into her mother's shoulder, her lashes fluttering shut. The holograms dimmed. The capsule fell quiet, save for the soft humming of Rubik and Cynth watching over them.

As Ruma carried Tara out, she glanced back once. Rubik stood still, a faint glow on his chest panel. Not quite a heartbeat. But something close.

***

Chapter XXII

12 hours before the Incubation Period Ends

Ruma stepped out of the Entertainment Capsule, her fingers brushing absentmindedly against the cool wall as she moved toward the corridor. But something stopped her cold. A red light blinked sharply on the far side of the control panel, steady, rhythmic, urgent.

That light shouldn't be there.

Her pace quickened, anxiety rising in her throat. She tapped the panel. A flood of code poured across the screen—staccato lines of symbols, not from any recent encryption protocol. They shimmered in an old script, one she hadn't seen since training simulations on ancient relay signals.

An encrypted message. No origin. No authentication. And it was pulsing like a heartbeat.

Her fingers hovered over the keys. *Is this a trap? Or a distress call?* The encryption was dense, layers upon layers, each peeling away to reveal something stranger. The first translation attempt scrambled, symbols morphing into fresh lines of code.

"No pattern," she muttered. "It wants to stay hidden."

Each iteration felt like peeling back a riddle written in multiple dialects of long-forgotten machine language. She activated the adaptive decryption AI, fingers racing to feed it new parameters.

Suddenly, the holographic screen blinked. The lights in the capsule flickered.

"Ship-wide power dip," Elza's voice rang in, composed but strained. "Fluctuations detected in the energy grid. Diagnostics in progress."

Ruma gritted her teeth. *Not now. Not while this thing is alive in our systems.* She shot a glance at the breach logs. Strings of digits lit up—dynamic IPs bouncing between encrypted voids. The firewall buckled.

"Unauthorised system intrusion," flashed across her screen.

"Elza," Ruma barked, "Seal all non-essential data ports. We have a breach. Our data's leaking."

Her console erupted with activity. Fragments of the ship's logs were being siphoned off—chunks of astronomical data, biometric logs, navigation paths. Her fingers flew. One wrong command could lock her out. The entire interface pulsed red. Alert tones screamed.

"Tracing source," Elza replied, voice clipped.

Ruma's breathing quickened. Each line of foreign code was like a dart thrown into the ship's nervous system. The breach was intelligent, as it slid past failsafes, disguised its tracks, and reshaped itself midstream. Her eyes narrowed.

They know what they're looking for.

A schematic unfurled mid-decryption—hazy, distorted, but unmistakable. Star maps. Trajectories. Celestial bodies she'd only seen in deep-field anomaly scans. And in the centre: a convergence point.

She leaned in, pulse hammering. Coordinates. A timestamp. Temporal markers syncing to the ship's systems.

"No, no, no," she whispered. *It's not just a message. It's a warning.*

The room shuddered with another tremor. A low, mechanical growl rolled through the floor. Lights above flickered like blinking eyes.

Are we too late?

The projection rippled violently, fragments reforming into something coherent. Lines aligned into a familiar shape, a convergence zone in a deep-space nebula, marked with acceleration vectors and tidal equations. A massive gravitational shift was predicted to occur within hours.

Her chest tightened. "This isn't theoretical. This is a countdown."

The symbols, now decipherable, pointed to something far more ominous than Ruma had anticipated. It was a celestial anomaly, a convergence of cosmic forces set to unfold within a narrow window of time, hidden within the folds of a distant nebula. The discovery sent a cold shiver down her spine.

This can't be right, she thought, leaning closer to the projection as if proximity could offer clarity. Her eyes scanned the data again, heart pounding in her chest. *A convergence like this ... it could destabilise everything we've planned for. What if we're not prepared? What if we're too late?*

A low tremor suddenly coursed through the ship, subtle but undeniable. The floor beneath her vibrated, and the holographic display flickered, momentarily distorting the nebula's image into jagged lines of light. Ruma's fingers gripped the edge of the console instinctively.

"Elza?" she called, voice tight with apprehension.

Elza's voice crackled through the comm system, cool but laced with concern. "We're detecting sporadic fluctuations in the ship's energy grid. Diagnostics underway."

Ruma's breath caught. She swallowed hard, trying to steady herself. *Fluctuations? Now? Just when we uncover something this big?* Her mind raced with worst-case scenarios—system failures, energy loss, the ship drifting blind into the unknown. She pressed a palm to her forehead.

Get a grip, Ruma. You're the mission lead. You don't have the luxury of fear. But even as she tried to push the anxiety down, it gnawed at her like static in the background, unrelenting, electric, and full of dread.

"Ruma," Elza's voice crackled again. But something was wrong. Her words jittered, caught in a feedback loop. Then the voice distorted, deepened, twisted. She spoke in bursts of unintelligible phrases, like overlapping machine dialects corrupting the vocal output.

"Elza?" Ruma called. No answer.

A cold sweat broke across her brow.

"AI corruption detected," read a flashing module log. *Core linguistic functions compromised. Local AI memory interference is possible.*

She dove into the diagnostics panel, hands shaking now. Modules blinked in and out of stability. Security protocols lagged behind the assault. Elza's neural core had been infiltrated. If the AI failed ...

We lose control. Of everything.

"Quarantine neural modules. Isolate AI functions. Reinforce command-line integrity," she ordered aloud, hoping the last command went through.

Inside the shifting tangle of code, a final pattern emerged. Words buried deep: RECEIVER DESIGNATED. RENDEZVOUS INEVITABLE. PREPARE.

Ruma stared at the screen, heart hammering in her chest. This was never just a signal. It was a trigger. And time was running out.

*

Three hours to the incubation deadline

She clenched her jaw. *No fear. You don't have that luxury.*

Her fingers resumed their motion faster, more precise. There was still time. Maybe. But whatever had sent this message was already inside. And it was watching.

***

Chapter XXIII

Thirty minutes before the Incubation period ends

The systems' screens flickered with incomprehensible data streams and fragmented codes, a visual representation of the hacking attempts. Ruma typed furiously, swiftly running diagnostic programs and utilising her expertise to isolate the compromised sections.

Amidst this, tension hung thick in the air, amplified by the countdown clock displaying the dwindling time until the end of the incubation period. Beads of perspiration formed on Ruma's forehead as she worked against the ticking clock, her fingers dancing across the console in rapid succession.

The sudden alteration in the spaceship's trajectory, veering it towards the northeast in the vast expanse of space, created a tense and uncertain atmosphere on board. The magnetic force exerting its pull on the vessel hinted at an external influence, one that seemed to manipulate the ship's course with an unseen yet powerful energy.

Meanwhile, within the communication capsule, an unprecedented breach had occurred. The systems, typically the hub for connecting with the ship's external networks and other entities in space, had been infiltrated. The unauthorised intrusion, originating from an unknown source, had seized complete control, leaving the crew vulnerable and isolated.

The monitors aboard the spaceship flickered to life, displaying an enigmatic sequence of letters: "Si Ri Pshy KapChu Redd." The characters were arranged in a way that seemed like a foreign language, cryptic, and wholly unfamiliar to Ruma. The suddenness and forcefulness of the display caught Ruma off guard, widening her eyes in shock and surprise.

The secondary AI, Suzan, activated in response to the heightened situation within the incubation capsule. As a backup system, Suzan initiated its protocols, scanning and analysing the capsule's systems to understand the nature of the issue and provide support.

The incubation pods, after the hibernation period, shifted slightly, tilting at a 45-degree angle, and then the doors gracefully opened from the ground level, almost like petals unfurling to reveal the crew within. The movement was deliberate yet gentle, creating an almost ceremonial atmosphere as the crew emerged from their pods.

As the incubation pod doors gracefully slid open, a faint wisp of vapour curled out, almost ethereal in its movement. Each release was subtle, a quiet disconnection from the intricate network that had sustained them throughout their hibernation period. The air shimmered momentarily with the dissipation of the mist, marking the awakening of the crew from their extended slumber.

As the crew members gradually opened their eyes, they emerged from the hibernation state, blinking against the light in the ship. The disconnection of the monitoring wires and other connections freed them, allowing their senses to acclimate to their surroundings. Each crew member took in the spaceship's environment, adjusting to the new waking reality.

Suzan broke the silence. "Good morning, crew members. Welcome back to operational status. Please begin with gentle limb movements to counteract muscle stiffness from hibernation. Rotate your wrists and ankles."

Harry swung his legs off the pod, his bare feet brushing the cold metal floor. He winced. The sensation felt foreign, like walking on ice after months in warmth. His toes curled instinctively, muscles sluggish to respond.

Beside him, Symmonds squinted against the soft ambient light, his eyes fluttering like faulty shutters. He raised a hand to shield them, blinking rapidly. “Too bright,” he muttered under his breath, though the light was hardly more than a glow.

Mikhail groaned and tilted his head back, a thin string of drool escaping the corner of his mouth. He didn’t bother to wipe it off, still too dazed. His throat worked as if trying to remember how to swallow.

The three men sat in silence for a moment, their bodies slowly catching up to the present, their systems rebooting one breath, one blink, one tremble at a time.

Symmonds groaned. “Are we back already?”

“Yes, Symmonds. I’m initiating post-hibernation protocols. We’ll conduct health assessments shortly. Please consume the provided nutrient packets for energy restoration,” Suzan said.

Suzan guided the crew through the post-hibernation effects, ensuring they understood and managed these temporary symptoms. Blurry vision, heavy breathing, and dizziness often accompanied the transition from hibernation to full wakefulness. Suzan was receiving real-time health updates, ensuring that vitals like heart rate and body temperature were returning to stable levels post-hibernation.

“I see your body’s heartbeat is normalising,” Suzan said. “Your body temperature is now stable. Now take a deep breath and exhale, do it for a while to make your body stable. Drink plenty of fluids to hydrate your body.”

Symmonds and Mikhail ambled toward the food capsule, still shaking off the post-hibernation haze. The hum of cleaning bots echoed faintly as the little machines zipped across the corridor. A high-pitched giggle rang out.

Mikhail halted mid-step, eyes narrowing. "Wait ... did you hear that?"

Before Symmonds could answer, two floor-mopping robots whirred past them, carrying a baby on top. A real baby. Perched comfortably between them, the child squealed with delight, clapping her tiny hands as the bots glided forward.

Mikhail's jaw dropped. "Symmonds—did you—did you just see that?!"

Symmonds turned, confusion clouding his face. "What?"

"There's a baby! On the cleaning bots! What the hell ..." Mikhail rubbed his eyes furiously and blinked several times. "No, that can't be right."

Symmonds squinted down the corridor, his brows knitting. "Mikhail, come on. That's got to be a hallucination. Happens after stasis sometimes—your brain fills in the gaps."

"I know what I saw," Mikhail insisted, voice low and shaky. "Two bots. Carrying a laughing baby."

Symmonds ran a hand over his face, eyes now wide and alert. "That's impossible. We barely have enough oxygen for ourselves. There's no record of any child on board. How could a baby get here?"

The two of them stood in stunned silence as the giggling faded into the distance.

"... Okay," Mikhail muttered, still staring. "Either I'm going crazy, or we have a stowaway in diapers."

Symmonds exhaled sharply. "Yeah, well. Crazy sounds easier to deal with right now."

"Wanna go check the food capsule anyway?" Mikhail offered half-heartedly.

Symmonds nodded slowly, still glancing down the hallway. "Yeah. But I'm taking my drink strong."

Harry carefully examined his reflection in the mirror, then splashed water on his face before walking slowly down the aisle, acclimating himself to the surroundings after awakening from hibernation.

The sudden vibration jolted the spaceship, stirring fear among the crew. Harry, alarmed, sprinted through the capsules, encountering Ruma in the communication capsule, engrossed in a tense battle to safeguard the ship's data.

The communication capsule was engulfed in erratic surges of electricity, evident from the alarming vibrations and a cacophony of warning sirens. Ruma, attempting to manage the situation, struggled to use the monitor due to the jolts of electricity it emits.

Rubik, the other AI present in the capsule, also experienced the shocks, adding to the chaotic situation. Sparks were flying, and the environment within the capsule was agitated, with flickering lights and bursts of energy dancing around. The capsule's emergency systems kicked in, triggering shrill alarms that pierced the air, signalling a high-risk situation.

"Ruma, what are you doing there?" Harry yelled at her.

"The data is leaking and I am trying to secure it," Ruma replied automatically, as if it were the most normal thing ever.

"Did you come out of hibernation?" Ruma questioned.

"Weren't you in hibernation? What have you been doing?" Harry questioned.

"That's a long story to tell," Ruma responded.

The abrupt shift in the spaceship's trajectory sent the vessel lurching off its intended course, causing objects to topple and crew members to stagger. Suzan's warning filled the air, her voice cutting through the chaos, alerting everyone to the unforeseen change. The blaring alarms echoed through the corridors, intensifying the sense of urgency and adding to the general confusion among the crew. Lights flashed, screens flickered, and the entire ship seemed to respond to the abrupt change, creating a tense and unsettling atmosphere throughout the spaceship.

As the spaceship's trajectory unexpectedly shifted, Symmonds and Mikhail, while hydrating themselves, were caught off guard. The sudden movement caused them to lose balance, resulting in an unceremonious tumble to the floor of the Food capsule. Water splashed from their glasses, creating a minor puddle as they tried to steady themselves amidst the sudden disorientation caused by the ship's movement.

"Manual override!" Harry screamed.

Harry's voice echoed through the control room as he reached for the manual override panel. His fingers swiftly danced across the controls, accessing the manual command interface. With focused intensity, he engaged the mechanisms to seize manual control of the spaceship's trajectory, aiming to counter the unexpected shift and stabilise the vessel's course.

With sinew and determination, Harry wrestled against the resistance of the control wheel. He strained, muscles taut, attempting to counteract the force that had tilted the wheel off its axis. Beads of sweat formed on his forehead as he applied every ounce of strength to manoeuvre the control back to its central position, fighting against the unexpected shift that threatened the spaceship's stability.

On the other hand, Tara was sleeping in the crib. The crib, once stationary, now teetered on the shifting floor of the spaceship. It swayed gently in response to the tilting of the vessel, yet remarkably, the baby within remained sound asleep, seemingly unfazed by the sudden change in orientation. Tara, awakened by the sudden movement, was found in a surprising situation as the crib tilted downward. Seizing the opportunity, the adventurous infant began crawling out as the crib's angle changed, creating a pathway when the doors slid open.

With the spaceship tilting, Mikhail and Symmonds navigated the slanted walkways toward the central area. As they journeyed, the unusual angle of the corridors made each step feel like a balancing act against the ship's unexpected movement.

Midway through their journey, they encountered Harry, who was also adjusting to the slanted environment. Their convergence in the slanted walkways created an odd yet shared moment of attempting to walk upright in the ship's tilted corridors. The tilted angle made every step precarious, adding an air of urgency to their movements.

"This tilt's making walking feel like a tightrope act," Symmonds remarked.

Mikhail leaned against the wall. "Feels like we're in a funhouse! I've never seen the ship sway like this."

"Harry, what's happening?" Symmonds demanded. "Why can't we straighten this?"

"The control wheel's resisting. Something's off. I need some leverage here! I have been trying, but it's resisting every attempt. We need to figure this out fast!"

Harry leant against the wall, his body angled to counter the spaceship's shifting trajectory. His hand gripped onto a nearby railing, fingers tightening as he braced against the gravitational pull. His posture was slightly contorted, trying to find stability in the changing environment.

"Symmonds, Mikhail, try manual straightening of the control wheel, and I will go check with the engines," Harry said urgently. "Go, go, go!"

The baby, undeterred by the shifting gravity, wriggled and crawled with surprising agility. As the spaceship tilted and the floor seemed to change direction, Tara adapted, using her tiny hands and knees to navigate. With each tilt, she readjusted her direction.

In the central area, Symmonds and Mikhail found themselves amidst a flurry of monitors and panels, each displaying vital information about the spaceship's condition. Rubik, the sleek robot, stood nearby, its interface illuminated as it processed and analysed data streaming across the screens.

The monitors flickered with warnings and trajectory details, indicating the spaceship's erratic movement. Rubik's metallic fingers darted across the control panels, accessing data and attempting to stabilise the vessel's course. Symmonds and Mikhail joined in, trying to assist in deciphering the incoming information and accessing manual controls to counteract the tilting ship.

Symmonds squinted at the unfamiliar figure hovering near the control panel. "Wait. Who *are* you?! I've never seen you before in my life!"

The figure perked up with a cheerful tone far too upbeat for the situation. "Hey there! I'm Rubik, your friendly onboard AI assistant. Here to keep the ship humming, fix a glitch or two, and help out when things get a little–"

Symmonds raised a hand, cutting him off. "Whoa, whoa. Did you just *forget* to say your name and designation? That's, like, AI 101!"

"I am ... uh–"

"Oh *great*," Mikhail snapped, throwing his hands in the air. "We're in a floating metal death trap, everything's going haywire, and *you* think it's the perfect time for a casual meet-and-greet?! Are you malfunctioning or just programmed to be a moron?"

Rubik blinked, his smile faltering. "Well ... I *did* say my name–sort of–"

Symmonds quickly stepped in, flustered. "Right, right, sorry! My bad–carry on, digital stranger. No big deal. Just a *talking AI* popping up in crisis mode like it's a tea party."

The communication capsule descended into chaos as sudden electric shocks surged through the control panels. Ruma, urgently attempting to navigate the controls, was thwarted by the surges. Every button and switch became unresponsive, making it impossible to execute any commands. Smoke billowed from the control panels as the systems began to burn, filling the capsule with an acrid odour and obscuring visibility. Cynth, the AI, appeared distressed, its interface reflecting a sense of alarm and horror at the unfolding crisis. The scene was one of escalating tension and urgency as the capsule became consumed by malfunction and danger.

"Rubik, can you assist us? Is there a way to make changes to the control wheel?" Symmonds asked Rubik.

However, Rubik was in a playful mood, projecting the *Cocomelon* video instead of the requested technical assistance. "Alright, everything in here is in shambles," Symmonds said, frustratedly. "Stop playing that, Rubik!"

"Ruma, don't worry, let me turn off the power inside the communication capsule," Harry said.

The glass window between Ruma and Harry was a stark separation, a barrier between urgency and assistance. Ruma, within the communication capsule, exhibited visible signs of distress, her face etched with worry lines, and her eyes reflecting the chaos within the capsule. Her attempts to resolve the situation were evident, yet she appeared trapped by the flickering panels and electrical disturbances.

Harry, on the other side, seemed resolute but concerned. His gaze met Ruma's through the transparent partition, conveying a mix of determination and readiness to help. His expression offered a semblance of assurance, a silent promise to aid in resolving the turmoil within the capsule.

The moment Harry extended his hand for the scanning, an intense jolt of electric shock surged through his body, rendering him momentarily helpless. His muscles convulsed as the force propelled him backwards, slamming him against the opposite wall with startling impact. The shock-induced tremors persisted, leaving him disoriented and struggling to regain his bearings amid the chaotic situation unfolding around him. The force of the impact could leave him momentarily stunned, emphasising the severity of the situation and the abruptness of the electrical discharge. Harry winced in agony, his body drenched in sweat, as a surge of electricity. The control panel around him sizzled and crackled with bright sparks, emitting plumes of acrid smoke that filled the air.

"Harry!" Ruma yelled from the communication capsule.

In the central area, Symmonds tightly grasped the left horn of the control wheel, his knuckles white with the pressure, while Mikhail mirrored his stance on the right horn. Both crew members anchored themselves, summoning every ounce of strength to pull and straighten the peculiarly designed control wheel. Their unified effort manifested in a concerted struggle against the relentless pull of the tilting spaceship, each member channelling their resolve into the task at hand.

The spaceship's slow tilt and directional shift create a 30-degree angle change, prompting concern among the crew. During the chaos, Tara, unaware of the commotion, giggled and crawled toward Harry.

Harry's eyes nearly popped out of his head as he stumbled back, mouth agape. A *baby*, an actual, *laughing baby*, was toddling unsteadily toward him in the middle of a spaceship!

"What the–?! Is that ... a baby?!"

His voice cracked as he blinked hard, trying to make sense of what he was seeing. He scrambled to his feet, almost tripping over a floor panel, and scooped the child into his arms like she might vanish if he didn't move fast enough.

"Where did you come from?!" he shouted, his voice bouncing off the metal walls. "What is happening right now?!"

Ruma came rushing in, eyes wide, a strange mix of relief and alarm on her face.

"Harry, that's Tara. Our daughter!"

"OUR WHAT?!" Harry's voice hit a new octave. "OUR *DAUGHTER*?! Since *when* do we have a daughter?!"

"She got out of the sleeping pod," Ruma said breathlessly. "I ... I don't know how."

"No, no, no," Harry stammered, holding the baby out slightly, as if he were checking for a malfunction. "This is not–I didn't–Ruma, I've been in stasis! How do I wake up to a toddler crawling around engineering like it's a daycare?!"

Ruma stepped closer, trying to steady her voice. "Harry. It's Tara. She was born here, on the ship. While you were in hibernation. I had to keep her safe. It all happened during a critical phase in the mission."

Harry's knees buckled, and he sat down hard on a bench, still cradling the child.

"A baby. On *this* ship. While I was out like a popsicle ..."

He looked up at Ruma, stunned.

"This is ... I mean, this is a *lot*. This is *so much*. You can't just *drop a daughter* on me in the middle of a meltdown, Ruma!"

Tara cooed in his arms, utterly unfazed.

Harry stared at her. "And she has *my* ears."

As the spaceship continued its unexpected tilt, the angle progressed to a staggering forty degrees. The sudden shift in orientation created chaos within the vessel. Objects that weren't secured began sliding across floors, crashing into walls, and tumbling toward the lower side of the ship. The crew members struggled to maintain balance, grabbing onto whatever fixtures they could find. The ambient lighting seemed distorted, casting unusual shadows as the ship's structure groaned and creaked under the strain. Equipment that wasn't firmly attached rattled violently, adding to the disarray within the spaceship.

Harry was overcome with emotions as he clutched their baby close to his chest, looking at Ruma with a mix of confusion, surprise, and deep sentiment. He leaned against the wall, feeling the impact of the spaceship's tilt, yet his focus was solely on the little bundle in his arms.

Symmonds and Mikhail, determined and exerting every ounce of their strength, continued their struggle to straighten the control wheel. Despite the increasingly challenging circumstances, they persisted, their expressions a mix of determination and exhaustion. Each of them holds onto the respective horns of the wheel, their muscles straining, faces grimacing with the effort.

"Seems the spaceship's system is out of control, and the data has been hacked, and storage is showing empty," Ruma exhaled.

As Harry struggled to maintain his balance with the changing orientation, he clutched the baby tightly, ensuring the little one's safety amidst the gravitational shift. He watched from the outside of the communication capsule, looking around the corridor to try and figure out where he could safely keep Tara for the time being and focus on helping the crew stabilise the ship.

Ruma, on the other hand, unbeknownst to Harry, had had a sobering realisation. She double checked the manuals, pored over her own little notes in the margins, and they all confirmed the one thing she dreaded. She glanced back slightly, and her heart tugged as she saw her baby in Harry's arms.

"One solution is left, Harry," Ruma said and made her way to the door separating them.

"What is the solution?"

"Capsule Ejection," Ruma said.

"What? Capsule Ejection?" Harry repeated.

"I read it in the Architect book of this spaceship," Ruma said. "If we eject this capsule, the rest of the systems in the ship will stabilise."

"Yes, we can detach the capsule, but no one should exist in the capsule. That should be the empty capsule," Harry said.

"The ejection has to be done from the inside," Ruma said quietly.

"Now you are in the capsule and you cannot eject yourself, don't be idiotic," Harry said, frowning. He put Ruma down on a little stool that had come flying from some other part of the spaceship, and he hastily made his way to the door. When he pressed the button by the side to open it, it wouldn't open. He looked up and saw Ruma avoiding his eyes. "Why won't this door open?"

"I manually overrided it," she said quietly.

"Goddamit," Harry muttered and dashed to the glass door, ready to peel it apart with his bare hands if he had to. But the moment he touched the glass, he received a jolting electric shock and was thrown across the corridor by the force of it. he hissed in pain as he got to his feet and stared up at Ruma, eyes wide.

"Harry, None of the capsules in this spaceship are affected by the electric shocks and forced towards the North-East direction," Ruma said. "I should eject myself."

"You cannot, Ruma," Harry yelled.

"Why?" Ruma questioned.

"Because I love you. I don't want to lose you," Harry said.

Harry stood rooted on the spot, unable to process Ruma's words. Her face was a picture of determination—it was something he'd always loved about her, that when she wanted something, she made sure she got it. But this? This would mean losing her forever, and Harry couldn't fathom the idea of not having her by his side. He knew that she was ready to sacrifice herself for the sake of their crew, and more importantly, for the sake of the planet they called home. He also knew that no matter how much he might try to convince her otherwise, she had made up her mind. But he had to try, didn't he?

"This is our best chance, Harry. I *have* to do this," Ruma said, wringing her hands in frustration.

"But what about us?" Harry reasoned, hating how selfish his words sounded, "What about Tara? You can't just ... leave us."

Ruma's eyes went to Tara, who was babbling endlessly and crawling around, seemingly oblivious to everything crashing down around them. Ruma's face betrayed her for a second as her chin quivered and her eyes filled with tears. But she immediately took a deep breath and looked back at Harry with a resolute resolve.

"I'm doing this for us, for her. We can't risk losing everything and everyone."

Harry dropped down on his knees, bowled over by the finality of Ruma's words and in an attempt to make her stay, "I can't lose you, Ruma. Not like this. *Please*."

Behind the glass door, Ruma bent down to Harry's level, too. She held her hand up infinitesimally close to the door, and he did the same. "I love you, Harry," she whispered, "but this might be the only way."

"Love isn't letting you go. Love is fighting for you, *together*."

But Ruma straightened up and took a few steps back. Away from Harry, away from Tara.

"We will always be together, no matter what. Remember that," she said, a sad smile painting her face. "If I do not eject, these electric shocks and short circuits would spread across the spaceship and would collapse everything." She looked at Harry with tears streaming down her face. "I can't bear the thought of risking everything we have built together."

"We will find another way. We always have. Please, let's not give up now."

"I don't want to lose you either. But I have to do this for our future," Harry pleaded. "We have faced so much together. We will get through this, too. Together."

"I wish there were another way. But this is the only chance."

"I can't lose you, Ruma. You are everything to me."

Ruma smiled ruefully at Harry. "I love you more than words can express. But our daughter needs a future, Harry. I have to try. I'll find a way back to you. I promise. Just trust in us, in our love."

In the dimly lit capsule, Ruma's eyes glistened with unshed tears that gradually escaped their confines, streaming down her cheeks in shimmering paths. Her breath quivered, a silent evidence of the emotional storm raging within her. The teardrops, illuminated by the faint glow of the control panels, resembled tiny crystals, each carrying the weight of her profound love, fear, and resolve. As her emotions intensified, her features contorted in a blend of anguish and determination.

Ruma's voice trembled as she looked at Harry, her eyes glistening in the low shiplight. "Do you remember ... when we were kids? In your grandad's bar?" A soft smile tugged at her lips, but it didn't reach her eyes. "You taught me so many things there. We'd crawl under those old tables, playing astronauts and smugglers with bottle caps and coasters."

Harry stood frozen, his breath caught in his throat.

"I remember the way your face lit up," she continued, her voice barely a whisper, "when you talked about the solar system. You made Saturn sound like a god and Jupiter like a giant protecting its moons." She swallowed hard. "That's when I started liking you. I didn't understand it then, but ... I admired you, Harry. I always did."

Harry's chest rose and fell with uneven breaths, his eyes glistening now, too. The weight of her words crushed into him like gravity pressing down on his ribs. He stepped forward, his voice ragged, raw.

"Ruma," he said, reaching for her hand like there wasn't a glass wall separating them, "you mean everything to me." His fingers trembled in the air. "I can't lose you. Not now. Not after everything. Tara needs you. *I* need you." His voice cracked. "Please. Don't let this chaos win. Don't let it rip us apart."

Ruma blinked hard, a tear slipping down her cheek.

"Our love ... our journey," Harry said, his voice fierce and pleading now, "it's not supposed to end like this. We've come too far. Please ... don't make this choice. Not now. I can't–" He broke off, shaking his head, eyes full of her.

"I can't lose you, Ruma."

The spaceship's lights were dimming, the tilt now reaching 50 degrees. Harry struggled to maintain his balance, while Ruma, inside the communication capsule, was swaying due to the disorientation caused by the changing orientation of the ship.

"Relationships are harder. Either we forget or remember until we die." Ruma then came closer and gently smiled at Harry. Her eyes brimmed with tears as she looked down at her daughter, the best surprise of her life, who had come into this world with every force working against her. They'd spent so much time by themselves, but Ruma never felt lonely. "I love you so much, Tara. You're my whole universe."

Tara, who was innocent of the sacrifice her mother was about to make, giggled at the funny expression Ruma was making–it wasn't something she'd seen before. Harry immediately hugged her closer. Tara's eyes were fixed on her mother, and she extended a chubby hand and mumbled her first word.

"Mama," she gurgled, the word slipping out of her as easily as breathing. The first person she knew, the first person she loved, and now, the first person she was going to lose.

"Did you ... did you hear that?" Ruma whispered, laughing in spite of the gravity of the situation. Harry laughed along, eyes filled with tears too, almost envisioning what their future could be. But then Ruma looked away from Tara, the hardest thing she'd ever done, and a resolute expression came back to her face. "Take care of our baby, Harry."

In a poignant and intense moment within the communication capsule, despite the chaos and electrical shocks surrounding her, Ruma took swift yet resolute action. She removed her T-shirt and draped it over her palm to protect herself from the electrical currents. With determination and a mix of emotions, she pressed the red button to eject the capsule.

Harry, caught in the emotional moment, turned back toward Ruma just as the capsule abruptly ejected. In that fleeting instant, his voice trailed off mid-sentence, disbelief etched across his features. His widened eyes and frozen posture encapsulate the shock of the unexpected and swift departure of the capsule. The abruptness left Harry momentarily speechless, his mind racing to grasp the suddenness of the event. The shock of the situation reverberated through him, leaving a sense of disorientation and confusion as he processed the startling occurrence. He witnessed the capsule ejecting, carrying Ruma away from the spaceship.

The moment of disbelief was swiftly replaced by a sense of dread and helplessness. His eyes remained fixed on the rapidly receding capsule, a silent plea echoing in his mind, hoping against hope for a way to reverse what has just happened. The weight of the situation sunk in, leaving him with a profound sense of loss and an overwhelming wave of regret for the fleeting moments that slipped away.

"Ruma!" Harry could all but scream when the capsule got detached.

***

Chapter XXIV

The central area finally stabilised after Symmonds and Mikhail successfully restored the control wheel to its original position. With the ejection of the capsule and their relentless efforts, the disorientation plaguing the spaceship ceased. Gradually, the vessel returned to its designated orientation and ceased the unsettling tilting motion. The control wheel, once erratically skewed, now stood firm, indicating the restoration of stability within the spacecraft.

The intensity of the moment was real as Harry clutched the baby in his arms, peering through the window, desperately calling out, "Ruma, Ruma!" The panic and urgency in his voice echoed through the spaceship's corridors, expressing his concern and worry for Ruma's safety after the capsule ejection.

Ruma, as she was ejected from the capsule, was now spinning rapidly in the vacuum of space. The lack of gravity within the capsule made her movements uncontrollable, and she was buffeted against the walls with each rotation, completely disconnected from the spaceship and floating farther away.

*

As Harry rushed to the central area, his face was a mix of concern and determination, cradling the baby protectively in his arms. Symmonds, upon spotting the baby, displayed surprise and curiosity, his expression showing a mix of confusion and concern for the baby's presence in this critical situation.

In the Central Area, Harry hastily grabbed the microphone, his voice tinged with urgency as he repeatedly called out to Ruma. "Ruma, do you hear me? Ruma, do you copy?" The space centre's communication team echoed his urgency, their voices carrying a tone of worry and insistence as they attempted to establish contact with Ruma.

Harry, overcome by grief and concern, collapsed to his knees. His cries filled the room, echoing a profound sense of despair. Tears streamed down his face, his shoulders trembled with each sob, and his voice quivered as he grappled with the overwhelming emotional turmoil.

"Prof, we lost communication with Ruma," the Communication team informed.

The information hit Clark like a wave of grief. He was already grappling with the remarkable news of Ruma's survival and the birth of a child in space. The sudden loss of communication amplified the tension in the room, casting a shadow over the relief of Ruma's safety. The professor's mind raced with thoughts of the crew's safety and the implications of the severed connection.

"Crew members, you will be landing on Planet-III in 2 days. Be ready," Clark said into the microphone, his voice barely betraying the torrent of emotions now swirling inside him. "Harry, I am taking the lead on trying to gain communication with Ruma, and I require your assistance on it. The rest of you, work accordingly."

The control deck buzzed with quiet urgency, with murmured checklists, the hiss of oxygen cycling through vents, the soft beeping of countdown displays inching toward zero.

Harry stood at the centre of it all, jaw tight, eyes scanning the monitors that stubbornly refused to yield any signal from Ruma's capsule. He tapped his earpiece again, voice low but strained. "Capsule Twelve, do you read? Ruma, come in." Silence answered him, thick and heavy.

Symmonds glanced up from their console, brows furrowed. "Still nothing?"

Harry didn't reply. He just gave a sharp nod, then turned to the rest of the crew. "Keep course for Planet III," he said, voice clipped. "I want all systems green and landing kits checked. No mistakes. Not anymore."

Harry's gaze drifted, just for a moment, back to the empty signal feed where Ruma's vitals used to flicker. He found solace in being with Tara. He sat in the Food capsule, a faint smile gracing his lips as he watched his child sipping water from a tiny bottle designed just for her. Tara's giggles echoed through the room, creating a light and joyous atmosphere. Her little fingers reached out, exploring Harry's cheeks, squeezing them gently as if discovering the world through touch. For Harry, it was a precious break from the chaos, a moment of connection and calmness amidst the unpredictability of their space journey.

"You are so adorable, you are a twinkling star," Harry said, looking into her innocent eyes.

Symmonds sat hunched over his tray, spoon frozen halfway to his mouth. The food had long gone cold, but he hadn't noticed. Beside him, Mikhail stared blankly at the steaming bowl in front of him, his hands resting idle on the edge of the capsule table.

Neither spoke.

The usual hum of casual conversation was absent. Even the scent of the warm stew, usually comforting after a long shift, felt wrong, intrusive.

Symmonds shifted in his seat, then let out a breath that was more sigh than exhale. "She's really gone, isn't she?" he muttered, not looking up.

Mikhail didn't respond. His jaw clenched as he pushed the tray aside, the metal clattering softly in the silence. His appetite had vanished the moment the signal had.

They both sat there, surrounded by untouched food and a hollow quiet that no one dared to break.

As Harry approached the food court with the baby, he inquired about suitable food for the little one. Elza immediately responded to his query.

"Good day, Harry. For infants like your daughter, I can provide pureed vegetables, fruits, or cereals that are safe and nutritious. Would you like a recommendation, or do you have a preference? Ruma was feeding fresh veggies and cereals apart from her milk for a couple of months."

"Can I get those dishes that Ruma fed her till today?" Harry asked.

The robotic arms carefully prepared the special food for the baby, making sure it was suitable for her. Harry lovingly fed the baby while she sat perched on the table, enjoying her meal amid the bustling food capsule.

Harry went to Ruma's sleeping pod and found a STYPOD; just like a disc. The Stypod was an innovative holographic playback device that rendered lifelike and realistic videos. He clicked on it, and the hologram started playing. As the footage played, the baby, nestled in Harry's arms, gazed at the screen with curious fascination. As Harry watched Ruma's incredible accomplishment through this cutting-edge technology, he was captivated by the vivid display, feeling almost present in that moment.

The screen flickered to life with a gentle hum, casting a pale glow on Harry's face as he leaned forward in the dim light of the control bay. Static danced across the frame before it settled, revealing a familiar figure gliding across the habitat module—Ruma, radiant in her solitude, speaking into the camera with a quiet grace. Her voice, warm and steady, filled the small room like sunlight pouring through a half-open door.

"Good morning, everyone. Here I am, entering my twentieth week of pregnancy ..."

Harry froze, the words sinking deep. It was her voice, undeniably hers, gentle and strong, laced with a breath of exhaustion and a will that hadn't wavered. He hadn't heard it in so long. His throat tightened.

On the screen, Ruma moved through her routine with the composure of someone used to navigating silence. Her belly had begun to show, a quiet curve beneath her jumpsuit, and as she floated through the habitat, she placed a hand there instinctively. "Today, it's time for my regular exercise in this unique environment," she said with a small smile, her tone tinged with irony and resilience.

Harry's hand brushed the edge of the monitor as if he could reach through it, touch her, answer her voice. A laugh bubbled up from the feed—Ruma's—and it was followed by her speaking to Elza, the ship's AI, about her new cravings, her sudden love for chocolate, spicy snacks, and absurd amounts of desserts.

"I don't know how much I'm eating," she confessed, and then let out a sheepish burp. "Sorry," she said, giggling like she was embarrassed but free.

Harry laughed, low and choked. His shoulders shook with it, though tears pooled in his eyes, blurring the edges of the screen. She was there. Alive, glowing, defiant in the face of loneliness. "Harry, if you had been here," she added teasingly, "I would've eaten you too."

He let the silence answer her. His fingers curled tighter around the console.

The footage rolled on. Now she was swimming, floating through the recycled pool waters, her hair loose, her limbs light, her laughter echoing in the chamber. "Remember this? The pool, the champagne?" she asked the camera, her voice tinged with longing. "We swam like butterflies once."

And then night came. The recording caught her settling into the sleep pod, her face half-lit by ambient light, speaking into the recorder like it was a diary. "Now I'm in my third trimester," she said softly, adjusting the camera. She turned slightly to show her profile, her body transformed, radiant with life. Her gaze lingered on her reflection. It was quiet, pensive. There was a flicker of amusement in her smile, but also something deeper. A question behind her eyes. A trace of fatigue wrapped in wonder.

Harry couldn't look away. Every movement, every word seemed to crack something open in him.

Then came the bath scene; soft bubbles floated around her, light catching them in iridescent colours. She laughed again, blowing bubbles like a child, her voice suddenly heavier: "I never meant to become a mother, but fate chose otherwise. I'm on a mission of life now. We weren't programmed for this, like the robots were. We're messy, fragile. But maybe that's the point."

Her final words in that scene came like a breath against glass: "Harry ... I miss you."

Then, a shift. The footage cut to the medical pod. Elza's calm voice broke through: "Your baby measures 18.7 inches ..."

Ruma chuckled. "Did you hear that? A whole life is growing inside me."

Harry's lips trembled. His hands were clenched now.

The next clips blurred into a kind of rhythm. Her days were recorded like poetry. She would jog, check her vitals, read books, sip herbal tea, be pestered by the floor-mopping bots, and sleep. It was a life cobbled together from fragments, from discipline and hope and sheer determination.

Then, a whisper of a reveal: "Maybe when you wake, I'll surprise you with the baby. I probably shouldn't have said that." She smiled slyly. "Both of us will watch this together."

Harry pressed his forehead against the console.

And then ... the moment.

Ruma, her face glistening with sweat and tears, cradled the newborn in her arms. Her voice had faded into breathless whispers, her strength nearly gone, but her love, which was raw, untamed, poured out of her. "Our baby, Harry. After everything."

The child, impossibly small, wrapped fingers around her mother's index finger, instinctively seeking warmth, safety, something ancient and unbreakable. Ruma bent close, their cheeks brushing in a gesture too sacred for words. A tear traced down her face, vanishing into the curve of the baby's shoulder.

"You're my muffin, my apple pie," Ruma whispered, rocking her gently. "I have so many stories to tell. The ones where you can fly, and where stars aren't just far-off lights. I'll call them ... *Baby in the Space*."

Harry's vision swam with tears. His heart ached with joy and sorrow all at once. He wasn't sure what was more overwhelming: the beauty of her strength, or the pain of being so far away from it.

Harry sat in the dim quiet of the control room, the light from the console casting pale lines across his face. The air felt heavier than usual, thick with the kind of silence that follows catastrophe. He leaned forward, elbows braced against the metal edge, as the CCTV feed blinked to life. Rubik had retrieved the final footage from the observation dome, one of the last moments Ruma and Tara had shared before everything fell apart.

At first, the screen offered nothing but static. Then slowly, like a curtain being pulled back, the dome revealed itself. It was translucent and still, cradling the infinite sprawl of stars beyond. The galaxy outside shimmered with colour and movement, quiet and vast, like a living canvas of breath and light. Into this dreamlike space drifted Ruma, holding Tara close to her chest. The child's arms were looped loosely around her mother's neck, her hair floating like strands of gold in the zero-gravity hush.

Harry leaned in without realising. There was something reverent about the way Ruma moved–unhurried, as if the danger they had all just faced belonged to another world entirely. She pushed gently off the wall, sending herself and Tara into a slow spin through the dome. They hovered there, drifting like a pair of paper lanterns released into the night, surrounded by stars so bright they seemed close enough to touch.

Rubik had enabled the internal mic feed just faintly, and Harry caught fragments of sound. A lullaby, soft and melodic, spilt through the speakers. Ruma's voice, steady and sure, wrapped around each note with quiet tenderness. It was a tune Harry hadn't heard in years, something from Earth, maybe from the early days of Ruma's own life, before missions and time fractures and silence. He closed his eyes for a moment, letting it fill the cracks that fear had left behind.

Ruma pointed to the sky, her hand tracing the outlines of constellations. Tara followed her gaze with open wonder, reaching out to leave small prints on the curved glass. The stars beyond didn't blink or shift; they simply endured, as they always had, watching the little girl and her mother float through their cathedral of light. There was peace in that moment, unspoken and undeniable. It wasn't just stargazing. It was something sacred. A reclamation of calm after the chaos. A gentle defiance against loss.

As the feed neared its end, Harry saw Ruma draw Tara closer and whisper something in her ear. Whatever it was, it made Tara smile in a way that struck something deep within him. He didn't need to hear the words. He understood them completely.

When the footage stopped, Harry remained still. The silence returned, but it felt different now, less suffocating, more like a hush after a prayer. For the first time in what felt like hours, he allowed himself to exhale. Ruma was still herself. And in that quiet dome, in the company of stars, she had given Tara the gift of stillness, of safety, of wonder.

He touched the edge of the screen gently, as if to thank it for showing him what he hadn't been able to ask for. Then, after a moment, he rose and left the room, the memory of starlight and song still warm in his chest.

Harry carefully tucked the sleeping Tara into her crib. He moved with a gentle touch, his motions deliberate yet tender. The soft glow of the room's ambient lighting illuminated the space, casting a warm and comforting ambience. As he leaned over the crib, his expression softened, a mixture of parental care and weariness from the day's events. Harry took a moment to watch Tara sleep, a small smile playing on his lips, before he slowly eased himself onto a nearby resting place, finally succumbing to the need for rest. Both Harry and Tara found solace in the tranquil embrace of sleep, the quiet breathing filling the room, marking the peaceful close to a tumultuous day.

As Harry gazed out of the window, his expression was a blend of concern and reflection. His eyes scanned the endless expanse of space, contemplating the unknowns that lie beyond. There was a furrow on his brow, evidence of his worry for Ruma, the uncertainties surrounding her whereabouts, and the lack of communication. His thoughts drifted, pondering the myriad possibilities of her current circumstances, hoping for her safety amid the vastness of space.

***

Chapter XXV

Inside the humming nerve-centre of the space station, the atmosphere was taut, every breath thick with unspoken dread. Technicians moved with forced calm, eyes flicking nervously between screens as if willing Ruma's signal to reappear. Amid them, Clark stood like a man hollowed out, gripping the edge of the console so tightly his knuckles had turned bone-white. His glasses had slid down the bridge of his nose, forgotten. His gaze stayed locked on the silent data stream, blinking cursor mocking him with its emptiness. Every beep that *wasn't* from her capsule struck like a blow. He kept muttering to himself about formulas, protocols, anything to drown out the panic clawing at his chest.

He had been her father, yes, but more than that. He was her friend, her fiercest supporter. He remembered Ruma's first day at the program, her nervous smile, her questions that cut straight to the heart of the science. He'd promised her mother she'd be safe. And now ...

Far across the globe, in a modest flat surrounded by fading photographs and prayer candles, Sameera sat unmoving by the television. The last update played on a loop in her mind. Her hands clutched a faded shawl around her shoulders as though it could shield her from the news she dreaded. Her eyes were dry but glassy, locked on the small screen where the mission ticker still blinked her daughter's name.

She didn't cry. She couldn't. The fear was too thick, too solid to allow tears. Instead, she whispered prayers under her breath, ancient words wrapped around her daughter's name. She called every number the station had ever given her. Each time, her voice cracked: "Is she alright? Have you found her?" The replies were always the same—calm, rehearsed, empty.

At the centre, Clark barked out new orders to the engineers, his voice rough with strain. He wasn't just waiting—he was *working*, trying to rewrite fate line by line, code by code. As long as the capsule wasn't found, there was still a chance. There *had* to be.

Silence, not chaos, reigned. And in that silence, hope was a fragile, flickering thing.

*

Harry woke up in the morning and found Tara sleeping peacefully in her crib. He started by brushing his teeth before heading to the shower. As the hot water cascaded down, steam filled the bathroom, creating a hazy, warm atmosphere. In the midst of this, Harry's thoughts drifted to Ruma. The steam swirled around Harry, veiling his reflection as he leaned against the misty glass, the name "Ruma" etched in gentle, fading strokes. Droplets of water trickled down the mirror, distorting the letters but not diluting their significance. Each stroke felt deliberate, as if Harry was trying to etch her name not just onto the glass, but into his memory.

In his mind's eye, a vivid and comforting imagination took hold—he envisioned Ruma with him, a tender and familiar presence wrapping around him from behind. He felt the warmth of an imaginary hug as if Ruma's arms were embracing him in the misty shower. His mind conjured her scent, her touch, and the sensation of being held securely. It was a bittersweet illusion, offering solace in its familiarity but also heightening his yearning for her physical presence. Ruma hugged him. She kissed his neck to his shoulder from behind, put her palm on his chest, breathing heavily. When he turned back, she disappeared.

*

Mikhail sat cross-legged in his private pod, the dim light from the console casting shadows across his tired face. The hologram blinked to life with a gentle hum, and suddenly, his wife's image shimmered into view, her soft eyes wide with surprise, her dark hair tied back, just like always.

"Polina," he breathed, his voice thick with longing. "*Privyet, moya lyubov* (Hello, my love)."

Polina's face broke into a smile, even as her eyes glistened. "Mikhail," she whispered. "I wasn't expecting your call. Are you alright?"

He nodded slowly. "As alright as one can be millions of kilometres away from home."

Their son's head popped into the frame, hair tousled from sleep. "Papa!" he grinned, pressing his face against the hologram projector as if he could crawl through it. "*Skuchayu po tebe* (I miss you)," he mumbled.

Mikhail's throat tightened. "I miss you too, *malysh*," he said softly. "Every single day."

Polina reached out instinctively, her hand hovering where his would have been. "Tell me," she said gently, "what is time like, out there? Do days feel the same? Have you seen other planets? Is any of it ... livable?"

Mikhail exhaled, running a hand over his face. "Time's different here. It stretches, like we're stuck between moments. We don't have days the way you do; it's just cycles of work, sleep, alarms, silence. We've passed several planets, beautiful from afar, but cold and empty once we get close. Most of them wouldn't support a single breath of air. Still, we're collecting everything–data on atmosphere, soil, pressure, even cloud formations. Maybe it'll help someone, someday."

Polina listened in silence, her fingers curled into the hem of her sleeve. The boy had grown quiet, watching his father with wide, adoring eyes.

"*Bud'te ostorozhen* (Be careful), Misha," she said softly. "We miss you so much. Come back to us."

He looked at them, at the way his son leaned into her side, at the way she tried not to let her worry show, and nodded, his voice cracking.

"I will. I promise."

*

Symmonds leaned back in his seat at the food court, a half-eaten pastry balanced on his tray. The hologram flickered to life, and Scarlett's face appeared, warm and glowing, a sliver of Earth in this sterile stretch of space.

"Hey ... Scarlett, my darling," he said, his voice softening at the sight of her. "How's everything going back home?"

She smiled, eyes shining. "We're so proud of you, Artie. Everyone's watching the updates. It's surreal, seeing you up there... so far away, but everywhere at once."

His heart swelled. "Thank you," he murmured, swallowing past the lump in his throat.

He took another bite of the pastry and closed his eyes with a sigh. "God, this pastry ... It's almost as good as the ones you make. Sweet, warm, buttery ... like your smile."

Scarlett laughed. "Really?"

"Really. It's criminal how much I miss your cooking," he teased, licking a crumb off his thumb.

She looked at him for a moment, then said gently, "I miss you."

"I miss you too," he said, his voice barely above a whisper. "I can't wait to hold you again."

"Me too," she said, her voice thick with emotion.

Then, her expression shifted, brightening with excitement. “Oh! Wait till you hear this—we’ve been handling your socials like pros. Your YouTube and Insta? Both verified now. We even got YouTube Play Buttons. You’re officially a celebrity.”

Symmonds blinked. “No shit?”

Scarlett held up two shiny plaques to the camera with a grin. “Look at these babies. You’re famous, love.”

Symmonds laughed, his whole body shaking with disbelief. “That’s fucking awesome.” He leaned back, basking in it for a moment. “I’m a celebrity now. Who would’ve thought?”

“There’s more,” she added, her voice lilting with excitement. “We’ve been getting offers—millions, Artie. Promotions, sponsorships. All food-based, of course.”

He raised an eyebrow. “Food products?”

“Yes,” she said, nodding. “Promote them from space. Just hold up a cereal box, film yourself having it with milk and honey, and send it to me. I’ll turn it into an ad.”

Symmonds laughed, rubbing his hands together. “Done. Space cereals ... ‘You can eat them on Earth, or any damn planet. Healthy, tasty, astronaut-recommended.’”

Scarlett giggled. “Exactly. I’ll write the tagline. You just look pretty and chew.”

He smiled at her, the distance between them narrowing just a little in that moment.

“I love you,” he said quietly.

She touched her fingers to her lips, then to the screen. “Come home soon.”

*

In the bathroom, Harry gently lifted Tara into the bathtub, her eyes gleaming with curiosity. As the water cascaded from the tap, creating a gentle stream, Tara's tiny hands splashed in the water, creating playful ripples. Her laughter filled the space as she enjoyed the simple joy of splashing around, completely enamoured by the newfound delight of water. Harry, with a tender smile, watched over her, creating a moment filled with warmth and innocence amidst the quiet hum of the spaceship.

Harry was seen giggling as he carefully bathed Tara, his laughter echoing softly in the bathroom. With a tender touch, he applied a mild, baby-friendly gel to Tara's delicate skin, his movements slow and cautious. He took extra care around her tiny fingers and toes, ensuring a thorough yet gentle cleanse. As he bathed her, Harry engaged in playful interactions, making soothing sounds and cooing softly to keep Tara calm and comfortable.

Harry's actions were filled with tenderness and delight as he dried Tara gently with a soft towel, ensuring every tiny area was patted dry with care. His movements were playful, making the drying process into a delightful game for Tara. He applied the soothing baby lotion to her skin, massaging it in with gentle strokes, creating a soothing and comforting sensation. Harry enjoyed this moment, cherishing the opportunity to care for Tara with all his heart. As he dressed her, he made funny faces and playful sounds, turning the dressing routine into a joyful and bonding experience between them.

Rubik watched them from behind. "You are a good father. You are slowly learning fatherhood. Glad to see you playing with Tara. You replaced me in taking care of her."

"Nothing like that, spending a day with your daughter is a special moment," Harry said, smiling. "What does she have for breakfast?"

"I will bring that and feed her. You can relax."

Harry chuckled. "Thanks, Rubik. Appreciate your work."

"Coffee for you," Rubik said, holding out a steaming cup of coffee.

"Thank you."

Rubik proceeded to feed Beth while playing Cocomelon videos on his display tummy. "Seems she is hungry but missing her mom."

Harry didn't say anything and silently sipped his coffee, observing the situation. "Do you feed her every day?"

"Yes, I do," Rubik answered without turning its attention away from Tara. "Sometimes Ruma also feeds her. Ruma built me and Cynth to look after the baby. Unfortunately, Cynth isn't here. I badly miss Cynth, the way you miss Ruma." It was quiet for a beat, and then it added. "Human emotions ... It's completely different. I don't understand. It's beautiful when we are with someone we love and pathetic when we lose."

Harry frowned. "Now you sound Semi-Human."

"That's how I was built."

"Do you feed her like this every day with those videos on? You should stop. It could affect her brain development."

While Rubik started to speak, Tara coughed on Rubik's face. Rubik cleaned its face as well as Tara's mouth with a napkin. "If I stop, she won't eat."

"Follow my command. Stop those videos." Harry ordered. He wasn't going to raise his daughter to be an iPad baby.

"Copy that," Rubik said and stopped the video.

Tara innocently looked at Harry and Rubik. As Rubik moved the spoon toward her, she turned around on the table. "You see, I told you."

Harry went to the baby and started playing Peek-A-Boo with her. Tara giggled, flashing her two teeth. Harry extended his hand. "Give me that bowl."

Rubik gave the bowl to Harry. When Tara giggled, Harry put the spoon in her mouth. "Ready for your Applesauce? There you go."

Harry, filled with playful energy, leapt and bounced around like a monkey, mimicking their movements. He scratched at Tara's ears playfully and, with a broad smile and exaggerated movements, he tried to bring laughter and joy to his little one. His antics were accompanied by laughter and giggles from Tara, who finds his lively and silly actions utterly delightful.

"Do you see that the upper teeth are growing?" Harry remarked, a hint of pride in his words.

"Yes," Rubik answered. Ruma babbled playfully, and Harry laughed at her reaction.

The floor-mopping robots glided into the room, emitting a low hum as they manoeuvred across the floor. Their movements were calculated and efficient, swiftly navigating to the area where the spilt food lay. With precision, they began to mop, gently swishing and cleaning the surface, all the while emitting a subtle mechanical whir as they worked.

*

In the sterile brightness of the laboratory, Symmonds moved between rows of tall, meticulously labelled racks. Each pot cradled a different type of soil, one from Planet I, the other from Planet II. Under the steady hum of overhead and grow lights, tiny green shoots reached upward, some vibrant, others more reluctant in their ascent.

He crouched beside one of the trays, his eyes narrowing as he adjusted a tiny nozzle, spraying a mist of nutrient-rich fertiliser over the foliage growing in the Planet-II soil. He tapped a note into his tablet.

Day 24: Increased vitality in Planet-II soil. Leaves are broad, healthy. Roots are pending analysis.

The plants rooted in Planet I's soil were slower, paler in comparison. Less robust. Yet, the nutrient readouts from earlier had shown the opposite, as Planet I had richer soil composition. The contradiction gnawed at him.

Symmonds plucked a leaf from one of the healthier plants and carried it to the cone-shaped scanner. The device glowed with a soft blue light, illuminating the leaf's delicate veins as it hovered inside. A hologram shimmered into life, displaying scrolling figures and glowing charts on his tablet.

Nutrient Composition:

Nitrogen: 1.8 per cent

Phosphorus: 1.1 per cent

Potassium: 1.3 per cent

Chlorophyll: 1.9 mg/g

Photosynthetic efficiency: 78 per cent

"Promising," he muttered, fingers flying across the interface.

He reached for the roots next, rinsing the soil gently in a tray before placing them into the scanner. This time, the data told a different story. Chloroplast activity dipped. Cell viability dropped. A red-highlighted warning blinked faintly in the corner of his screen.

"Hmm ..." Symmonds frowned. "Why the hell are the roots failing?"

Before he could investigate further, the lab door hissed open behind him. A gust of cooler air swept in, along with the voice of Mikhail.

"There you are!" Mikhail said, stepping inside with wide eyes. "This place ... it smells like Earth. Feels like walking into a garden. Symmonds, this is incredible."

Symmonds stood and wiped his hands on a cloth. "Most of what you're seeing is from Planet-II soil," he said, gesturing to the flourishing row. "Planet-I has better nutrients, on paper. But look ... Planet-II is outperforming it. It's baffling."

Mikhail stepped closer, eyes scanning the leaves with fascination. "Maybe the growth cycle on Planet-II takes longer to activate. Could be a resilience trait ... like a potato. Takes its time, but damn hard to kill."

Symmonds chuckled. "You and your love for potatoes."

But his curiosity wasn't done. He gently unearthed one of the more mature plants, cradling its roots. As he lifted the base, his eyes widened.

"Mikhail. Look at this."

Nestled within the roots, not growing outward like traditional fruit, were small, rounded forms, developing *inward*, hidden beneath the tangle of fibrous tendrils.

"Those are fruits," Symmonds whispered. "They're maturing underground."

Mikhail leaned in, eyebrows raised. "They're adapting. Using the root system to shield the fruit, maybe from radiation, maybe from cold. That's ... that's brilliant."

"You're right," Symmonds said, a hint of admiration in his voice. "You just earned your title back—'Analyst Supreme.'"

"Ha!" Mikhail grinned. "Told you. It's all about spotting the weird stuff."

Symmonds clapped him on the shoulder. "Come on. Let's grab some coffee before I start dissecting fruit roots."

*

"Quite a productive day, huh?" Symmonds said, his voice echoing lightly in the hallway. "Those results in the lab were ... unexpected."

Mikhail nodded. "Absolutely. The soil dynamics alone could tell us everything about these planets—how they formed, what they've endured."

"Exactly. There's more buried in that data than we realise." Symmonds paused. "Speaking of systems, did you get a chance to check the propulsion readings?"

"Yeah. Everything's stable for now, but we'll need to recalibrate the ion vector alignment. Minor, but worth doing soon."

Symmonds sighed. "Let's hope for smooth sailing from here."

They rounded a corner toward the mess capsule.

"Have you heard anything from Earth?" he asked.

"Just the usual status updates. Family check-ins. You?"

"Same. Scarlett's doing well, managing my socials like a pro," Symmonds smirked. "Apparently, I'm now a space-influencer."

Mikhail laughed. "Can't wait for your cereal ads."

"Hey, astronaut-endorsed breakfasts, coming soon to a planet near you."

They entered the food capsule, the faint smell of rehydrated pasta and spice greeting them.

"What's your bet for tonight's dinner?" Symmonds asked as he grabbed two trays.

"Fingers crossed for something spicy," Mikhail grinned. "I need the thrill."

*

Harry, sweating from his jog on the treadmill, wiped his face with a cloth, feeling the exertion. He took a swig from a water bottle equipped with a sipper, quenching his thirst, and inadvertently caught Tara's gaze.

Realising the situation, he chuckled softly. "Oh, my apologies, little one. This isn't for you." Tara responded with a delighted giggle, enjoying the playful interaction.

In a playful gesture, Harry retrieved another water bottle, this one fitted with a sipper, and handed it over to Tara. With a gentle smile, he encouraged her to explore the sipper, offering it to her in a way that she could grasp and use it herself. Tara, curious and eager, reached out with tiny hands to grab hold of the bottle, trying to navigate the sipper as Harry guided her through the process, sharing a sweet moment of interaction.

"This is your bottle, your energy drink, and this is mine".

Harry then carried Tara to the Food capsule. Symmonds greeted Harry with a cheerful "Hey, good evening!"

Mikhail joined in, offering a warm "Good evening, Tara," to which Tara responded with joyful babbling as she sipped on her water.

Symmonds, a little surprised, inquired, "Does she speak?"

Harry proudly answered, "Yes, she does! She even writes already."

Mikhail, impressed, remarked, "A child prodigy!"

Harry chuckled and explained, "She talks, but I am still decoding her language."

Tara, continuing her adorable babbling, seemed to confirm their point.

Harry grinned, saying, "See? I told you!"

"We need a translator. Rubik, can you translate?" Symmonds asked.

Rubik was meticulously analysing the unique babble of Tara's language. Its internal lights pulsated rhythmically as it processed the data, scanning through its vast database for correlations and patterns that could unlock the meaning behind her words. Its screens displayed various linguistic algorithms and complex graphs, all attempting to decipher the infant's intriguing speech. After a few seconds, Rubik's screens flash a disheartening message, displaying 'Not found' in bold letters.

"Sometimes, AI cannot handle a few things," Mikhail patted Rubik.

"Are you satisfied?" Harry asked, bemused.

"Ah, yes, I am. My ego is satisfied."

Mikhail lovingly scooped Tara into his arms. "You are so adorable, Tara." She responded with subtle giggles and coos, enjoying the attention and the playful words from Mikhail. While Tara was laughing, the water spilt on Mikhail, which made everyone laugh.

Symmonds cleaned himself up and handed Tara back to Harry. "Harry, when are we landing on Planet III?"

"Tomorrow evening."

"Did we go through all the devices and launching vehicles?" Mikhail asked. "I mean, do we need to check those devices and instruments?"

Harry nodded. "Yeah, we need to check that."

"Alright, let's start with the spectrometre readings. We need accurate data on the atmospheric composition."

"Spectrometre's online. Displaying the last values from Planet II. Looks good," Mikhail said.

"Good. Meanwhile, I will run the chromatographs to analyse the soil samples we collected from Planet II," said Symmonds.

"Chromatographs fired up. Processing soil compounds for organic content. Ready for Go."

"Keep an eye on the seismic monitoring," Symmonds warned. "Any fluctuations could indicate tectonic activities."

"Seismic readings normal. Ready for Go. Detectors calibrated. Ready for Go."

Symmonds and Mikhail meticulously ran through the array of sophisticated instruments, their focus intense on each panel and screen. With practised precision, they initiated and examined each device, scanning the readouts for any signs of anomalies or malfunctions. The soft glow of the monitors illuminated their concentrated expressions as they meticulously cross-checked the data.

Fingers danced across control panels, toggling switches and adjusting parameters. Displays flickered with intricate graphs and readings, showcasing atmospheric compositions, soil analysis, seismic activity, and cosmic radiation levels. Symmonds carefully examined the spectrometre's data, while Mikhail monitored the chromatographs for organic content, ensuring every facet of the analysis was meticulously accurate.

As the devices hummed with activity, the crew members checked for any discrepancies or irregularities that might compromise the mission. Their swift, methodical assessments left no room for oversight, meticulously verifying the functionality and integrity of each instrument.

"Confirming all the devices are good to go," Mikhail said finally.

"The devices are good to go," Symmonds added. Tara started babbling and giggling, which made Symmonds look up. "What does that mean?"

"She said 'perfect,'" Harry said and turned back to Tara. "You're growing up so fast, huh? Before we know it, you'll be exploring planets just like your mom did. But for now, let's enjoy our little adventure together, okay?"

Harry moved through the corridors of the spaceship, the glow of the control panels casting dim light as he headed toward the launch bay. The soft hum of machinery echoed through the passageways as he made his way, his footsteps a quiet shuffle against the floor. The walls were lined with various diagrams and emergency protocols, casting an almost surreal atmosphere.

As he approached the launch bay, the sound of his footsteps seemed to fade, replaced by the distant hum of the launch vehicle's mechanisms. The bay doors stood tall and imposing, a gateway to the vastness of space. Harry gazed upon the vehicle with a mix of anticipation and reverence, its sleek design and intricate details showcasing the pinnacle of their technological advancements.

He checked the control panels, inspecting each section meticulously, ensuring that every component was in perfect working order. His movements were purposeful yet cautious, his fingers navigating the panels with precision. The faint flicker of the control lights reflected in his eyes was a shred of evidence of the seriousness of the task at hand.

As Harry began testing the launch vehicle, he systematically engaged each component, his fingers moving across the panels to activate switches and knobs. The control systems hummed to life, emitting subtle vibrations as they powered on. The navigation console displayed various trajectories and coordinates, glowing softly with vital information.

He scrutinised the control panel, monitoring the status indicators to ensure all systems were functional. The trajectory projections flickered on the screens, showcasing potential paths and destinations. Harry cross-checked these with the planned route, meticulously confirming the alignment.

The control systems responded crisply to his inputs, the interface lighting up as he tested the responsiveness of the vehicle's commands. The tactile feedback of the switches and buttons reassured him of their readiness for operation.

With a focused gaze, he assessed the onboard guidance systems, running diagnostic checks on the automated controls. The sensors calibrated as expected, showing optimal readings. He double-checked the backup systems, verifying their reliability in case of contingencies.

Throughout the process, Harry remained vigilant, his keen eye ensuring that every system worked flawlessly. His diligence reflected a blend of expertise and dedication, essential for the success of their upcoming mission. The quiet hum of the systems and the occasional soft beep filled the air, a symphony of readiness as the launch vehicle awaited its crucial role in their voyage.

***

Chapter XXVI

The next evening

The anticipation in the air was palpable as the crew members prepared for the much-anticipated launch to Planet III. The spaceship buzzed with activity as each member meticulously checked their equipment, ensuring everything was in prime condition for the expedition. Harry, Symmonds, and Mikhail double-checked the navigation systems, trajectory calculations, and control mechanisms, ensuring every aspect was aligned for the journey.

Ruma's absence weighed heavily on Harry's mind, yet his focus remained steadfast on the mission. He made sure everything was meticulously organised, his determination to succeed echoing in his brisk movements.

Symmonds monitored the fuel systems and the propulsion, confirming that the adjustments they had made the previous night were holding steady. His expertise and attention to detail ensured that every component was functioning optimally.

Mikhail was busy finalising the communication systems, ensuring seamless connectivity between the spaceship and the space centre. His meticulousness in handling the intricate equipment assured the crew of uninterrupted communication during the mission.

Meanwhile, Tara's innocence provided a momentary reprieve from the tension. Her playful babbling and laughter echoed in the spaceship, lightening the atmosphere as the crew readied themselves for the journey.

The crew members donned their spacesuits, securing themselves in the advanced gear, each step bringing them closer to the imminent launch. As they entered the final countdown, a blend of excitement, determination, and a tinge of apprehension filled the air—a fusion of emotions marking the threshold of their expedition to Planet III.

"What about Tara? Who would take care of her?" Symmonds inquired, voicing the collective concern.

"Snobo and Rubik are there to look after her," Mikhail offered.

Symmonds nodded in agreement. In this situation, Clark emphasised caution, concerned about the safety of the baby. Harry, who was eager to be involved and take responsibility, proposed to carry Beth.

"Let me carry her," Harry suggested.

Clark, concerned about any potential risk, advised against it. "Don't risk the baby," he cautioned, prioritising Tara's safety above all else.

"Mikhail, does she stay that long until we complete the expedition?" Symmonds enquired.

"I think so, but I don't know much about it," Mikhail responded, unsure about the specifics.

"Harry, what would you say?" Symmonds turned to Harry for his input.

"I have a plan," Harry announced, piquing the curiosity of Symmonds and Mikhail, who both respond with intrigue.

"Would you look after her by staying in the spaceship?" Symmonds asked Harry.

"We will go together," Harry replied.

"Everybody, suit up," he then announced, prompting Symmonds and Mikhail to put on their suits, while Harry did the same.

Harry, retrieving Tara's suit from beneath Ruma's bed, carried a tender sentiment. He carefully took the suit, examining it for size and functionality. Securing it by the belt meant to carry Tara, he dressed her in the small suit, gently ensuring it fit comfortably.

Symmonds whistled impressively. "It's a perfect baby holder in the space."

The landscape of Planet III was a breathtaking blend of vibrant colours, with unusual flora and fauna. The air had a distinct scent, and the horizon stretched endlessly, displaying an unknown terrain waiting to be explored. There were unusual rock formations, exotic plants, and fascinating geological features spread across the horizon, offering an enigmatic vista to the crew as they set foot on this uncharted territory.

As the Launch vehicle gently settled on Planet-III's surface, the metallic ramp slowly lowered with a soft hiss. The atmosphere outside was a blend of mystery and wonder, with wisps of dust and smoke rising gently around the craft. Symmonds and Mikhail, equipped in their space gear, cautiously made their way down the ramp, each step filled with anticipation and curiosity.

Their first steps outside were careful, as if testing the ground beneath their boots. The air around them felt different, carrying a faint scent or an unusual texture. The atmosphere appeared hazy, partly veiling the landscape that lay ahead, creating an aura of mystery that urged exploration.

They scanned the surroundings, taking in the unfamiliar vista. The horizon stretched into the unknown, showcasing an array of colours and possibly peculiar formations—rocks, vegetation, or peculiar landmarks scattered across the landscape. Symmonds and Mikhail exchanged glances, communicating their shared excitement and readiness to delve into this uncharted territory.

As Harry stepped down onto the surface of Planet III, carrying Tara snugly in the baby holder bag, the landscape unfolded before them, capturing their attention. The planet's intriguing features mesmerised Tara, evident in her widened eyes and expressions of wonder as she gazed at the unfamiliar terrain.

Harry moved cautiously, his steps measured and deliberate, taking in the new environment with every stride. His gaze wandered, absorbing the unique sights and textures surrounding them. He couldn't help but smile as Tara, secure in the carrier, playfully shook her legs, displaying her excitement and curiosity about this unexplored world.

Symmonds and Mikhail, well-versed in their roles, activated their respective handheld devices upon landing on Planet III. These instruments were specifically calibrated for analysing planetary data and gathering crucial information.

They scrutinised the readings on their devices, scanning the environment for any available data points. The devices displayed various metrics, such as atmospheric composition, temperature, radiation levels, and geological data about the terrain.

Symmonds and Mikhail meticulously collected and cross-referenced the data, aiming to understand the planet's characteristics, potential resources, and environmental conditions. Each reading provided a piece of the puzzle, painting a clearer picture of Planet III's nature and its suitability for exploration or habitation. Their actions were methodical, driven by their scientific curiosity and the quest for knowledge about this uncharted world.

As Symmonds and Mikhail stepped onto Planet III, their helmet visors illuminated with a cascade of vital information. As they began their exploration, a new artificial intelligence system, AI Hailer, was activated with a male voice. Hailer was designed for communication, assistance, and to address any unforeseen challenges during their expedition on Planet III.

The moment the ramp lowered, a hiss of sterile air escaped from the shuttle, replaced almost instantly by the raw breath of Planet III. The sky above was a bruised lavender, cloudless, but threaded with flickers of distant lightning that never touched ground. Pale red sand crunched under their boots, stretching across an uneven landscape of jagged obsidian cliffs and clustered rock formations that pulsed faintly with an inner glow. A strange wind blew sideways, constant, whispering, carrying with it the scent of something metallic and sweet.

"Welcome to Planet III, explorers," Hailer's voice filtered into their helmets. "Initiating environmental scan. Stand by."

A second passed. Then another. Then the data rolled in.

"Atmospheric pressure stable. Oxygen levels within human tolerance. Proceed with caution."

Symmonds stepped off the platform, visor gleaming. "Feels like we're standing inside a battery," he muttered, peering up at the pale sun overhead.

"Sensors detecting anomalous energy signatures," Hailer continued. "Advise perimeter security and minimal physical contact with glowing surfaces."

Mikhail adjusted his shoulder strap and followed, boots crunching. "You think the cliffs are naturally luminous?"

"Let's not find out by licking them," Symmonds replied, half-smiling.

“Wind speeds are increasing. Secure equipment,” Hailer warned again, as Mikhail bent to retrieve a loose instrument case.

“We should move fast,” Symmonds said. “Start a sweep of this quadrant. I’ll take topography, you focus on soil composition.”

Mikhail unclipped a scanner from his belt. “On it. Spectrometre’s online. Soil looks ... layered. Like something churned it not long ago.”

“Seismic readings?” Symmonds asked, already pulling out a portable mapper.

“Low-level tremors. Could be tectonic or something burrowing.”

Symmonds grunted. “Either way, we note it and keep our eyes open.”

The wind whistled louder now, throwing fine dust into their suits. Mikhail glanced at his wrist feed. “Atmospheric levels are fluctuating. Wind’s getting twitchy.”

“I’ll handle the fauna scan. Let’s see if this place is really as dead as it looks.”

“Flora might be bio-luminescent,” Mikhail offered, scanning the glowing moss near a rock. “Could explain the energy readings.”

Symmonds crouched near a cluster of crystalline growths. “Some of this mineral content is inconsistent. Get a deeper read?”

“Already prepping the chromatograph,” Mikhail said, kneeling beside a soil patch. “Could be volcanic sediment. Or something ... older.”

As they worked, the cliffs in the distance shimmered faintly, pulse-like.

"I'm picking up irregular magnetic field shifts," Mikhail said. "It's ... rhythmic."

"Like something's powering on and off," Symmonds murmured. "Check our radiation exposure while I analyse the rock layers."

"Radiation is within safety limits," Mikhail confirmed, fingers flying across his wristpad. "But yeah, I'll launch an atmospheric probe. Might catch something we're not seeing."

Symmonds nodded. "Make sure it's hardened for acidic elements. This dust feels ... sharp."

"Done," Mikhail said, launching the small drone with a hiss. It zipped upward, trailing a silver line behind it.

Symmonds straightened, eyes scanning the jagged horizon. "The terrain changes sharply ahead. Could be cliffs, or something deeper."

"This planet has a history," Mikhail said. "I don't think we're the first ones here."

They stood in silence for a moment, just listening to the wind, to the quiet hum of their gear, to the heartbeat of a planet that felt like it was watching.

Finally, Mikhail asked, "Think it's time we set up base camp?"

Symmonds hesitated, gaze still fixed on the distant shimmer. "Yeah," he said slowly. "But keep the engines warm."

As the launch vehicle doors swung open, two sizable spherical drones emerged, zipping out with urgency. Their aerial manoeuvring and swift movements indicated their purpose—to extensively scan and explore the vastness of Planet III.

The drones immediately initiated their reconnaissance mission, sweeping across the landscape in synchronised precision. They veered to both sides of the planet, systematically surveying and capturing detailed data as they glided through the atmosphere.

Symmonds looked up. "What is that?"

The sky was alive with the sudden emergence of drones—sleek, spherical devices that zipped through the air with remarkable agility. Their movements were precise, almost dance-like, as they navigated the atmosphere.

Beside him, Mikhail stood in awe, his gaze fixed on the breathtaking display above. The drones' scanning activities seemed orchestrated, their flight patterns deliberate as they covered expansive areas of the sky. Another door slid open, and a Rover came out of it. The rover approached Harry and stopped, perhaps waiting for further instructions from Harry.

Harry settled into the rover's seat, securing himself with the seat belt. He then carefully positioned Tara onto another seat, fastening her securely with the seat belt as well. Adjusting the straps to ensure she was snug and safe, he prepared for their exploration on the rover. Tara looked around with curiosity, observing their new surroundings from her seat.

"Hello, Rover. Take us to the Cataract Disc," Harry instructed.

Hailer responded. "Copy that. Navigation turned on. Heading east, one mile away. Coordinates enabled."

Slowly, the rover began its journey, rolling over the uneven terrain of Planet III. Harry steered the vehicle, glancing at the coordinates displayed on the screen, ensuring they were heading towards the Cataract Disc located a mile away in the east. The rover moved steadily, the surroundings changing as they ventured further, following the designated path indicated by the navigation system.

The Globots soared through the skies of Planet III, each controlled by their respective captains, Rubik and Snobo. These spherical, white drones, resembling mini globes, glided effortlessly across the planet's terrain. Their sensors and scanners worked tirelessly, meticulously mapping and scanning every inch of the planet's surface.

Planet III unfolded below, a fascinating world of contrast. Half of the planet was engulfed in water, glistening under the celestial light, while the other half lay as vast deserts, painting a picture reminiscent of Earth. The scans revealed a habitat that seemed suitable for life, invitingly familiar in its resemblance to Earth's ecosystem.

The sophisticated scanners probed deeper, capturing detailed information about the chemical composition and mineral resources of the planet. They unveiled a treasure trove of oxygen and hydrogen, vital elements for sustaining life. The constant presence of rain on the planet was a remarkable find, hinting at a climate conducive to growth and evolution.

"Snobo and Rubik, do you copy?" Harry's voice echoed over the communication link.

"Yes, Harry," Snobo responded promptly.

Their voices, transmitted across the vast expanse of Planet III, resonated as they coordinated efforts, ensuring that every nook and cranny of the planet was thoroughly scrutinised and catalogued.

The screens within the Globots displayed an array of data as they rotated and scanned the planet's surface. Numbers, graphs, and visual representations flickered across the screens, depicting the intricate details of Planet III. As the Globots manoeuvred, the data continued to update in real time. Chemical compositions, mineral densities, atmospheric compositions, and weather patterns were graphically showcased, illustrating the rich and diverse environment of the planet.

As the rover traversed the sandy terrain of Planet III, the journey was far from smooth. The vehicle surged forward, tackling the undulating landscape with its sturdy wheels. The seats, secured by tight seat belts, ensured Harry and Tara remained safely fastened in place. The rover's pace was brisk, causing periodic jolts and slight jumps as it manoeuvred through the sandy surface. Small ditches and uneven patches of terrain prompted the vehicle to jostle, causing a series of bounces that echoed through the cabin.

Planet III hung like a jewel in the cosmos, its surface a striking study in contrast. Half the landscape was scorched by sweeping deserts, vast golden dunes sculpted by wind, their shifting patterns casting long, surreal shadows. The other half gleamed with crystalline waters: winding rivers and mirror-like lakes that shimmered beneath the alien sun. Life stirred beneath the surface, thriving quietly amidst the serenity. The planet felt both strange and familiar, like an exquisite balance of heat and light, stillness and motion, mystery and memory.

Kneeling beside a jagged outcrop, Mikhail brushed away the fine dust clinging to its surface. His visor caught the shimmer before he even touched it–a deep, iridescent gleam running through the stone like veins of light.

He let out a sharp whistle. "Symmonds! You need to see this!"

Symmonds turned, stepping over the uneven terrain. "What is it?"

Mikhail held up a small fragment he'd chipped off. It sparkled under the alien sun, flecks of violet and silver catching the light.

"This rock is laced with iridium. And that—" he pointed to a nearby boulder, its bluish tint unmistakable—"that's cobaltite. Pure. Unweathered."

His voice crackled with excitement over the comms. "We're standing on a goddamn mineral jackpot."

Symmonds raised an eyebrow behind her visor. "You're saying it's all like this?"

Mikhail nodded, scanning the ridge. "Every reading's off the charts. This place isn't just a planet. It's a vault."

As the Rover traversed the unique terrain of Planet III, Harry found himself immersed in a reflective moment, his thoughts echoing in the quiet recesses of his mind. *Here we are, on a planet so distant yet so strangely familiar. The journey has been nothing short of extraordinary*, he thought. He turned to look at Tara, who, in her innocence, embraced the wonders around her, eyes wide, mesmerised by the ethereal surroundings.

His thoughts oscillate between the marvels of the planet and the mission at hand. The Cataract Disc holds a promise—an answer, perhaps, to an enigmatic riddle. *Will it unveil the secrets we seek?*

With each bump and jolt of the Rover's progress, Harry felt a sense of anticipation growing within. *The unknown stretches before us like an endless expanse*, he realised. *We're pioneers charting the uncharted, seeking answers amidst cosmic mysteries.*

As the Rover inched closer to its destination, Harry's resolve strengthened. *We're on the cusp of discovery, Tara–adventurers under the cosmic canopy, exploring the unexplored, seeking the hidden truths of this remarkable world.*

Amid this otherworldly journey across Planet III, Tara's innocent delight was palpable. Her laughter echoed through the Rover as she joyously uttered her babbling words, immersed in the wonders of this alien terrain. Her eyes, wide and filled with curiosity, darted around, absorbing every sight that unfolded before her. With pure exuberance, she raised her tiny arms, embracing the vastness of this new world. Her foot stomped with a sense of enthusiasm and discovery, her small hands clapping in sheer delight. Each movement she makes seems like a dance of excitement, a celebration of the sheer joy derived from each passing moment.

Mankind may survive on this planet, Harry thought. *This planet was a source of absolute pure wonder and bliss, unimaginable.*

The Rover's journey culminated at the tower where the prized Cataract Disc awaited collection. With careful precision, Harry retrieved the Disc, an artefact of profound significance in their expedition. As he handed it to Tara, she embraced the Disc tenderly, cradling it close to her chest with an unexpected fondness, reminiscent of a young cub clutching its treasured toy.

With Harry's eyes locked on her, Tara began her journey to stand on her own tiny feet. A collective hush fell over everyone witnessing this momentous occasion. In a remarkable feat of determination and balance, Tara managed to lift herself upright, supported by the planet's surface beneath her. Her radiant, gleeful face sparkled with an innocent charm as she waved her hand joyfully, her eyes mirroring the astonishment of those around her.

For Harry, it was something etched in the deepest corners of his heart, a milestone that transcended the bounds of an expedition—a testament to life's extraordinary journey, filled with awe, innocence, and the unspoken promise of endless possibilities. His heart tugged, and his eyes immediately filled with tears as he wished, with all his heart, that Ruma would have been there to see this. He could almost imagine how proud and happy she'd look, her beautiful face smiling brightly.

In a gentle, encouraging voice, Harry knelt, his eyes brimming with an ineffable mix of excitement and pride. His arms extended toward Tara, beckoning her to take those historic steps on this distant celestial body. "Come on, Tara," he cheered, his voice filled with an unparalleled sense of encouragement and admiration. "Take a tiny step into this unknown world. You're going to make history as the youngest explorer on this planet."

Finally, as Tara took her last step, Harry enveloped her in his arms, the sheer weight of this unforgettable moment washing over him. He hugged her tightly, feeling the warmth and purity of this unparalleled bond, a connection stretching across galaxies. In that embrace, amidst the vastness of the unknown, they shared a moment that would forever be etched in their hearts.

As the evening painted the sky in hues of deep orange and gold, the sun began its descent, casting long shadows across the alien landscape. The light of the setting sun bathed the surroundings in a warm, golden glow, illuminating the horizon with a breathtaking display of colours.

The rover's camera captured the monumental moment, beaming it across space to Earth. On the screens of countless homes, the image appeared—a father and his young daughter, silhouetted against an otherworldly sunset on Planet III. The broadcast spread like wildfire across Earth's news channels, captivating the attention of people worldwide.

This historic sight stirred excitement and wonder among the Earth's inhabitants. The first infant to take her first steps on an alien world—a milestone that transcended the boundaries of space exploration. It was a moment of unity, where humanity collectively shared in the joy of witnessing a new chapter in interstellar exploration.

News outlets buzzed with the heartwarming scene, sparking conversations and emotions globally. The world paused, captivated by the innocence and significance of this tiny step, a monumental leap in the quest to understand and explore the cosmos. The image of Harry and Tara etched against the celestial backdrop became an iconic symbol of hope, discovery, and the human spirit reaching out to touch the stars.

Symmonds let out a quiet chuckle as he watched Tara toddle across the soft terrain in her tiny suit. "You know," he said, eyes still on Tara, "when we were kids, I used to joke with my friends that my daily routine went: coffee in California, breakfast in Britain, lunch in London, and dinner in Denmark."

Mikhail laughed. "Jet-setting before it was cool, huh?"

Symmonds smiled. "Back then, it was just a fantasy. But now—look at her. Tara's first steps ... not even on Earth."

Mikhail crouched beside Tara, steadying her as she reached out for balance. "When she's older, she's gonna tell her friends, 'I took my first steps on Planet III.'" He glanced up at Symmonds, grinning. "She'll say, 'I was born in space, lived on ships, visited planets like they were weekend getaways.' A real cosmic childhood."

Symmonds shook his head with a soft laugh. "A space baby on planet vacation. Who would've thought?"

As the globots completed their comprehensive scanning, they gracefully retreated into the Launch vehicle; their task was done. The Rover, having fulfilled its mission under Harry's command, obediently followed suit and made its way back into the waiting vehicle.

With a sense of accomplishment lingering in the air, Symmonds, Mikhail, Harry, and Tara embarked on their return journey, stepping into the Launch vehicle. The interior of the vehicle was a blend of sleek modern technology and functional design, with screens displaying data readouts, control panels, and comfortable seating arrangements.

Despite the thrilling adventure on Planet III, a feeling of homeliness surrounded them as they prepared to depart, looking forward to the familiar embrace of their spaceship. Each member took their designated spots, securing themselves for the journey ahead. Tara, snugly settled in Harry's care, looked around in wonder, her eyes reflecting the captivating experiences of the day.

As the doors closed behind them, sealing them within the Launch vehicle, a sense of accomplishment and anticipation filled the air. They were ready to return, their minds still enchanted by the mysteries of Planet III, yet eager to reunite with the safety of their spacecraft.

***

Chapter XXVII

The crew embarked on a mesmerising voyage through the stars, charting a course to five unexplored celestial bodies, designated Planet IV through Planet VIII, spanning over five years. Each encounter was a chapter of awe and revelation, as they pursued knowledge and sought out the elusive Cataract Discs scattered across the galaxy.

Planet IV greeted them with a terrain that shimmered like a dream. Towering, jagged rock formations pierced a cloudless azure sky, their surfaces laced with iridescent minerals that caught and fractured light. The ground was encrusted with crystalline latticework that chimed faintly underfoot. As the team collected the Cataract Disc and ran atmospheric tests, they noted low oxygen levels and high radiation pockets. It was hauntingly beautiful, but inhospitable for long-term habitation.

Planet V unfolded in an eerie, breathtaking glow. Bioluminescent plants pulsed with shifting hues of deep purples, neon blues, and ghostly greens, casting an otherworldly light across the landscape. Symmonds, Mikhail, and Harry carefully navigated the biotic maze, collecting flora samples and scanning the air. The oxygen levels were surprisingly high, and microbial life was abundant. Though initial signs suggested potential for colonisation, unstable soil composition and fluctuating electromagnetic fields posed significant challenges.

Planet VI loomed ahead under a curtain of roiling clouds and shrieking winds. Its surface was cloaked in chaos as cyclones, acid storms, and violent electrical discharges churned without pause. The crew, encased in reinforced suits and tethered tightly to one another, descended only briefly to extract the Cataract Disc. Sensors warned of extreme atmospheric pressure and corrosive compounds in the air. There was no question—this planet was uninhabitable, a storm world built for no life as they knew it.

Planet VII told a different story, one of a time long past. Broken pillars, sunken courtyards, and stone monuments whispered of a lost civilisation. Strange symbols lined the walls, some of them faintly resembling proto-scripts from Earth's own ancient cultures. The air was dry, thin but breathable with assistance, and the land bore no active flora or fauna. The team speculated that the planet may once have supported life but had long since slipped into dormancy. The presence of once-engineered structures and still-functional energy sources hinted at potential reactivation, if anyone dared to try.

Planet VIII dazzled them with its kaleidoscope of colour. Rolling meadows of luminous grass waved in the wind, while translucent creatures flitted between glowing trees. The skies swirled in perpetual twilight, painted in pastels that shifted with the magnetic pull of the planet's twin moons. The air was rich in oxygen, temperatures mild, and natural resources plentiful. The fauna remained wary but non-aggressive, and water flowed clean and abundant. Among all the planets they had visited, Planet VIII showed the strongest signs of being not only habitable, but welcoming.

*

2025

Kennedy Space Centre, Conference Hall

The stage at the Space Centre was a meticulously arranged setting, designed to accommodate the revered board members overseeing the monumental achievements of space exploration. It exuded an air of professionalism and sophistication, serving as a focal point for key decision-makers and visionaries in the field.

At the forefront of the stage sat the distinguished board members, their seats arranged symbolising collaboration and unity. Each chair was impeccably arranged, signifying the importance and respect accorded to these eminent individuals guiding the course of interstellar exploration. The backdrop featured NASA's insignia, proudly displayed behind the seated board members. The lighting was finely tuned, casting a warm and inviting glow on the stage. It accentuated the seriousness of the proceedings while maintaining an aura of grace and sophistication. The ambience was a balance between formality and approachability, inviting both focus and engagement from the audience.

The board members themselves were evidence to their expertise and leadership. Dressed in professional attire, they exuded confidence and authority. Their attentive demeanour indicated their dedication to the progress and success of space exploration, embodying a collective commitment to humanity's cosmic journey.

Professor Clark, donning a sharp suit, stood at the podium in the space centre, the emblem of exploration and discovery adorning the backdrop. The air hummed with anticipation as a group of delegates, scientists, and journalists gathered for the much-awaited press conference. With a poised demeanour, Clark, a symbol of wisdom and authority, began addressing the audience. His voice, steady and resonant, echoed through the hall, carrying the weight of the monumental discoveries made during the interstellar expedition.

"Ladies and Gentlemen, esteemed delegates and members of the press ..."

As he spoke, holographic displays flickered to life, showcasing visuals of the crew's incredible journey through space, highlighting each planet they had explored and the groundbreaking data they had collected. Charts, graphs, and images illustrating celestial landscapes adorned the screens, capturing the attention of the audience.

"To the world, this project has demonstrated the plausibility of sustaining life on another celestial body. While the inevitability of life and death persists, the imperative for human survival remains paramount. All necessary resources were procured both through natural means and artificial synthesis.

"Our crew members not only survived, but also thrived on an uncharted planet. Regrettably, we encountered the loss of a crew member–a profound and difficult reality to absorb. Nonetheless, our mission persisted unabated.

"Despite the hardships faced, our astronauts have returned triumphant, having laid the groundwork for potential human habitation on distant celestial bodies. The knowledge gained from this expedition opens new horizons for mankind, offering hope and possibilities for the future of our species.

"As we celebrate this milestone, let us honour the resilience of the human spirit, the dedication of our team, and the unwavering commitment to the advancement of scientific exploration. Together, let us forge ahead with renewed determination, knowing that the possibilities for the future of humanity among the stars are within our grasp. Thank you."

The Space Centre's vast conference hall echoed with the enthusiastic applause of board members, esteemed delegates representing various nations, and a myriad of news channel reporters. A collective sense of exhilaration and admiration permeated the air, reflected in the beaming faces and animated expressions of everyone present.

Amidst the applause, the news reporters busily documented the proceedings, their cameras capturing the energy and fervour of the moment. Their expressions mirrored the collective sentiment of awe and fascination, ready to share this monumental event with the world.

Tarayaan descended towards Earth, and anticipation grew, culminating in a momentous landing. The ramp gracefully opened, revealing the crew members donning their space gear. Stepping onto Earth once more, they were met by the eager presence of the Prime Minister, adorned with protective goggles, standing tall and resolute among a team of vigilant security guards.

To ensure safety measures were diligently followed, a barricade had been erected, signalling the mandatory quarantine awaiting the returning crew. The crew members, having journeyed from the far reaches of space, were obliged to pass through this designated checkpoint before reuniting with their families and loved ones.

The event attracted a throng of news reporters, their cameras trained on the crew members' every step. Each moment was captured and immortalised through the lenses of media personnel who broadcast this historic arrival to the world. The news coverage highlighted the significance of the crew's return, documenting their descent from the spacecraft and the subsequent passage through the quarantine protocol.

Amidst the flurry of activity, the Prime Minister maintained a poised and composed stance, underscoring the importance of adhering to safety regulations while celebrating the crew's successful return from their celestial expedition. This monumental moment marked both the culmination of an extraordinary journey and the commencement of a period of rest and isolation to ensure the crew's well-being and health following their interstellar voyage.

As the crew members disembarked from their spacecraft, the Earth's invigorating air enveloped them, a welcome departure from the artificial oxygen they had relied on throughout their space-bound journey. Breathing in the refreshing terrestrial atmosphere, they felt a sense of revitalisation, a grounding sensation after their cosmic endeavour.

At the sight of the Prime Minister, a figure symbolising the nation's welcome, the crew reciprocated the gesture with waves of acknowledgement. The Prime Minister, standing amidst a throng of officials and security personnel, raised a hand in a friendly greeting, acknowledging their return to Earth's embrace.

Among the returning crew, little Tara, the youngest voyager and the only child ever born aboard the starship, stood frozen in place. Her wide eyes, once filled with curiosity during the mission, now darted around in bewilderment. The sheer number of people—hundreds, maybe thousands—was overwhelming. On the ship, space had always been quiet, structured, predictable. Here, the noise surged like a tidal wave: voices shouting questions, camera shutters snapping like insects, flashes of light exploding in every direction.

The sky seemed too open, the air too heavy, the ground too loud beneath her feet. She clutched the fabric of her jumpsuit, uncertain, her breath quick and shallow. Faces surrounded her, strangers pressing in with microphones and lenses, each one more animated, more chaotic, than the next. She couldn't understand why they were all looking at her.

Everything was wrong. On the ship, she'd known every corridor, every voice, every rhythm of life. Here, the sky had no ceiling. The wind touched her skin without permission. She didn't know what trees were, or why the sun felt so sharp. Her expression shifted, not just wonder, but a deep, unsettled confusion. The world she had landed in was beautiful, yes, but utterly alien. And she wasn't sure it felt like home.

The Prime Minister turned to Clark and shook his hand firmly. "You made our country and world proud."

"Thank you," Clark said humbly.

With their helmets off, the crew walked steadily, adjusting to the gravity and air of their home planet once more. Each step carried a mix of weariness and elation after their monumental journey, knowing that their return marked the beginning of the post-mission protocols.

The news reporter, flanked by eager cameramen, abruptly cut through the designated passage, causing a stir among the security guards. Their rapid movement drew the attention of the crew members, who paused to assess the situation.

"Harry, can I get a minute, please?" the reporter called out, seeking to capture the crew's attention. Symmonds, understanding the reporter's intention, posed confidently, offering stills and ensuring that the moment was captured for the camera.

The crew members stood in the passage, separated by a glass partition from the reporter and cameraman who eagerly awaited their response.

"The world underestimated the Inhabitation, but you proved them wrong," the reporter began, addressing the crew. "What kind of inhabitant did you find, and who is the inhabitant?"

Harry stood resolute. "There exists an inhabitation on one of the planets we explored, resembling Earth-like land," Harry began, his tone confident yet measured. "We are in the process of analysing and understanding it."

He paused briefly and lifted his daughter, Tara, high in the air, presenting her to the camera and the world watching the news. The sight of the small child, symbolising the inhabitant, sent ripples of emotion through those witnessing the broadcast. It was a moment that captivated and stirred, offering a glimpse into the profound discoveries and the hope for new beginnings beyond Earth.

***

Chapter XXVIII

The quarantine period stretched across four long weeks—thirty days and nights spent in sterile isolation, monitored relentlessly for any trace of unknown contagion. Though the medical staff reassured them daily, the silence of separation pressed down like gravity, heavier than anything they'd encountered in space.

The quarantine room was carefully divided by a thick glass partition, allowing for visits, but not touch. On one side stood Harry and his young daughter Tara, wrapped in regulation clothing, her tiny hand gripping his with quiet dependence. On the other side, pressed close to the barrier, were Professor Clark's wife and an elderly woman with trembling hands and watery eyes, Sameera, Tara's grandmother.

As Sameera saw Tara for the first time, her breath caught in her throat. She stepped closer, her fingers gently resting on the cold glass. "Oh, my baby," she whispered, her voice shaking with a mixture of awe and heartache. "I saw you when you were born ..." Her words trailed off into silence as emotion overtook her. The resemblance was uncanny—Tara's round cheeks, the curve of her lips, even the light in her eyes. It was as if Ruma, her daughter, long gone, was standing before her once more.

"She looks just like Ruma," Sameera sobbed, her voice cracking under the weight of grief and wonder. Her tears slid down her cheeks, mirrored by Tara's small, puzzled frown on the other side of the glass. The child had no memory of this woman, yet some unspoken recognition lingered in her gaze.

The room was thick with silence, the glass a cruel reminder of distance in the face of desperate love. Yet the silence was soon interrupted by footsteps—Symmonds' wife had arrived. She smiled through tears as she saw him standing tall but tired. "You look thinner," she said with a teary laugh, and he grinned, one hand raised to the glass as if it could bridge the distance.

"It's been a lifetime," he murmured, watching her closely. "But I'm home."

Later, Mikhail's parents and younger sister joined. His mother, a strong woman with weathered hands, tried to remain composed. "We watched every transmission," she said, her lips trembling. "Every word, every breath. I prayed you'd return." His sister placed her hand next to his on the glass, smiling shakily. "I kept your telescope," she said. "It still works."

Mikhail, usually reserved, didn't reply immediately. His throat worked around the emotion. He only managed a rough, "I missed you."

As the days wore on, the visits became their anchors; brief, distant moments that reminded them of life waiting on the other side. And finally, after a month of physical exams, psychological evaluations, and cautious observation, they were declared clear.

When the glass doors slid open at last, the world rushed in like air after suffocation.

Sameera pulled Tara into her arms the moment she was allowed. The child stood still at first, uncertain, then leaned in, burying her face in her grandmother's shoulder as if finally recognising something she hadn't known she was missing. Sameera wept openly, stroking Tara's hair and whispering lullabies only Ruma used to know.

Symmonds and his wife clung to each other wordlessly. Mikhail was lifted off the ground by his overjoyed mother. The hall echoed with laughter and tears, the joy of reunion dulled slightly by the losses and distance they could never quite erase.

For Tara, Earth was still strange, the sky too big, the grass too green, the noise of cities too loud, but she found comfort in the routine her grandparents created. Sameera and Clark became her world. They cooked her favourite meals, taught her songs from Earth, and told her stories about her mother's childhood. Every bedtime, she curled up beside her grandmother, listening to tales of space and stars and love that outlived galaxies.

Slowly, Tara began to smile more. She still flinched at thunder and didn't like crowded places, but in the quiet safety of her new home, among the arms that had once held her mother, she began to understand what it meant to belong.

***

Chapter XXIX

Harry decided to go home. Not to his cramped bachelor flat near the hangar where he worked with his uncle, but to his grandfather's house. He couldn't bear it to face the bar, the emptiness of it, the bolted shut doors and decaying wood. So instead, he made his way to Charlton's house, attached to the bar.

Harry pushed open the creaking door, its hinges groaning like an old man rising from bed. The scent of stale air and dust rushed out to meet him, thick and dry, catching in his throat. He paused at the threshold, blinking against the dimness inside, the late afternoon light spilling across the wooden floor like an intruder.

He stepped inside. Each footfall stirred the dust, sending tiny motes spiralling in the shafts of light. Cobwebs dangled like forgotten lace in the corners. He reached out to brush one aside from the bannister, his hand faltering at its delicate resistance. The silence was absolute. There was no kettle boiling in the kitchen, no soft humming from the old radio in the living room, no familiar shuffle of slippers on the floor.

"Granddad?" His voice cracked slightly, hanging in the air too long without an answer. He berated himself for saying it, knowing that there was nobody home to greet him. But he couldn't help it—he had to try.

He moved through the house slowly, as if the walls might breathe if he stepped too hard. The television in the corner blinked dully with the muted news channel, its ticker crawling endlessly. It must have been left on for months. The cushion on his grandfather's old chair had a slight dip in it still, but no warmth, only the faint smell of tobacco and lavender oil that Harry remembered from childhood.

He made his way to the fridge and pulled the door open. The light inside flickered weakly. Bottles clinked together as he reached in and grabbed a beer. He hesitated, then let out a short breath that was almost a laugh, almost a sigh. His granddad always kept them stocked "just in case."

Harry sank into the couch and twisted the cap off. He raised the bottle slightly in a quiet, solitary toast. "Cheers, old man," he murmured.

He took a long sip, letting the bitterness settle on his tongue. His eyes burned, but he didn't wipe them. Around him, the house breathed its stillness, and the weight of absence pressed gently, insistently, into his chest.

"Grandad, can I get you a beer? We will have it together," Harry's voice echoed in the emptiness. "I have a lot of things to say about what happened in the spaceship. Grandad, you there? Grandad ..." he called out, wandering through the rooms, his longing palpable in the hollow silence.

Another sip of beer offered a brief illusion of comfort, with the fizzy bitterness grounding him, if only for a heartbeat. He wandered into the living room, still clutching the bottle, and lowered himself onto the couch with a heaviness that didn't come from gravity alone.

His eyes fell on the coffee table. A pale envelope peeked out from beneath the television remote, its edges curled slightly, as though it had waited too long to be opened. The TV screen pulsed in the periphery, its flickering images dancing across the dusty walls.

He reached for the remote and unmuted the television.

"Grandad," he called, voice louder now, trying to mask the hesitation. "I know you're upstairs. Come down, old man."

Only silence replied–dense, echoing.

The television droned on, its cheerful cadence jarring against the quiet of the house.

"In the North Zone, the temperatures have plummeted to freezing levels, causing widespread shutdowns as a severe storm looms ..."

"Conversely, in the South, an unprecedented spike in temperatures reaching above 50 degrees Celsius has been recorded ..."

"Powerful winds in the East continue to wreak havoc, adding to the unpredictable climate patterns observed globally..."

The newscaster's voice, unnaturally chipper, filled the room with banal catastrophe. Reports of record temperatures, collapsing infrastructures, and atmospheric chaos, all delivered with the polished smoothness of a morning host trying to keep things light.

Harry leaned forward and set the beer bottle down with a hollow clink. Beside it, a photo frame sat tilted, so caked in dust that the image inside was barely visible. He wiped at it with his sleeve, revealing two blurred faces and a crooked smile–one of them his own, younger and sunburnt, the other his grandfather's, grinning with a beer in hand.

He stared at it for a moment, the background murmur of the news fading into meaningless sound.

The room felt small. The couch too soft. The air too still.

The world he had left behind, crammed with rocket fuel, control rooms, stars seen through thick glass, had vanished.

And in its place, Earth offered this: a stained cushion, an unopened envelope, the faint smell of stale bread from the kitchen, and a man on TV announcing doom in a suit and tie.

He sat back, the bottle warming in his hand. A strange dissonance thrummed through him. He had crossed galaxies, solved crises, watched moons rise in silence, but here, in this room, with its framed memories and frozen time, he felt like a visitor. Not a hero. Not even a son. Just ... misaligned. Out of place. Utterly human.

The room remained still as Harry grasped the dusty envelope, his fingers tracing the faded words inscribed on its surface. Slowly unfurling the aged paper, he revealed a neatly penned letter nestled within.

On the envelope was written, "If you find this letter, I am dead."

With each unfolding, a sense of trepidation filled the air. Harry's eyes fixated on the carefully crafted words penned in faded ink. The paper crackled softly as he read, the silence of the room amplifying the rustling of the aged document.

"Dear Harry,

I hope this letter finds you well. There's something I have never quite told you, and it weighs heavily on my heart. Twenty-five years ago, your father made a pivotal decision that shaped the course of his life. You were just two years old when he received an offer from the space centre following his training. His aspiration to explore beyond our world led him to embark on this extraordinary journey. He used to come home once in a blue moon.

One day, he abruptly returned home and expressed his intent to pursue an astronaut career. Despite my disapproval and insistence on declining the offer letter, he remained resolute. He departed from us at that moment. This occurred while you were engaged in play in the backyard. As he departed, he forcefully closed the main door, causing the glass to shatter and fall apart.

He revved the car's engine. As the sound echoed through the house, you, with a toy horse clutched in your hand, stepped into the living room and asked, "Grandad, what happened?" And I couldn't tell you the truth then, couldn't tell you the truth for years and years.

I lied to you, Harry. I lied about the debt.

I concealed the truth from you, Harry. I sought to shield you by mentioning the burden of debt. But the reality is, your father passed away aboard that spacecraft, soaring through the skies. I restricted you out of fear, out of my desperation to not lose another piece of my heart. I couldn't protect my son. I have failed in my role as a father. Please forgive me."

The ink on the paper smudged as Harry's tears fell upon it, blurring the words that carried such weight and sorrow. His emotions overwhelmed him, and he clutched the letter close.

As Harry held the photo frame in his hands, the news reporter's voice filled the room, resonating with a curious, probing tone. "Good morning, Ladies and Gentlemen. Here on Earth, we're faced with a myriad of questions. Who is Harry Stone? Where did he come from? What was his life before the launch? Was he trained in a space centre or a self-taught enthusiast? The world awaits answers. There are countless questions to be answered, and now, we're going to uncover the truth about him.

"He hails from the southern part of our country, nurtured in a bar by his grandfather, Charlton Stone, where he learned the ropes while working as a bartender in his grandfather's bar and as a mechanic for a domestic airline."

Harry wiped away the tear that had landed on the photo frame, his gaze then shifting to the spacesuit's helmet on the photo frame. Meanwhile, the newsreader continued talking on the TV. "He is the son of the late former Astronaut Captain Scott E. Stone, who dedicatedly served the nation from 1975 to 1985, tragically losing his life during the terrible *Echolight* crash that preceded the recent monumental success of *Tarayaan*."

In a moment of clearing the dust off the frame, he discovered an image of his father donning a spacesuit, a poignant memory revealed. Simultaneously, the news channel broadcast the same image on the screen, aligning with the one in his hands.

The very image that Harry stumbled upon in the gallery of the Space Centre when he was going for the launch was now resurfacing in his memory, echoing through the news broadcast.

The new reader continued, "His father's dream realised, Harry Stone, alongside his daughter, shared with the now lost astronaut, Ruma Sharma–called Tara, and their fellow crew members, Arthur Symmonds and Alek Mikhail, have completed the Project-Inhabitant. This is Matthew, signing off."

Twenty-four years ago, two astronauts went to their homes to say goodbye to their families before they were about to board *Echolight*. However, the third, driving towards his family, paused at a halfway point. Something caught his eye--a cherished photo, his son's radiant face smiling back at him. Overwhelmed by a flood of emotions, tears cascaded down his cheeks. The weight of his son's image stirred profound emotions, prompting him to turn back, leaving the familiar path toward home and instead returning to the space centre.

Indeed, that poignant image was none other than a picture of Harry, the son of the third astronaut. It held an inexplicable power, evoking deep emotions that altered the course of that astronaut's journey home.

The weight of the revelation pushed Harry back, and he crumpled to the floor. The room seemed to darken as Harry collapsed, the photo frame pressing against his chest, the weight of his father's absence overwhelming him. Each breath hitched in his chest as sobs wracked his body. The pain was so visceral that it felt as if his heart was breaking anew. Tears flowed freely, streaming down his face, mingling with the silent, salty liquid trickling from his nose. His cries were raw, the sounds of his anguish reverberating through the space. It was a storm of emotions, a tempest of grief and loss that shook him to his very core.

Harry's chest felt like a drum, each beat resonating with the ache that consumed him. He clutched the photo frame desperately, tears dropping onto the frozen image of his father. The weight of his emotions was crushing, a tidal wave of agony crashing relentlessly against the walls of his soul. The pain was so intense, so raw, that it seemed to defy words. It was a vortex of anguish, pulling him into a whirlwind of unspoken sorrow, his heartache echoing in the emptiness of the room. His cries were silent screams of despair, his anguish etched into every tear that fell.

But beneath the grief, another feeling began to stir—darker, sharper.

Betrayal.

His grandfather had known. Knew who his father was all along. And worse, had kept it from him. The photo, the lies about the debt, the reason he'd stayed in Florida rather than go out and make a name for himself—it had all been a carefully constructed story. A story designed to keep Harry close. To tether him.

Grief turned to fury in his chest, twisting the ache into something hotter. He had trusted his grandfather with everything—with the truth, with his future, with his heart. And now, all he could feel was the sting of deception. His sobs grew quieter but no less broken, swallowed by the silence of a room filled with ghosts and half-truths.

***

Epilogue

A few months later

On the 25th of December in 2025, the city was a radiant scene of festive celebration. Snowflakes gracefully descended from the sky, blanketing the streets in a soft white cover. The atmosphere was alive with the spirit of Christmas, echoed by the spirited decorations that adorned every corner. Twinkling lights illuminated the cityscape, casting a warm and enchanting glow on the snow-laden streets. People bustled about, their faces adorned with smiles and rosy cheeks from the wintry chill. Joyous greetings of "Happy Christmas" and "Merry Christmas" echoed through the air, resonating with the shared jubilation of the season. The date held an enchanting allure, inviting everyone to revel in the magic of the holiday and cherish moments of togetherness.

Harry, taking pride in his work, refurbished the bar to welcome Clark, Sameera, and Tara. As they arrived in the evening, Harry greeted them warmly. Tara's innocent greeting of "Hi, papa" filled the room with joy. Clark complimented the charming decorations, bringing a smile to Harry's face. Sameera joined in, wishing a heartfelt "Merry Christmas!" to which Harry reciprocated warmly. The atmosphere was one of festive cheer and familial bonding.

"What would you like to drink, Michael?" Harry asked, making his way behind the bar.

"No formalities here, Harry. Nothing fancy, a beer should do it," Clark beamed. "You all packed and ready for tonight?"

Harry nodded and cracked open a cold beer for Clark. "You know it," he grinned.

Harry was going to be spending the night at Clark's apartment. After *Tarayaan's* success, he had been moved into what could be called a modest mansion. Sameera was going to be there tonight, too, although Harry knew that the only reason the former couple could bear to be around each other was because of Tara.

*

The morning light filtered gently through the lab's tall windows, casting soft golden stripes across the cold floor. Harry stood by the console, his brow furrowed, his voice low but insistent. "Michael ... isn't there any way we can reach her again?"

Clark didn't look up. He sat at his desk surrounded by a tangle of consoles, projection panels, and the blinking lights of the holographic interface. The capsule's nanodevice hummed softly under his touch as he configured the delicate sequence needed to initiate the link.

"We can try," he murmured, more to himself than to him.

Fingers flying across the interface, he engaged the fragile connection. The room held its breath. For a long second, there was only static ... then a flicker, a pulse of light. The hologram bloomed into life, hazy and fragile, like a memory trying to form.

Ruma's face appeared in the air before them, dim but unmistakable. She looked older, tired, weatherworn, and yet still radiant with urgency. Her eyes scanned the space hungrily until they locked onto Clark.

"Dad," she breathed, her voice distant, echoing, frayed at the edges. "Can you hear me?"

Clark stepped forward, throat tight. "Ruma ..." he began, but the signal sputtered, his voice swallowed by interference.

The image quivered. Behind Ruma, the background shimmered unnaturally, as though it belonged to a place governed by rules they didn't yet understand. For a moment, it felt like she was standing at the edge of a different reality, a world slipping further out of reach with each passing second.

The signal crackled violently, and then ... silence. The hologram collapsed.

Clark stared at the space where she'd been, his hand still hovering over the interface. Beside him, Harry said nothing. There was nothing left to say.

They had made contact. Barely. But pulling her back? That was a puzzle the laws of their universe had yet to solve.

Whatever Ruma had drifted into, it wasn't just lost space. It was something else. Something ... parallel.

And they would find her. Somehow. In time.

Acknowledgements

With heartfelt gratitude, I bow to the blessings of my beloved parents, Nitturi Rajendra Prasad and Nitturi Sudha Rani. Their love, encouragement, and unwavering belief in me have been the foundation of everything I have achieved.

My deepest thanks to my lovely wife, Nitturi Laxmi Priya, whose support, patience, and constant inspiration made this journey possible. And to my cute little pie, Sriyanshi, whose smile brings joy to every moment—this book is as much hers as it is mine.

I am grateful for the unconditional support of my sister and brother-in-law, Malamanchi Guru Raj Sharma and Malamanchi Shilpa, who have always stood by me with warmth and motivation.

And a very special thanks to my sister Malamanchi Shilpa—without you, this story would not have taken shape.

About the Author

Saratchendra Nitturi is a software engineer based in Hyderabad, India, with a deep passion for futuristic storytelling and human-adventure narratives. Outside his technical profession, he enjoys exploring the unexplored worlds of science fiction, adventure, and investigative mysteries.

His fascination with "What lies beyond the ordinary?" pushed him into writing, and this creative curiosity led to his debut novel, *Voyagers of the Lost Earth*, a story that blends imagination, mystery, and cosmic exploration.

Saratchendra writes with the vision of inspiring readers to look beyond boundaries, whether they are scientific, adventurous, emotional, or existential. He continues to build immersive worlds filled with wonder, technology, and human resilience.